AF270762

Wrapped Up in Christmas Love

A Wrapped Up in Christmas Romance

Janice Lynn

TULE
PUBLISHING

Wrapped Up in Christmas Love
Copyright© 2024 Janice Lynn
Tule Publishing First Printing, November 2024

The Tule Publishing, Inc.

ALL RIGHTS RESERVED

First Publication by Tule Publishing 2024

Cover design by Lee Hyat Design

Quilt pattern design by Nancy Cann for the Quilts of Valor Foundation (QOVF)

No part of this book may be used or reproduced in any manner whatsoever without written permission except in the case of brief quotations embodied in critical articles and reviews.

This is a work of fiction. Names, characters, places, and incidents are products of the author's imagination or are used fictitiously. Any resemblance to actual events, locales, organizations, or persons, living or dead, is entirely coincidental.

AI was not used to create any part of this book and no part of this book may be used for generative training.

ISBN: 978-1-965640-30-2

Wrapped Up in Christmas Love

Dedication

To The Quilts of Valor Foundation. Thank you to every person who contributes to this wonderful organization and as always, to every military service member past and present.

Chapter One

Our flag does not fly because the wind moves it. It flies with the last breath of every fallen soldier who protected it. ~ UNKNOWN

STARING AT THE garland-draped courthouse monument, Master Sergeant Zach Dawson's own breath caught. Memories of his brothers—and sisters—in arms who had given their all threatened to buckle his knees. Unbidden, his right hand flexed. Just to the other side of the marble inscription, a flagpole's halyard clanged from the crisp November wind. Heart pounding, Zach lifted his gaze to the red, white, and blue sashaying high above the courthouse lawn.

No one loved that flag and what it represented more than he did.

The Army had been his life for so long that almost two years after his medical discharge, Zach was still trying to figure out who he was in the civilian world. He longed to be where the action was, not on a forced vacation in the middle-of-nowhere, baseball-and-apple-pie, already-decorated-for-Christmas, Pine Hill, Kentucky. He'd had almost a year's *vacation* when he'd been lying in a hospital bed, then confined within a rehab facility. Being busy kept him sane.

Trying to shut out the chinking metal, Zach took a few deep breaths and glanced around Pine Hill's revitalized town square. His stomach growled at the scents wafting from a mom-and-pop, oven-baked pizzeria. Garland with twinkling lights and shiny red bows framed windows and doorways. Trendy shops lined the streets, including the one his army buddy Bodie Lewis had disappeared inside to buy dog treats. Paw Parties? Seriously? Then again, Zach would cut his pal some slack since it was Zach who'd been helping Bodie's wife make snowflakes that morning. Sarah had been so kind since his arrival a few days before that he hadn't had the heart to say no when she'd needed help with a church project.

Across the square, an arm-laded blond stepped out of a shop with an artsy sign featuring a sewing needle with a string curling around to write, THE THREADED NEEDLE. Shifting her wares, she paused to speak with a granny wearing a red Santa sweater, candy-cane leggings, and black boots that came up to her knees. A large cloth bag with the store's emblem hung from the blond's shoulder and her hands gripped the box overflowing with shiny green and red fabric. Chatting only a moment, she smiled with genuine affection, then crossed the street to a gray sedan parked on the opposite courthouse corner from Zach. She reached for the door handle just as the wind's greedy fingers pilfered a paper from the box she finagled on her hip. The breeze twirled the pale green sheet this way, then that, dancing its lifted prize to the noisy flag's beat.

"No!" She shoved her bag and box into the car, then chased after the sheet, almost comically, as the wind toyed with her, appearing to let go, only to snatch it away just when the page was almost low enough to reach. She'd been too far away for Zach to readily help, but a strong gust zoomed the page across the courthouse lawn and would have plastered the sheet to his face had he not caught it.

The blond rushed to him. "Oh, thank you! I was afraid I'd lost that. How my list came out of my notebook is craziness."

"No problem." Zach met her blue-as-the-sky eyes.

Around him the wind calmed, but the otherworldly force blasting his body had his feet bracing to keep from being blown back. Stunned and thinking his reaction must have to do with how the inscription had gotten inside his head, he glanced down at what he held. WEDDING CHECKLIST headlined a neatly written list bordered with colorful Christmas lights. Throat tightening, he looked up. "You're getting married?"

Why his insides felt strangled at seeing a few items checked off made no sense. Nor did his desire to crumble and toss the list back to the wind.

"No. Definitely not me." Laughing, she held out her hand. "Thank you."

Zach should give her the paper and be done with little miss blue eyes. Instead, curiosity got the better of him. "If you aren't getting married, why do you have a handwritten wedding checklist that you chased as if it revealed your deepest secrets? Better yet, how do you make your letters so perfectly shaped and sized? I'm not sure if I'm impressed or scared that this could have been typed."

"There is nothing wrong with good penmanship." Still holding out her hand, her gaze narrowed. "Do I know you?"

Zach's lips twitched. "No, but you should."

Rolling her eyes, she harrumphed. "I seriously doubt that, but you should definitely ask Santa for a new book of cheesy pickup lines because that one is so middle school."

"Was I trying to pick you up?" he wondered out loud. Beyond the occasional dinner date, he'd not been interested in dating since prior to his accident. Even then, cheesy pickup lines had never been his thing.

"You said I should … oh, never mind." Pink splashed across her cheeks. Then with obvious annoyance, she gave him a look worthy of the burliest drill sergeant. "Give me my list and I'll be on my way so that you can attempt to impress someone else with your lackluster smarm."

Give her the paper, Zach, then walk away. No need to rebut that lackluster smarm. Especially since she was right. His comment had been lackluster. He forced his fingers to release their hold.

"Thank you." She didn't meet his gaze, just stared at his chest, mumbled something under her breath, then, paper in hand, turned to leave. The wind acted up anew, slowing her trek to her car and plastering her clothes to her five-foot-four-ish frame. The gust pulled at her shoulder-length hair, making the strands dance about her, and tugged at the light purple number she wore loosely about her neck. Just as the scarf worked itself free, she grabbed hold and, in the process, lost her death grip, allowing Mother Nature to once again dance her list through the air.

His gaze zeroed in on the paper's aerobatics, Zach leapt to action. Turning, seeing he yet again held her list, the blond lifted her chest with a deep inhalation.

"Lose something?" he teased, surprised by how glad he was that her departure had been delayed.

She was not similarly amused. Her fiery gaze shot daggers as she marched back. He was positive he died a thousand deaths in her mind and all of them painfully torturous.

With a frustrated huff, she snatched the paper. "Thank you."

"If you want to spend time with me, Blondie, you don't have to fake losing your list again. I'll give you my phone number." Usually only the heat of battle triggered the adrenaline rushing through him. "*If* you ask nicely."

Make that a thousand-and-one deaths he'd died in her mind.

"There you go not trying to pick me up again." She placed her free hand on her hip. "Congratulations. You succeeded and completely failed to impress. Again."

Her words might have stung, except something more than annoyance flickered in her gaze. Intrigue. Interest. *Attraction?*

Fascinated by both the fire in her eyes and the burn in his chest, Zach grinned. "Sorry about earlier. I'd take your advice about asking Santa for that book, but it wouldn't do me any good. Would you believe Santa stuffs my stocking with coal each year?"

"Oh, I'd believe that."

He chuckled. "Can we start over?"

Shaking her head, she met his gaze head-on. "There's no need. Hopefully our paths will never cross again."

"That would be a shame." He wanted their paths to cross.

Pine Hill had suddenly become a lot more exciting than just burning up vacation time while visiting the Lewis family.

"I can only hope to be so shamefully lucky, then." Blondie glanced at her watch, then gave another look of irritation. "But if our paths do cross, don't feel the need to say hello or any other non-pickup lines."

"I'll keep that in mind."

Pivoting, she fought the wind to her car, got inside, and shot him one last look, one that appeared to be full of curiosity until she realized he was watching her. Then, expression pinched, she drove away with a little squeal of her tires.

Watching the car disappear, Zach crammed his hands into his jeans pockets. He'd say hello and a lot more if—no, when—their paths crossed again. No doubt he'd come off with another bad pickup line just to see her eyes ignite. Blondie was likely more bark than bite, but either way, he'd never shied away from danger. Quite the opposite.

She'd been carrying a bag with the quilt shop's logo. Pine Hill wasn't that big. He was there another week and would figure out who she was. That part would be easy. But it was going to take a whole lot of Christmas magic to get her to stop looking at him as if he were at the top of Santa's Naughty List.

"I'D LIKED TO tell that man a thing or two," Isabelle Davis mumbled under her breath as she carried a box of Christmas sashes toward the Pine Hill high school music room. "Like how he wasn't nearly as amusing as he thought he was and how just because he looks like some super-buff movie star, that doesn't mean—"

"Did you say something, Izzy?"

Ordering her facial features to relax, she smiled at her eighteen-year-old beauty queen cousin who looked a lot like Isabelle's younger sister, Sophie. They shared the same brown hair and sparkly eyes that were family trademarks. Isabelle was an outlier with her blond locks and blue eyes. Unfortunately. How many times had she wished she'd inherited the darker features of her mother's family rather than having any resemblance to her father?

"I was talking to myself." Isabelle willed the tall man with his army emblazoned T-shirt, slightly wavy brown hair that was much too long for him to be active military, and laughing hazel eyes out of her head.

Who was he? She'd lived in Pine Hill all her life, minus college and a year where she'd worked for an accounting firm in Nashville. Mr. Muscled Up Paper Snatcher wasn't from Pine Hill. Men who looked like him stood out as surely as if they had a HUNK neon sign flashing over their head. Ha, men like him would stand out in Times Square, no sign needed. Santa might have him on the naughty list, but he topped the nice looks list.

"Don't mind me." She hugged the box to her chest. "Being in these halls where I spent my teenaged years makes me feel over-the-hill." The tiled floors and painted walls looked exactly as they had when Isabelle had been preparing for her own senior year events.

Even the various handmade poster boards advertising

upcoming Christmas events had a familiar feel. How had more than a decade passed since she'd graduated from this very school? Her thirtieth birthday loomed. That wasn't old, but she sure was nothing like the youthful, idealistic teen smiling at her, either. Then again, had she ever been like that?

The teen gave her an odd look. "You're not old, Izzy. You're young and beautiful, not to mention the smartest person I know. I'm sure glad you're helping with my Christmas choir concert. Can you believe it's my last one? I can't imagine not being in Mr. Reeves's music classes or in this building when so much of my life centers here."

Exactly. Isabelle wouldn't point out that life wouldn't slow down but would continue rushing by, and soon enough it would be Annabelle musing about past glory days. Not that Isabelle expected Annabelle to be like her. No doubt, her cousin would be swept off her feet, just as Sophie had been two years ago by firefighter Cole Aaron. Isabelle was much too practical to get swept away. She could walk just fine all by herself. The annoying army shirt guy popped back into her mind. Was his shirt why he'd instantly set her on edge?

"I love helping with anything you need." She smiled at the teen over the box she held as they stepped into the music room. "So does Sophie. We adore you."

"There you are!" The early-thirties choir director crossed the instrument-and-teen-filled room. Pushing his wireframe glasses up the bridge of his nose, his gaze met Isabelle's. "We're excited about the concert Christmas sashes you made. They're going to add a fun pop of color."

"We're grateful we were able to help." Handing the box over, Isabelle smiled.

Trevor Reeves had been with the school a couple of years and had done wonderful things, expanding the band and choir programs. Friendly, he always made a point to say hi at church or social gatherings. She'd gotten the impression he'd liked Sophie, but that interest had been useless as her sister was head over heels for her fiancé.

"I can't believe you finished them so quickly." He pulled out a few of the red and green sashes with their festive sequins. "They're amazing. Not that I expected anything less, but you and Sophie shouldn't have pushed yourselves."

"It wasn't a problem." As busy as they were with the up-coming holidays and Sophie's wedding, Isabelle had enjoyed staying late with her sister and working on the project. The one-on-one time they'd always had an abundance of had become a scarcity. "We're getting things done early to try to keep Sophie as stress-free as possible leading up to her wedding."

"Does Sophie get stressed?" Trevor laughed. "I've never seen her that she wasn't bubbling over with sunshine."

Exactly. Isabelle worked hard to make sure her sister stayed that way. Long ago, she'd vowed to protect Sophie from things that stole her happiness. What was a little pre-wedding stress if it kept Sophie smiling? Wasn't that Isa-belle's job as big sister and maid of honor? To make sure her big day went perfectly?

"You're a bit of sunshine, too." Trevor smiled, then shot an embarrassed glance toward Annabelle.

His face pinkening, he unnecessarily pushed his glasses

upward again. Had he forgotten the teen was there? Isabelle fought snorting. Compared to Sophie, she was a cloudy day.

Uncomfortable that her grinning cousin was glancing back and forth between her and the music teacher, Isabelle cleared her throat. "Check these and if you need more, let Annabelle know." There, she'd made it clear that he didn't have to contact her directly, just in case he'd decided since Sophie wasn't available, she'd make do. "We want her senior year Christmas concert to be perfect. Not only is she family, but she's also the quilt shop's star part-time employee."

Annabelle leaned forward and kissed her cheek. "Thank you, Izzy. You and Sophie are the best. I'll see you at The Threaded Needle after school."

"Maybe I could stop by and—"

"Oh, look at the time," Isabelle interrupted the still blushing teacher, glancing pointedly at her watch.

No need to encourage him when she had no time for such nonsense. Other than with Greg during the time she'd lived in Nashville, she never had. It didn't bother her. She had a wedding to plan, a quilt shop to run, and she'd never give a man a chance to do to her what her father had done to her mother.

"HOW DOES A tiny hole-in-the-wall town have such good food?" Zach took another bite of his Pine Hill burger. Although he'd always been fine with eating whatever, he enjoyed good food. Lou's topped some of the finest he'd ever sampled.

"Quality basic ingredients and a talented cook." Across the booth, Bodie grinned. "You should stick around to have some of Lou's chili that he serves at the annual Christmas Festival. My mouth waters just thinking about it."

"I'll be long gone before Christmas festivals." Or maybe not, since even the diner already had silver tinsel garland and a two-foot artificial tree at the cash register counter. Advertisements for local Christmas activities were taped along the front and a Triple B Ranch Toy Drive drop-off bin was prominently displayed. A bit early to be so holidayed up, but whatever tinseled up this small town's Christmas float.

"This forced vacation is ridiculous." Zach snorted his disgust at being shackled by his current *restrictions*. After his injuries, he'd been in a low, dark place and climbing out of that despair had taken a while, but he had overcome. "My accident was almost two years ago. That I blacked out two weeks ago had to do with my not eating while undercover, not my head injuries. Lukas should know that."

Bodie looked skeptical. "You think?"

"I'm fine." The intense throb that sometimes hit was killer, but what were a few lingering headaches when compared to what many of his comrades dealt with? What they'd sacrificed? Zach was one of the lucky ones.

"The building you were in exploded. You were unconscious for weeks, had surgery after surgery removing shrapnel, including the piece that paralyzed your right arm and hand." Bodie unnecessarily reminded. "The moment you left the rehab facility, you dived into working for iSecure and have pushed nonstop. A few weeks' vacation isn't going to hurt you."

Zach's hopefully last surgery scar burned his upper back just below his T-shirt's collar.

Willing it to stop, he stuck the last of his burger into his mouth, but what had tasted delicious a minute before now had to be forcibly swallowed with a gulp of water. "Is that how you felt after your medical leave when your hip was busted up? That a few weeks of R and R wasn't a bad thing?"

"Point taken." Bodie's gaze didn't waver from Zach's. "But that time off ended up being the best thing that ever happened to me."

Those few weeks between his pal's discharge from the rehab facility in DC, the same one Zach had been at less than a year later, and his starting work for iSecure had led Bodie to Pine Hill to thank a woman for a patriotic quilt that had been a catalyst to his turnaround.

"I'm happy you found where you belong in the civilian world, but the thought of staying in one place makes me feel as if my air supply is being cut off. It's why I couldn't just sit in DC for the next month. I need to get back to what I do best—making a difference."

Zach had been good at his job. The best. But not quite good enough. Not that he remembered much about that horrific day. Could he have prevented their mission from being compromised? Have prevented unnecessary loss? If so, could he live with himself that some of those sacrificed last breaths had been his fault? Was that why no amount of therapy had been able to recover whatever his brain had locked away? He curled his fingers into his palms, his nails digging into the callused flesh. Most of the feeling had come back months ago, and after the numbness, he welcomed the physical discomfort.

Bodie's brow arched. "That wasn't what you were doing last night on Sarah's computer? Making a difference?"

"More like your wife had me working the bugs out of her embroidery program." Sarah's computer was a dinosaur. He'd half expected to hear a dial-up noise when he'd turned on the beast. Zach wouldn't be bypassing any major security walls with that snail system. "You can thank me for the extra time she'll have to watch Jeannie, freeing you up from babysitting duty."

"Thanks for helping Sarah, but watching Jeannie is a privilege, not a duty."

Zach eyed his friend. "It's hard for me to reconcile that the tough soldier I served with now gets up in the middle of the night to change diapers."

Bodie's grin said he wouldn't trade doing so for the world. "Best job I ever had."

Zach wrinkled his nose. "Diaper duty?"

"Dad duty," Bodie corrected.

The sincerity on his friend's face had Zach shaking his head. Bodie had been one of the best soldiers Zach had ever served with, which was likely why they'd become such good friends during their deployment together. To see the soldier so domesticated boggled the mind, but Bodie appeared happy playing house and chasing down lead-footed grannies in his sheriff's deputy SUV. Then again, the IED explosion that had left Bodie hospitalized for months provided a powerful impetus. Zach knew that power, knew how it could bend a man into anything it chose, sometimes dragging one's mind to the pits of hell.

"Better you than me." Zach picked at the grilled vegetables on his plate. "Not that I know much about babies, but I'll admit yours is cute when she smiles."

"Which she does a lot around you." Bodie's tone implied that he didn't understand why.

Zach chuckled. "Kid has good taste, even at five months."

"Or is just too young to know better than to be charmed by the likes of you," Bodie countered. "The ladies always did fall for you. Even my wife is taken in, especially because you're interested in her quilting."

How a quilt could change his pal's life had been a ray of light when Zach had been in a dark place and given him something to focus on during his therapy. Quilting had become his therapy.

"Sarah showed me the Quilts of Valor quilt she's working on." The red, white, and blue quilt pieces had called to him, and he'd worked with her for several hours the previous night. "That such a work of art will welcome our brothers and sisters home"—Zach dragged in a deep breath—"well, that's an awesome thing."

Understanding shone in Bodie's eyes. "Gets you in the feels, doesn't it?"

The diner door opened, and a new customer bell chimed as something else—someone else—who got Zach in the feels walked in. Adrenaline surged. Blondie stepped up to the counter, brushed a strand of stick-straight hair behind her ear, then spoke to the cashier.

Turning to see who he looked at, Bodie snorted. "You may as well get that look off your face. You'd have better luck convincing Lukas that you don't need a break than you do of wooing Isabelle Davis."

"You know her?" *Isabelle Davis.*

Taking another drink, Zach let her name settle into his mind, rolling it around, liking it. Isabelle fit. Belle meant beautiful and that she was, especially when her full lips curved upward in a smile. Not that she'd smiled at him, but given time, she would. Blondie might have been all blustery but there had been something more in her gaze, too. Daggers, he recalled, suppressing a chuckle. If she freely smiled at him, it would be because he'd gotten trampled by the reindeer he'd met earlier at Harvey Farm.

"There aren't many folks around here I don't know. Three years and the whole town thinks we're family." Bodie chuckled. "Pine Hill is a friendly place."

Zach's gaze didn't leave where Isabelle chatted with the cashier. "I wouldn't mind being friends with her."

"I don't think even you can make that happen, but you'll get your chance soon enough. She and Sarah go to church together and Isabelle attends most of our get-togethers at Hamilton House." The massive, renovated old Victorian had belonged to Sarah's late aunt and was now a bed-and-breakfast. "But I wouldn't mention that you're staying in our Beds for Vets suite, and I'd lose the army shirt."

"Why's that?" Why would it matter to Blondie what he wore or which room he stayed in while visiting his friend?

She glanced at her watch as the cashier took off toward the kitchen.

"Isabelle is polite, but she isn't a fan of anything to do with the likes of you and me." Bodie dabbed a condensation ring on the table with his napkin. "Sarah says it's to do with her military dad leaving when she and her sister were little kids."

Curious as to what leaving entailed, Zach's gaze met his friend's. "That turned her against everything military?"

Dropping his crumbled napkin to the tabletop, Bodie shrugged. "Seems so."

"Also seems unfair."

"You and I learned long ago that life isn't fair but is more about making the best with what opportunities you're given."

"Good point." Zach's focus returned to where Isabelle tapped her foot with impatience while she waited for her to-go order. "Excuse me a minute."

"Because?" Bodie asked, although his friend knew good and well where Zach was headed as he slid his six-foot-three frame out of the booth.

"I'm making the best of a given opportunity."

STANDING AT THE cashier counter just inside Lou's Diner, Isabelle toyed with a stray piece of silver tinsel that had come loose from Lou's countertop tree. That the restaurant was running behind with her order fit the way her day had gone thus far. She needed to get back to The Threaded Needle. Sophie's new Christmas quilt kits needed uploading onto their website, plus half a dozen other things required attention before Aunt Claudia and her friends arrived at closing. The older ladies were bringing Sophie's wedding dress. Or what would be her wedding dress once finished. The Butterflies, as the group of her aunt's lifelong friends called themselves, had insisted upon making the gown as their wedding gift. Having Sophie's wedding attire ready was a big item Isabelle would like to mark off her wedding checklist. At least, they'd finally see what the women had come up with from Sophie's descriptions. Hopefully, they'd not made any too over-the-top changes, but the Butterflies weren't known for being conventional.

"Look what the wind blew in," an amused male voice drawled from behind her, sending shivers over Isabelle's skin.

Without looking, she knew it was Annoyance Himself.

His smooth baritone rolled out like the finest silk and his amusement was just as irritating as it had been on the square. "Are you following me, Blondie?"

Her cheeks burned and her stomach gurgled loud enough he'd likely heard. Maybe if she ignored him, he'd go away. Hoping to distract herself from the fact that he stood right behind her, she looked for more stray tinsel, didn't see any, so read Lou's joke of the day.

What do you call a snowman with a six-pack?

Yeah, that wasn't helping because she'd bet her Christmas morning goodies that Prince Annoying was sporting a six-pack under his army T-shirt.

The abdominal snowman.

"Can't say I blame you for making sure our paths crossed," he continued in that *I'm hot and we both know it* drawl.

Crumbled candy canes and threadbare stockings! He wasn't going to go away, not without torturing her first. Face tightly pinched, she turned, hoping he accurately read how much she wished he'd disappear. Maybe *the abdominal snowman* could gobble him up so she could get her lunch in peace and forget he existed. Her gaze collided with broad shoulders that had her gulping. There was a toughness about him that said anything trying to gobble him up would be in for a run for their money and would lose.

"I recall mentioning not to bother saying hello if our paths did cross again."

Disappointment hit that she hadn't imagined how good-looking he was. Or how tall. He towered over her five foot four inches. And if there was ever a competition for an abdominal snowman, he'd win. Scolding herself for noticing how his T-shirt clung to his muscles, she upped her glare game. Maybe he'd take the hint and leave.

"Yep." His lips twitched, almost as if he knew he made her insides jitter like a shaken snow globe. "That's why I didn't say hello."

Isabelle looked upward at Lou's tiled ceiling, counted to six, and winced when she couldn't think of the next number to save her life. Not good for someone with an accounting degree.

"Oops, sorry. I didn't realize that I should have been more specific. I meant for you not to say anything at all," she clarified.

"Not say anything and let all your effort in following me be wasted? *Tsk. Tsk.*" His eyes twinkled brighter than Lou's shiny Christmas tree lights. "I'd hate to disappoint you that way."

"Seeing you again is disappointing." *Exhilarating,* her

inner voice corrected.

Why, oh, why, did being near him make breathing difficult? It was as if he sucked up all the oxygen and what air was left made her head spin.

"Disappointing?" He gave an exaggerated fake sigh. "I thought you were happy to see me."

"*Pfft*. Wrong again." Annoyed was what she was.

At him because he'd occupied all her thoughts since their windy encounter. But even more so, at herself, because excitement surged at the way merriment danced in his eyes when they looked in hers. Approval shone in their hazel depths, as if he enjoyed their verbal sparring and that she had no qualms in standing up to him. Not only did he not mind; he seemed to appreciate that she wasn't falling at his boots.

"If I didn't know better, I'd think you didn't like me." He sounded as if he didn't believe anyone capable of such a feat. His ego alone could power Santa's sleigh, no reindeer needed.

"Ahh, you finally got something right." She kept her eyes narrowed, possibly to block out some of his maleness.

Seriously, Santa should package up his pheromones and spread the overabundance on Christmas morning. He had more than enough to spare.

"Given long enough, it was bound to happen." Grinning, he added, "Name's Zach, by the way. Zach Dawson."

Zach. Strong and to the point, like him.

"That matters to me how?" Harsh, but she wasn't budging an inch to his swagger and smiles. Her self-preservation skills had been finely honed years ago and he'd already dinged them enough for one day.

"You know you were wondering." His teasing was doubly worse in that he was right.

She was curious as to who he was and why he was in Pine Hill. Perhaps he consulted with one of the factories in their industrial park or had been hired to do something in preparation for the On-the-Square Christmas Festival in a few weeks. They always had a few out-of-town vendors. If he could package up his smile, he'd have a best seller.

"What your name is doesn't matter to me. I couldn't care less if—"

"Hey, Blondie?" he interrupted, causing her to pause. "You're protesting too much."

Irritated that he was right about that, too, she tapped her boot against the floor. "Don't call me that."

"What would you prefer for me to call you?" The corner of his mouth curved upward, digging a dimple into his cheek that had probably been adorable when he'd been young. *It's adorable now,* the annoying voice in her head pointed out. Adorable seemed the wrong adjective to use when describing someone so … so … masculine.

"That's the point. I don't want you to call me," she managed.

The gold flecks in his eyes flickered as if warm flames, inviting her to relax and cozy up. "Fair enough. If that's what you want, I won't call."

"Good. Don't." Had she really just crossed her arms?

Someone watching would think she was throwing a temper tantrum. Not even as a child had she done that. Just ask her mother. Darlene would be the first to say that Isabelle had always been responsible, a rule follower, and never caused a bit of trouble.

Zach's irritating, knowing smile made Isabelle want to cause so much trouble Santa would permanently strike her name off the nice list.

"But if you change your mind—" The twitch of his lips drew her gaze.

She'd never really thought about mouths having genders, but Zach's was all male. Strong, full, and ... annoying.

"I won't," she assured, relieved as Bessie returned, bag in hand. "Oh, look, there's my order." She gave him a dismissive, squinty smile. "I can't say it's been pleasant, but maybe my luck will change, and seeing you won't happen again. A girl can hope."

Because being around Zach made her painfully aware of just how gorgeous he was. Seriously, a manly mouth? The wind must have carried a little Christmas crazy that morning as she couldn't think of another reason for why she'd had to take another peek at those lips before rushing out of Lou's with her food and on-fire cheeks.

Zach's laughter followed her from the diner, mocking her flight. Once inside her car, she sank back into her seat and took a big breath, as if she'd been fleeing for her life.

Maybe she had. From the abdominal snowman.

Zach, the abdominal snowman.

She burst into laughter, not sure what she found so funny, or even if she found anything funny, but perhaps she laughed from stress and a bit of hysteria.

That had to be it. Dependable, always rational, Isabelle Davis was now nuttier than Ruby Jenkins's award-winning fruitcake.

Chapter Two

"I s Cole planning to wear his fuzzy red Santa suit instead of his military uniform to your wedding, Sophie?"

Despite the exasperation Isabelle hadn't been able to shake after her lunchtime encounter with the full-of-himself stranger, she smiled at Rosie Hudson as she paced back and forth from one fabric display to another while they waited on Sophie to model her gown.

"You think we could convince him to?" Isabelle straightened a display that Rosie had bumped into on her last spin around.

Waiting in the quilt shop's Christmas section had been easiest due to the wooden rocking chair that Sarah occupied while nursing her five-month-old daughter. Left up to Isabelle, her soon-to-be brother-in-law would wear his Santa suit rather than his Marine uniform. Not that Isabelle was as big on the holidays as Sophie, but military uniforms reminded her of things she would just as soon not be reminded of on her sister's wedding day.

"Cole's not wearing his Santa suit," Maybelle Kirby assured, her tone brooking no argument from where she browsed Christmas embroidered kitchen towels. If the

Butterflies had a leader, Maybelle would be it. The regal, older Grace Kelly look-alike with her no-nonsense attitude and ability to whip a room into shape made Isabelle partial to the woman. Isabelle appreciated order. Maybelle held up a MERRY CHRISTMAS towel. "These are lovely."

"Maybe Cole could wear his firefighter uniform," Ruby suggested, moving next to Isabelle to browse through the holiday fabric she'd just straightened. "Cole and my grandson look so handsome in their uniforms." The older woman beamed. "Andrew's coming home from California to be the best man, you know?"

"We know," Maybelle and Rosie said simultaneously, as if they'd heard Ruby make the comment a few times previously.

Unfazed, Ruby just smiled at her five decades-plus friends. Ruby was an iconic grandma. She cooked. She sewed. She loved with all her heart. "I can't wait to see him, Morgan, and Grayson. It feels as if it's been forever since they got married this summer. I know Claudia thinks the same about her granddaughter and great-grandson. I'm glad they chose to spend their honeymoon in Pine Hill, so we got to spend time with them."

"Not much of a honeymoon." Rosie fluttered her fake lashes. Rosie was the life of the Butterflies' party. Always had been and always would be. Just ask her and she'd tell you while tossing Christmas-colored confetti to prove it. "They should have left Greyson with Claudia and gone somewhere exotic."

"Morgan wanted to stay here after their wedding." Ruby gave her friend a don't-you-go-hating-on-my-grandson look.

The marriage of Ruby's grandson to Claudia's granddaughter had officially cemented the Butterflies into family. Not that it mattered. The women were closer than most blood relatives. Isabelle had thought of them as family long before her second cousin had married Andrew.

While Isabelle decided to redo the fabric display, putting each bolt into order by theme, the group chatted about Andrew and Morgan a few minutes before Cole's Santa role came up again.

"How Sophie transforms that hunky man into a plausible Santa amazes me." The large diamond wedding set on Rosie's left hand sparkled as it caught the quilt shop's lights when she fluffed her short, punk rock blue hair. The style might appear ridiculous on some sixty-something women, but Rosie pulled off the look. Everything about the exuberant woman was larger than life and made Isabelle feel dull and plain. Or maybe it was lingering thoughts of Zach that had her questioning her stick-straight pale locks cut into a no-nonsense, shoulder-length bob.

Isabelle forced herself away from Zach thoughts for the four millionth time that day to thinking that at the rate they were selling the festive holiday fabric, she'd have to order more soon. Santa patterns here. Holly patterns there. Reindeer patterns next to the Santa ones. A happy snowman print caught her eye, and she sighed as Zach's teasing gaze popped back into her mind. She'd not felt dull or plain when she'd been staring into those sparkly eyes. She'd felt … alive.

Not alive, she corrected herself. Annoyed. That was what she'd felt. Annoyed. Irritated. Livid. Prickly. *Breathless*.

Frustrated, she shoved the snowman fabric as far back

between the other bolts as it would go, not caring what order it was in, just proud that it could barely be seen. Maybe she'd nix snowman orders of any kind for the rest of the season.

"Oh, that one is perfect for what I'm looking for." Ruby rescued the hidden material.

Of course it was. Isabelle stepped back to give Ruby room to examine the fabric. In the process, she bumped against a holiday-themed sewing items display and knocked a few pieces to the floor. Stooping to pick up the dropped goodies, she realized what they were and fought screaming. Seriously? Of everything in the shop, she'd hit the silly snowman pincushions Sophie had been so tickled with when she'd unboxed them.

Mumbling under her breath, Isabelle stewed. Would the ladies notice if she opened one of the plastic packages and took out her frustrations on one of the smiling fellow's round bellies with as many stray pins as she could find? She wished she'd never read that joke at Lou's. Or ran into her own personal abdominal—um, make that abominable— snowman.

"I knew the first time my Andrew brought Cole over that that young man was a good one." Ruby brushed her fingertips over the cotton blend as she unwound the fabric bolt to better see the pattern.

Isabelle swore the merry snowmen were taunting her.

"Agreed." Maybelle gave her verdict, and the ladies sang more of Sophie's fiancé's virtues.

Initially, Isabelle hadn't been convinced, but Cole had won her over. Now, Isabelle trusted him with Sophie's future happiness and well-being. Mostly. She'd keep vigilance on protecting her impulsive sister long after Sophie had walked down the aisle. Ha, she'd likely still be slaying dragons on Sophie's behalf when they were Butterfly-aged. It was what she'd always done to protect her prone-to-getting-into-situations younger sister.

Rising from where she'd gathered the snowman pincushions, Isabelle slid the packages onto their metal hooks, repeatedly glancing toward the EMPLOYEES ONLY door at the back of the shop. What was taking Sophie and Aunt Claudia so long? All they'd had to do was slip the dress over Sophie's head and zip the zipper.

With a Butterfly-made pink quilt draped over her shoulder, Sarah cooed at the five-month-old baby she nursed. "I can't wait to have this little sweetie's picture made with Santa Cole. Bodie and I will treasure pulling it out to display each Christmas."

"Of course you will. Now, finish feeding my god-granddaughter so I can love on my Jeannie May," Maybelle pointed out, pursing her lips and giving Sarah an expectant look.

Sarah had named her daughter after her belated Aunt Jean and Maybelle. Maybelle and Jean had been best friends right up until Sarah's aunt had passed from pneumonia a few years back. Maybelle and the Butterflies had taken Sarah under their wings and were doing the same with Jeannie. Ha, the ladies seemed to have the entire town under their matronly wings. Thank goodness Isabelle managed, for the most part, to stay on the outskirts of their good-intentioned, but interfering, ways.

"What makes you think you get to hold Jeannie first?" Rosie frowned at Maybelle, flashing her diamond as her hand went to her hips.

"That cutie pie doesn't want to look at your Jack Frost-colored hair right after she eats."

"*Humph*." Rosie gave Maybelle a down-her-nose sneer. "I'm like a Rockefeller Center Christmas tree with a beautiful blue star on top and you're that pitiful one branch, no leaves twig from that seventies dog cartoon." She batted her long lashes. "Of course, Jeannie prefers me."

"Rosie's got a few cobwebs in that tree she's comparing herself to, as well," Ruby teased, still eyeing the snowman fabric that Isabelle wished she'd hurry and put back on the rack.

The fabric wasn't even of the abominable snowman, so it shouldn't remind her of Zach. He looked nothing like a rounded snowman, not with his chiseled jaw, dimpled cheeks, broad shoulders, and those abs ... ugh. *No more Zach thoughts.*

Isabelle added NO MORE ZACH THOUGHTS to her to-do list, then crossed it off. There. She was so over thinking about him.

"Sarah, tell old blue there how you chose me as Jeannie May's godmother."

"Sophie revamped Cole's Santa suit. It looks and feels real with the new padding, and she's gotten really good with doing his face and wig." Isabelle rushed to distract the two women from their lifelong bickering habit.

For as long as she could remember, Rosie and Maybelle had been exchanging barbs, with the other two Butterflies often egging them on. Yet, without a doubt, they loved each other. Theirs was a friendship that had lasted, and would continue to last, a lifetime. Still, Isabelle wasn't risking a Butterfly smackdown in the quilt shop. She could just imagine fabric and thread flying every which way. Not that she'd mind the snowman material being shredded.

"Sophie has an artistic gift. It's part of what makes your quilt shop so successful, your business acumen and her creativity." Giving Rosie one last glare, Maybelle put the MERRY CHRISTMAS towel back on the shelf. "Cole gets a big kick out of being Santa for the kids."

"Cole knows it's better to give than to receive." Ruby finally tucked the snowman fabric onto the rack and pulled out a reindeer print. "From the moment he moved to Pine Hill, he's been a giver. That's why he and Andrew get along so well. Two birds of a feather."

A commotion sounded from the back of the shop. Peeking through the doorway, Aunt Claudia cleared her throat, then made a drumroll sound. "Ladies and Butterflies, I present to you the loveliest of brides wearing a one-of-a-kind gown."

Smiling so big she looked as if she might burst with joy, Sophie stepped through the door and floated into the quilt shop. A vision in antique white satin and lace, she stopped in front of a Christmas tree decorated with big red bows and various sewing items for sale and turned to three-sixty showcase her mermaid-style dress. When she faced them again, her gaze met Isabelle's, obviously wanting reassurance that she wasn't imagining the dress's exquisiteness.

Isabelle's eyes watered. "Oh, Sophie, you look beautiful."

"This dress makes me feel beautiful." Sophie lifted the hem, revealing a thin underlayer of fluff. "See the adorable butterflies in the lace's pattern? It's perfection."

The women glowed at the compliment and converged on the bride-to-be.

"It's going to be." Maybelle moved in for a closer look, turning Sophie. "It's not finished yet."

"Just wait until we get the remainder of the lace and pearls attached," Aunt Claudia said. Maybelle had overseen the making of the gown, but Aunt Claudia had been the one to assure the design was the way Sophie described her fantasy dress.

"You're going to be the talk of the town," Ruby promised, her expression dreamy.

Rosie tugged at the zipper seam to make sure there was no give. "I still think you should have worn my wedding dress as your something borrowed."

"Right." Maybelle rolled her eyes heavenward. "As if anyone wants to wear the wedding dress an old clown wore a year ago in her circus-act ceremony."

Aunt Claudia cackled as she studied Sophie. "She could have borrowed your hair for her something blue."

Isabelle suppressed a giggle, as did Ruby, Sarah, and Sophie, based on how their hands covered their mouths.

"Don't mind Rosie. She can't stand not being the center of attention. That's why she keeps offering her dress." Maybelle measured various points on the back of the dress. "Mark down twenty inches. Rosie's wedding is last year's old news. *Old* being the key word."

"You're just jealous because you couldn't convince John

to marry you if you got down on one knee and begged him." As she spouted her accusation about the gentleman Maybelle had been spotted around town with over the past year, Rosie made a note on a clipboard while the others fluttered around Sophie.

"If any of us got down on one knee, we might never get back up." Ruby slapped her thigh. "You thinking about marrying John, Maybelle?"

Maybelle gave a horrified look. "Absolutely not. I'm a once and done bride. My Robert was the love of my life. John is a good friend whom I go to dinner with when I'm not busy with one of our projects or helping Rosie look for her reading glasses yet again."

"If that was a dig at my age, might I remind you that I'm not as old as you?" Rosie asked.

Isabelle wasn't sure of what the real age difference between the women was, but Rosie frequently let it be known that she was younger than Maybelle.

"No worries, Rosie. Nothing is ever going to outdo your wedding last Christmas." Isabelle smiled at the blue-haired newlywed. "I mean, an ice-skating rink and snowman building at a wedding reception? That'll be impossible to top."

Isabelle immediately had to kick the thought of making a six-pack snowman out of her head. Crossed off her list or not, Zach's flirty grin popped into her head, and she fought frowning. Why wouldn't he stay out of her thoughts?

"Isn't this just the best dress ever?" Sophie's happy sigh drew everyone's attention.

Watching Sophie turn, her smile so brilliant she outshone the angel topper on the Christmas tree behind her, Isabelle embraced her sister's happiness. *This*, she thought. Seeing her sister happy. That was why she'd moved back to Pine Hill. Sophie had the best heart and deserved every good thing. Isabelle intended to make sure she had it and that her wedding was everything Sophie had ever dreamed.

"Yes, I do believe it is." Aunt Claudia's eyes filled with pride, then she turned to Isabelle. "Just as your maid of honor dress will be. Don't think we've forgotten that we're in charge of making it, too."

Isabelle had insisted the women finish Sophie's gown first. What Isabelle wore wasn't important. She could always find something that would work in a pinch.

"I just appreciate that Sophie isn't going with Rosie's ugly Christmas sweater bridesmaid dresses." Isabelle's reminder earned glares from Maybelle, Claudia, and Ruby.

Rosie had made sure her bridesmaids hadn't overshadowed her. Sophie seemed to want the opposite, insisting that Isabelle's gown be glamorous, whimsical, and feminine. Her sister should know that she preferred practical. As silly as some of the things had been, Rosie's wedding had been special in so many ways, not the least of which was that Cole had proposed to Sophie there.

"The whole fiasco was more like a three-ring circus than a wedding," Maybelle grumbled, moving the measuring tape over a smidge. "Poor Lou. You know the man wonders what possessed him to marry our Rosie."

"No one asked you." Rosie lifted her chin. "Lou is a very happily married man who wakes up to every day feeling like Christmas morning thanks to our perfect wedding."

"Your perfect mess, you mean." Maybelle snorted. "The man thought he was getting sugarplums and instead he got lumps of coal."

Coal. Zach's grin danced through Isabelle's mind again and she swallowed.

"My wedding is going to be a simple Christmas ceremony at Pine Hill Church." Sophie's face glowed. "I want the whole world to know Cole is mine, but for our vows, it'll just be us and close family and friends with Sarah's dad officiating."

"Oh, the world knows. Anyone who sees that man around you knows he's all yours." Aunt Claudia's face expressed approval as she made another mark on the clipboard where they were making notes about the dress.

Isabelle agreed that anyone who saw them together would know how Cole felt. How they both felt. Cole loved Sophie, and her sister was all twinkly lights whenever he was near.

"Fifty years together and everyone who sees us knows my Charles is mine, too." Ruby beamed. "He looks at me the same way and I just adore looking right back. He's such a wonderful man."

Rosie made a gagging sound, then pointed to an area just beneath Sophie's waist. "The back needs pearly sequins, ladies. A row added right there on both sides. A few pearls, too, the luxurious tiny ones, and it'll be perfect. Not as perfect as my dress, mind you, but close."

"Nonsense." Maybelle frowned as she studied the gown's back. "What we have planned is just the right amount to catch the light and add a hint of sparkle without being *gaudy.*"

"We don't want to shadow Sophie's inner glow." Ruby studied the dress back.

"As if you could." Isabelle smiled as she caught her sister's eye. "Sophie doesn't need artificial shine. She sparkles from the inside out."

It was one of the things she loved most about her sister. Sophie found joy in everything. Her pureness of heart never saw the negative in anyone or anything.

Sophie just smiled. Then, with a gush of pre-wedding emotions, her eyes watered. "I'm so grateful to each of you for all you're doing to make my wedding so special."

"Then stop your crying," Isabelle ordered, not able to stand Sophie's tears.

She'd never been able to and did whatever was needed to put the joy back onto Sophie's face.

"Sorry, I'm happy, it's just…" Sophie's voice trailed off and she sniffled.

Isabelle's stomach plummeted. Was something wrong? Had Cole said or done something that was making her sister have second thoughts? She struggled to believe it, but something sure had Sophie upset.

"Just?" Maybelle prompted.

"All of this is wonderful," Sophie began, a trembly forced smile marring her lovely face. "A dream come true. I've so much to be thankful for, and feel guilty for wanting more, only—" She hesitantly looked Isabelle's way. "As wonderful as everything is, the day won't be complete without Daddy to walk me down the aisle."

A strangled cry clawed its way free from Isabelle's throat.

Of all the things she might have guessed Sophie would say, wanting the father they hadn't seen in over twenty years to walk her down the aisle hadn't been one of them.

"You can't let that man ruin your wedding day," Isabelle urged.

Their father had already ruined enough of their days when they'd been children and unable to do anything about it. Long ago, Isabelle had determined to take that power away from him and had never looked back. If only tender-hearted Sophie could do the same.

The others in the room averted their gazes, even Maybelle, who usually had no qualms at tackling awkward situations. Isabelle couldn't imagine a more awkward situation than one involving Cliff Davis. The man was a menace to all things good. No wonder the usually chatty women were silent.

"It's just … I wish Daddy could be there." Sophie swiped at a tear that ran down her cheek before it could drip onto her dress. "I know you think I'm silly, but what little girl doesn't dream of having her father escort her down the aisle to her Prince Charming?"

"Little girls whose father walked away from his wife and two young daughters." Isabelle battled the urge to wrap her arms around her sister to hold her the way she had when Sophie cried when they'd been small. She also fought walking out of the shop to scream so loudly it shook the garland wreaths right off the courthouse windows. She and Sophie had very different takes on their father. For all Isabelle cared, he could stay gone.

"Don't you ever wonder where he is and what he's doing?" Sophie's brown eyes glistened.

"No." Isabelle rarely thought about their father and when she did, it was never in any way good. Her thoughts ran more along the lines of what she'd like to do to him for how he'd abandoned their family and caused so much pain to her sister and mother.

"I'd do anything if he could be at my wedding. I've always prayed he'd come home and believed he someday would. Wouldn't that just be the perfect Christmas miracle?" Sophie gave a wobbly smile. "For Daddy to be at my wedding to walk me down the aisle to Cole? Oh, Isabelle, can you imagine how wonderful that would be?"

Wonderful? It would be a nightmare. Isabelle fought making a gagging sound similar to the one Rosie had made earlier.

"He's been gone over twenty years, Sophie. Twenty. Years." She stressed the words, because Sophie was acting as if their father had just left last month and might pop back into town at any moment. "His showing up for your wedding isn't something Santa can just stuff in his bag and deliver to you."

Sophie's lower lip went out, more in quivery disappointment than a pout. Guilt hit, but before Isabelle could say anything, Maybelle did what she did best and took charge.

"That's a nice thought, Sophie. Now, let's get you out of this dress before it gets stained. Plus, much to my disappointment about not getting to smooch on my Jeannie May this evening, Sarah needs to get home. She's got to get ready for the special tree decorating at Hamilton House in honor of our little darling this Friday evening."

"Come on, Sophie," Rosie jumped in. "Claudia, Ruby, and I will help you get out of your wedding gown. Maybelle, you come, too, in case we need to make note of any last minute needed tweaks."

Hands shaking, Isabelle fiddled with a bin of on-sale button packets, straightening the display. Were the Butterflies rushing Sophie off because they thought she had been too harsh? She normally indulged Sophie's every whim, just not when it came to their father or the military. It was why Isabelle had little to do with the local Quilts of Valor Foundation group that Sophie headed. The less Isabelle had to do with anything military, the better.

When the Butterflies and her sister disappeared to the back room, Isabelle met Sarah's empathetic gaze and winced. "You think I'm terrible?"

Cradling Jeannie, Sarah shook her head. "No, I think you love Sophie with all your heart and truly believe what you said."

Sarah's comment eased the guilt at how deflated Sophie had looked when the Butterflies led her to the back. Sophie would realize Isabelle was right, that Cliff Davis had no place at her wedding, much less deserved the honor of walking her down the aisle. *Surely.*

Sarah propped Jeannie onto her shoulder. "I also know that you're going to do it."

Isabelle frowned. "Do what?"

"Give Sophie her Christmas miracle." Sarah's gaze didn't waver. "You saw how much it means to her, just as the rest of us did. You have to find your father."

No, Isabelle really didn't have to do that.

But rather than point that out, she exhaled the breath she hadn't realized she'd been holding. Heaviness weighed on her shoulders. "How would you propose I do that? Call the North Pole and tell Santa my sister has been extra good this year and needs Daddy home for her wedding?"

"Or you could talk to Bodie."

"You think the sheriff's department will track down a man who willingly left his family over twenty years ago?" Isabelle shook her head. "I don't think so."

Sarah kissed the baby's temple. "I doubt it, too, but if you wanted to find your father, Bodie may be able to help. When he first came to Pine Hill, he never intended to stay, but had planned to work for his friend Lukas's company, iSecure. They specialize in everything to do with security and all kinds of secretive stuff. If anyone can track down what happened to your father, it's them. Plus, Bodie has a friend who—"

"Our father has known where we are all along." Isabelle was not going to hunt for her father, not even for Sophie. "He hasn't come back. He doesn't want to be found. He forgot us a long time ago."

"You don't know where his mind has been," Sarah gently reminded, patting her baby's back.

Isabelle snorted. "I think it's safe to say not with his wife and two daughters or he wouldn't have left us."

"Maybe he wanted to come home but didn't know how or if y'all would welcome him home. Maybe he's just been waiting for a sign. Give him one."

Sarah was as bad as Sophie. They both saw the world

through their bright and shiny Christmas-goodness goggles. Santa probably struggled to know which of their names to put at the top of his nice list each year and ended up with them in a perpetual tie.

"I'm not tracking down my father, Sarah. Not even for Sophie." Not even if it meant being left off Santa's list. "Let's talk about this weekend. What can I do to help with the Christmas tree decorating at Hamilton House?"

As HAMILTON HOUSE'S front door opened, Zach jumped up from where he checked light strings on the living room floor. Before he'd left for his shift at the sherriff's department, Bodie had asked Zach to make sure all the bulbs worked.

"Down, Harry," Sarah told the Australian shepherd-blue heeler mix that bounced all around her in a voice so gentle she could have been talking to the baby she carried. She used her hip to push the heavy wooden door closed, shaking the already-in-place outdoor Christmas wreath against its beveled glass center. "Just a sec, and I'll let you have a peek at your favorite person in the whole world."

She bent enough for Harry to have a gentle nuzzle of his snout against the baby's cheek. Jeannie responded by making a gurgling sound, then happily stuck her middle and ring fingers into her tiny mouth.

"Satisfied that I brought her back safely?" Laughing, Sarah straightened from having let Harry see her daughter.

Apparently, the dog was satisfied as he let out a yelp.

"Hey," Zach greeted, admiring how protective Harry was

with Jeannie and how great Sarah was with including the dog, even when her arms were full. Had she brought anything home that needed unloading from her car still? "Can I help you?"

Sarah gave him a bright smile, the kind that made Zach feel truly welcome in her and Bodie's home. He liked that meeting Sarah in person had lived up to the person he'd imagined from Bodie's phone descriptions.

"Oh, that would be great. Here. Hold Jeannie while I love on Harry a minute."

Not what Zach had in mind, but Sarah had already shoved the baby at him and was crouched before he realized what was happening. Panic hit that he was holding a baby. His urge was to grasp her as tightly as he could, to make sure he didn't drop her. She was too fragile for that, so he just stood frozen.

"Who's a good boy?" Sarah scratched Harry behind the ears and nuzzled her face against his. "Harry is, that's who's a good boy. The best. You're such a good big brother to our sweet Jeannie. Yes, you are. Did your daddy leave you here to keep Zach company while he was at work tonight, keeping Pine Hill safe?"

His entire body focused on the baby in his hands, Zach suspected that was exactly what his friend had done when he'd realized Zach would be at the house alone. The bed-and-breakfast had been full the night before, but everyone had checked out earlier that day and the next guests wouldn't arrive until the following morning.

With the awkward way he gripped Jeannie's middle, her tiny legs wiggled back and forth from where they dangled in his outstretched reach. Her big blue eyes stared at him with forgiving wonder, and he'd swear she'd just batted her long lashes and given him a gummy smile. Warmth spread through Zach with the same force as if he'd been awarded a Medal of Honor. Cute kid, but that didn't mean he wanted to hold her.

He didn't want to hold her. Sure, he smiled back at her from a safe distance, but that wasn't the same thing as having someone so tiny and fragile within his palms. *What if his hand failed and he dropped Jeannie?*

"She's not going to bite you."

Nervous to take his eyes off the baby, Zach hesitated to look toward where Sarah loved on Harry. "Because she doesn't have teeth?"

Sarah laughed. Standing, she moved next to him. He assumed she planned to take the baby, because she really should. The sooner, the better. Instead, she began teaching Baby Holding 101, as if he needed to add that skill to his arsenal.

"Here, move your hands like this and put her against your body like that," she instructed in a firm, and yet somehow gentle, voice.

"You should take her." He pushed the baby toward her, but Sarah shook her head.

"You offered, and I really need you to watch her while I run to the bathroom."

Zach winced. It wasn't as if he could insist that she bring the baby into the bathroom with her. Well, he could, but what kind of houseguest would he be if he did that when she and Bodie had taken him in during his *vacation?*

"Fine. Go," he mumbled, thinking he liked held-out-away-from-him Jeannie better than close-against-his-chest-warm-and-snuggly Jeannie. Still, she was safer in his arms than in his palms. "Hurry."

"Of course." Sarah's tone had Zach wondering just how long her daughter was going to be stuck with him.

He took a deep breath, then eyed the poor baby. Not that Jeannie seemed to mind his awkwardness. She just stared up at him with her much-too-trusting eyes.

"Looks like it's just you and me, kid."

She blinked.

Okay. He could do this long enough for Sarah to run to the bathroom. No big deal. But when he just stood there, hoping he didn't drop or break her, her heightening-in-color face crinkled.

"Uh, don't do that," he begged. "Your mom will be back soon." *He hoped.* "We don't want her wondering why you're all red-faced and unhappy."

At his voice, the quivering stilled. But apparently, she wanted him to keep talking because when he didn't, her lower lip went out into the world's most heart-wrenching pout. Nervousness grew in Zach's belly. What did a burly soldier say to a five-month-old?

"You have a good mom and dad."

Jeannie's lower lip retreated a bit and her blue eyes stared up at him expectantly. Okay, he needed to keep talking. Anything. *Just talk.*

"Your dad was one of the baddest soldiers I was ever privileged to serve with, and I mean that in the best, most complimentary way. We'd been on a search and rescue when our company was surrounded. There wasn't a way out. We all knew it was likely our end and it's nothing short of a miracle that we survived. There's no one else in the world I'd rather have had by my side that day than your dad, Lukas, Matt, and Riley."

Jeannie made a noise that might have been a happy coo. *Keep talking, Zach. Just keep talking.*

"Lukas got out and started iSecure. He's made a fortune catering to the rich and famous, and who knows how many governments' security needs? Me? I'd do anything if I could get medical clearance to reenlist. Or, currently, get back to work for iSecure. One little blackout spell and Lukas decides I can't take on any new assignments until January because I need a vacation. I thought the spells were gone. I hadn't had one since prior to going to work for Lukas, but maybe not?" He sighed. "Can't say I blame him, since Doc says I have to go thirty days without another spell before I can drive."

That one hurt. Big time. For months, he'd been incapacitated and not able to do for himself. Numerous surgeries and painful hours of therapy had helped him get some semblance of his life back. Not the military life he craved, but he enjoyed his work at iSecure. Jeannie gurgled something and Zach drudged on, saying whatever popped into his head. The kid liked being talked to. He was a highly trained soldier. He could do anything for a few minutes to get a job done.

"Your mom is a good cook. Those cookies I pilfered out of the kitchen are worth you growing in your teeth." Growing in her teeth? Was that what babies did? Why didn't he know these things? It wasn't as if he thought Santa delivered a full set of incisors and molars on one's first Christmas. "She makes a mean beef stew, too, but since that's for the guests tomorrow, we won't mention how the container may be two bowls short of where it started."

Harry gave a yelp, as if agreeing on the tastiness of the soup he'd shared a little of. Or maybe the dog was warning him they both should stay out of the stew? Keeping a tight hold around Jeannie, Zach glanced at where the dog eyed him. Shared soup or not, Harry was ready to leap to action should Zach do a single thing wrong with the baby. If he headed toward the door with Jeannie in tow, he suspected he'd be fighting for his life.

"Good dog," he praised and meant it, grateful Jeannie would grow up with Harry to keep a watchful eye. Zach would have given the dog a pat, but both hands were full of baby. He wasn't loosening his grip in case Jeannie decided to give an unexpected jolt. Plus, he probably should wait until Jeannie was safely back in her mother's arms prior to petting the on-alert dog. "In addition to having a good mom and dad, you've got a great dog. Harry is one smart guy."

The dog gave a single bark that sounded a lot like, *Yep*.

Knowing he needed to keep talking as every time he got quiet for more than a few seconds Jeannie's lip went out, Zach rambled on, mentioning the weather when he could think of nothing else to say. Of course, that led to him saying how windy the day had been, and that led to Blondie, aka Isabelle Davis.

"I don't think she liked me very much," he told the baby, deciding she was a decent listener when she stuck two fingers in her mouth and happily began sucking them, all the while keeping her eyes trained on Zach. "Maybe you could use some of your baby magic and put in a good word for me at your Christmas tree decorating party."

"Who?"

Had Sarah purposely snuck up on him to check out how his babysitting gig was going? Even if she had, how had he missed her presence? That he had made his right temple pound. He'd always prided himself on being completely aware of his surroundings. Maybe he was having more of a head trauma relapse than he wanted to admit.

"I was talking with Jeannie about the wind." He thrust the baby toward her.

"You were asking Jeannie to put in a good word for you with the wind?" Sarah wasn't buying his cover.

No wonder. But she did take Jeannie. Giving her back had him feeling off-kilter, which was odd since holding her had felt so strange.

"Doesn't the wind whisper into every woman's ear?" he said flippantly, while debating whether he wanted to discuss Isabelle.

Would Sarah point out that he'd only be there for a week and should stay away from her friend if he admitted that he found Isabelle fascinating?

Sarah shifted the baby in her arms to where now both she and Jeannie stared at him. "But you're hoping the wind whispers into one particular woman's ear?"

Why not tell her? It wasn't as if he'd hid his interest when he'd seen Isabelle at Lou's, nor did he expect Bodie not to mention the run-in to his wife. He doubted his brother-in-arms kept anything from Sarah. There might be a few things he hadn't told her for her own protection, but he'd guess Sarah knew more about his friend than anyone. The evidence was in how they looked at each other.

"I met someone today." At Sarah's interested and lack of horrified look, he continued, "The wind blew us together. Or, more accurately, blew her wedding checklist to me from across the courthouse."

Sarah's eyes widened. "You met Isabelle?"

"You guessed who I meant based upon a wedding checklist?" His stomach knotted with a similar intensity as it had when Sarah had handed him the baby.

Sarah laughed. "It doesn't take your background to figure that one out. You mentioned the courthouse. Isabelle works across the street and is the ultimate list maker."

Impressed, he nodded. "I bumped into her again at Lou's when Bodie and I ate lunch. By the way, Bodie said to tell you that Lou sent goodies for you and that he left them in the fridge."

"Yum. Now, tell me more about meeting Isabelle."

"There's not much to tell. She didn't seem keen on our being friends."

"She wouldn't." Sarah hugged Jeannie closer and kissed her cheek. "But obviously you were."

There was no denying it. If he hadn't been, he wouldn't have brought her up to a five-month-old and her doting mother.

"It's just as well she wasn't interested. I'll only be here a week." He was positive Isabelle wasn't the type of girl to knowingly go into a relationship destined to only last a few days. Relationship? He wasn't the type to knowingly go into a relationship, period.

Sarah eyed him, then gave a smile that made him as nervous as holding her baby had. "There's no reason you can't stay longer than a week, Zach. You're off work until the new year. Bodie and I both want you to stay. Jeannie, too. Isn't that right?" She glanced at the baby as if she expected an answer and wouldn't you know, Jeannie cooed, making Sarah smile before returning her gaze to him. "See? She adores you. The timing couldn't be better as there's not anyone coming to stay in our Beds for Vets suite until January. The room is yours until she arrives. Please stay."

"I can't." Clamminess coated Zach's skin. His gut instinct said he should get out of Pine Hill as quickly as he could, while he still could.

"Why not? Bodie said you weren't going to your family's, but just headed to the Keys for some deep-sea fishing with Matt. Fishing over Thanksgiving and Christmas?" Her nose wrinkled as if that was the worst idea ever. "Seriously, who does that?"

Not him, but he'd thought to give it a go since his bachelor buddy had a boat he kept docked there and had invited him down for some single bro time on the water. Zach had thought it a good idea to not linger at any of his friends' places too long. He'd considered visiting his parents, but he'd dismissed the idea almost as quickly as it occurred. If this vacation was supposed to de-stress him, he definitely needed to stay away from Atlanta.

"Why not spend the holidays with us?" With a determined look, Sarah lifted her chin. "You've a much better chance of a white Christmas here than in the Keys."

"Sand's white."

Sarah frowned.

"I can't stay, Sarah, but thanks for the offer."

"You keep saying you can't, but you can." She glanced down at the gurgling baby in her arms, then back up at him with a resilient look. "And you are. I insist upon it. You deserve a magical Christmas surrounded by friends who love you, and you've come to the right place."

Zac started to point out that Bodie was his only friend in Pine Hill, but that wasn't the case. Apparently, any friend of Bodie's was a friend of Sarah's. Bodie had been partially right about the folks in Pine Hill treating you as if you were long-lost family. Sarah sure did. Isabelle, on the other hand...

"I'll think about it," he promised.

He would, but he'd leave as planned. Amongst his other reasons, he didn't want to intrude on Bodie and Sarah's first Christmas with their daughter.

Besides, he didn't believe in magical Christmases, much less deserve one.

Chapter Three

Visiting at Hamilton House, Isabelle arranged Christmas tree cookies on a tray on the kitchen's island countertop, admiring the colorful icing and containers of candy decorations as she summoned the question that had burned in her mind all week.

"So, that thing we were talking about Tuesday evening. Do you really think Bodie could find my father?"

Sarah turned from where she pulled mini poppyseed ham sandwiches from the oven. "Yes, but even better, Bodie has a friend visiting who works for iSecure." Sarah paused to spatula the sandwiches onto the large Santa serving platter. "He's a computer genius. He sure helped me set up my embroidery program fast right after he arrived at Hamilton House. I bet he'd love to help find your father."

Isabelle was glad someone would love finding Cliff Davis. She wasn't looking forward to the effort. Why, why, why did Sophie want their father at her wedding, much less to walk her down the aisle? Isabelle wondered for the thousandth time since Sophie's dress fitting. As horrific as she found the idea of searching for the man who'd abandoned them, the tear that had run down her sister's cheek haunted Isabelle.

Between that and the buff stranger with the awful pickup lines, Isabelle had slept very little. She'd barely done anything that one or the other wasn't weighing on her mind. Stupid laughing man. Stupid runaway father. Stupid cookie she'd just accidentally broken and now had to eat to cover up the evidence. She poked a piece of the tree cookie into her mouth, letting the sugary sweetness comfort her. What if Sarah had been right and, by some miracle, Isabelle could arrange for her father to escort Sophie down the aisle? If that would make Sophie happy, and their mom was okay with it, then Isabelle would suck up all her misgivings. As far as their mom, she didn't plan to mention it to her until she knew whether finding Cliff Davis was even a possibility. Why bring up past hurts if she didn't have to?

Sarah rinsed off the now empty baking pan. "Plus, Zach really needs something to occupy his time while Bodie's at work."

"Zach?" The name clicked and, heart pounding, Isabelle blamed her lack of sleep for not putting two and two together sooner. "As in six foot plus, solid wall of muscles, laughing hazel eyes with melted gold flecks, hair too long, gorgeous Zach Dawson?"

Sarah turned from the sink, an amused look on her face. "That's not exactly how I'd describe him, but yes, Zach Dawson."

"Yeah, well, I'd rather him not be who helps track down my father." Why did the idea of Mr. Annoying knowing her most humiliating and hurtful childhood memory bother her so much? The last thing she wanted was *him* prying into her past.

Drying the pan, then sliding it into a cabinet, Sarah arched a brow. "Am I missing something? Why would you turn down help to make Sophie's wedding dreams come true?"

"I'd rather not talk to someone I don't know about my father."

"You should at least consider." Sarah surveyed the smorgasbord of goodies on display for her guests. "With his past, Zach probably understands your father better than most."

"He's military?" Of course he was. No wonder all the warning bells had clanged when she'd first looked up into his laughing eyes. His army T-shirt had been his own prideful patriotism, not a family member's.

Sarah nodded. "He's staying in our Beds for Vets suite. We're honored to have him visit."

"He's here to rehab?" The suite was for helping veterans get back on their feet when they returned to civilian life.

"Bodie and Zach have been friends for a long time. Zach's here to visit." But even as Sarah said it, Isabelle knew there was more. "He went to work for iSecure after injuries prevented him from continuing in the army. He's been with the company just over a year."

Zach had been hurt? Why did that knot her belly?

"He didn't look like anything was wrong with him." He'd looked strong, healthy, full of life—*Thank God*. But only *thank God* because Isabelle didn't wish ill upon anyone. Not even *him*.

"Zach has worked hard to regain his strength and life." Sarah's soft tone conveyed deep empathy that likely had to do with Bodie's past. "Some injuries can't be seen."

Isabelle knew all about those injuries. The ones that couldn't be seen. She'd lived with them for the first part of her life.

"That's more reason for me to stay away from Zach. Maybe Bodie will help."

"Help with what?" Bodie asked, joining them in the kitchen with Jeannie in his arms.

Sarah filled her husband in while Bodie removed a teether from the refrigerator and handed it to the baby he held. Immediately, the blue-eyed cherub raised it to her mouth and began gumming the pink ring.

With every detail Sarah gave, Isabelle's stomach twisted tighter and tighter. "If we can't find him, Sophie will be devastated. I don't want that, not right before her wedding, so this has to be kept quiet. Who knows where our father is or what he's been doing? I refuse to let that man disappoint her again."

Jeannie waved the teether at her father, smiling up at Bodie.

He grinned at the baby, then, expression serious, met Isabelle's gaze. "That man being your father?"

"He wasn't much of a father. Not like you already are."

"Sarah makes it easy." Bodie shot an appreciative look toward his wife, who kissed his cheek, then went to check on her guests. "But not a day goes by that I don't question my ability to do a good job raising our daughter. Sometimes the demons one battles in one's head convinces a person that the best thing for his family is for him to stay away. Those demons make it easy to believe that they are better off without you being in the picture."

"You sound as if you're speaking from experience." Isabelle didn't buy that her father's decision to leave had been anything other than selfishness.

He hadn't been thinking about his wife or two young daughters when he'd skipped town.

"I am. Make no mistake, I'd always do what's best for my wife and child, no matter the cost to myself." The steely look that came into Bodie's eyes assured there was nothing he wouldn't do to protect them.

"You wouldn't leave them." Isabelle knew she spoke the truth.

"Never that my being with them wasn't putting them in harm's way. If it did"—his hold on Jeannie tightened, causing the baby to glance up as he took a deep breath—"if it did, then I'd do whatever was necessary to keep my family safe."

Bodie was the type of man who would always do the right thing. Leaving his family would never be that. He didn't understand the difference in her father's abandonment and what he was describing. "You would, but that isn't my father."

"You'd know better than me."

Isabelle did know. Painfully so.

Bodie's gaze went beyond her to whomever had entered the kitchen, then back to Isabelle. "You want to find your father? Sarah just returned with the perfect guy."

"Don't believe a word he says about me, Blondie."

Isabelle had known who he was looking at before Zach had said a word. The hairs on the back of her neck had alerted her that he was near, but she refused to acknowledge his comment.

She focused on Bodie. "I prefer you or a professional. I recall meeting Lukas and his family at your wedding. I'd like to hire his company."

Bodie didn't look sure. "No offense, but I'm not sure you can afford iSecure. On the low end you'd be looking at..." He told her an amount more than what she made in three months.

She winced. "That much?"

Sarah took Jeannie from Bodie. "It's so lucky that one of iSecure's top guys is in Pine Hill and willing to help you."

Isabelle had never shirked from uncomfortable situations. Usually, she was the one who dealt with them so that her mother and Sophie never had to. But she didn't want to talk to Zach about her father's abandonment. She didn't want to turn and come face-to-face with him again, either. She knew those hazel eyes would be more twinkly than all the gorgeous Christmas lights Sarah had strung around Hamilton House.

"Much as your ego might find it difficult to believe, we weren't discussing you." She avoided meeting Zach's gaze when he joined them at the kitchen island and stared directly at her.

"Actually, we were," Bodie reminded and Isabelle's face heated.

Oops. They had been.

Zach grinned. "Oh? What were you saying? Asking for my phone number or just wanting to know all my deepest, darkest secrets?"

If only. Instead, she was about to tell him hers.

"BODIE THOUGHT YOU might be able to find someone for me."

"No need to look any further. I'm right here." Zach waggled his brows.

He'd caught a glimpse of Isabelle earlier when she'd first arrived, but she'd immediately disappeared into the kitchen with Sarah. He'd wanted to follow her, but Lukas had called. Due to the noisy party festivities and Christmas music playing in the background, Zach had headed to his room.

Lukas had just been checking on him. When he'd come back downstairs, Harry had wanted to go out and thought Zach was just the guy to take him. Not that Zach minded. Crowded parties for Christmas tree decorating weren't exactly his thing. Hadn't his mother just arranged for some interior decorator to spiff up the house to a magazine replica of whatever was the latest Christmas fad? Zach sure couldn't recall tree decorating parties or the loving way Sarah displayed her aunt's antique ornaments.

Isabelle shot Sarah a see-what-I-mean look, then toyed with her sweater's zipper. "Not interested."

Bodie snorted, then nudged Zach's arm. "On that note, Sarah and I are going to leave you two to discuss this while we go find the Fruit flies. I imagine they're cooking up some holiday mischief and need to be reined in before they get out of control."

Fruit flies? Oh, yeah, Sarah's group of old-lady friends. Bodie was always calling them by some insect name. Earlier in the week he'd called them hornets, then gnats. The one

Zach had met at Lou's seemed harmless enough, more like a blue ladybug if he'd had to give an insect name.

Sarah smiled, then the trio left the kitchen, leaving Zach alone with Isabelle. Her color heightened, her pulse pounded at her throat, and she was going to rip that zipper tab off any moment if she didn't quit jerking it back and forth.

He grinned. "I can tell you're excited to see me again."

At Sarah's advice, he'd held off on going to the quilt shop, but Tuesday seemed longer than three days ago. Finally, Isabelle's gaze lifted, blue fire sparking with annoyance.

"Is that what you call the sudden urge to be ill? Excitement?"

Zach laughed. "When are you going to admit that you like me, Blondie?"

"I asked you not to call me that." She gave him one of her pinched-face scowls. "As for the other, I'll tell you what ... you just hold your breath until it happens."

"That bad, eh?"

Eyes still narrowed, she sighed. "If you'll excuse me, I'm off to find my sister."

That same sinking feeling hit that had when she'd driven away from the square. Just as she stepped into the large rectangular foyer in the middle of Hamilton House, Zach reached for her hand, momentarily staying her.

"Wait." Electricity flared where their skin touched.

Not so long ago his hand had been dead, unable to move or feel. How sad if he'd never experienced the zings coursing through him?

Her gaze dropped to where he held her, and he wondered if she felt it, too, or if his nerve endings were just misfiring from some missed piece of shrapnel still lodged near his spine. Taking a deep breath, she pulled free. He hadn't been holding tight, just enough to temporarily stay her. At the loss, he shoved his fingers into his jeans pocket to keep from reaching out again.

"Don't go. Please." Heart pounding all the way to his throat that their conversation wasn't going as he'd imagined a thousand times that week, that he didn't know when he'd see her again if she left Hamilton House, Zach latched onto the one thing that might give her pause. "What did you mean about me helping to find someone?"

Frustration flickered across her beautiful face. "It's nothing."

The tension pouring off her as she sucked in a deep breath said otherwise.

"I'll just ask Bodie," he pointed out, a bit in awe at how much he wanted to brush her hair away from her face and assure her that whatever had her wound tighter than the stripes on her candy cane sweater, he'd help. "You know he'll tell me. We're brothers." At her confused look, he added, "We served in the army together. He's my brother in every way that counts. Serving with someone, being willing to die next to them, for them, creates a bond every bit as strong as blood. Stronger in many cases."

Much stronger than the bond Zach shared with his blood relatives. They'd never understood him, and truthfully, he didn't understand them, either. He imagined the longer he stayed away, the happier they were.

Rather than respond, Isabelle looked around the Christmas-decorated foyer. Her gaze lingered on the thickly wrapped garland twisting around the curved staircase's railing. White lights twinkled from beneath the greenery, snow-covered pinecones, and silver ribbons. Matching garland and lights were strung over the oversized openings that led into the living room on the side opposite of them and, on the side where they stood, into a dining room that was as elaborately decorated as any his mother's decorators had ever done.

"Bodie probably will tell you since it's not necessarily a secret from anyone other than my mother and my sister and her fiancé. I'm looking for"—Isabelle's face scrunched—"my father."

The word was so tortured sounding that Zach's heart squeezed. "He's missing?"

Pink stained her cheeks. "For the past twenty years."

Zach studied the angle of her jaw, the way her fingers clenched and unclenched, the I-don't-care-about-this expression she was trying so hard to pull off—and failing. Bodie had said that her father left when Isabelle was young. What had Zach missed?

"That's a long time." Would she knee him if he hugged her? He wasn't a hugging kind of guy, but she sure looked as if she needed comforting, and his arms itched to hold her.

"Tell me about it." Her fingers curled into her palms. The skin stretched taut over her knuckles. "Or I guess it's me who will tell you, since Bodie believes you can track him down." Her blue eyes pierced him. "Can you?"

Pain shone even as her chin tilted upward. Zach took it all in—her tough bravado on the outside, the hurt that gripped her insides, and the sappy sensation in his chest.

"I need to know more." Not that he'd say no. He'd help her find her father. He'd go to the North Pole and drag Santa to Pine Hill if it was what he had to do to earn a smile from her.

"I figured you would." Glancing into the living area, she focused on a pretty brunette who practically bubbled as she chatted with a small group huddled around her in the open living room. A man came over, handed her a drink, then slid his arm possessively around her waist.

"Someone you know?"

"That's my sister and her fiancé."

Zach had figured as much. "The ones you don't want to know that you're searching for your father?"

"My only sister, my only sibling, and yes, Sophie can't know. Neither can Cole. He might tell Sophie."

Curious, Zach asked, "Why can't she know? Seems as if she'd want to know something like that."

As if she suddenly worried that he planned to clang a bell and announce it to the room, fear entered her eyes. "You can't tell her."

Nor would he, but her reaction stung.

"Why would I tell her? I don't know her."

Isabelle humphed. "If you're in Pine Hill very long, you will. Sophie's a friendly sort and wants to wrap the whole world in warm fuzzy happiness."

"Unlike you?" He'd meant the comment as a tease, something to ease the tension oozing from her every pore, but her face blotched.

"I'm friendly enough when I want to be friends with

someone."

"Point taken." There were too many people in Hamilton House to have a private conversation, unless they headed to his room, and he was one hundred percent she'd have him singing Christmas carols with the sopranos if he suggested they go there. "How about we meet for lunch tomorrow and you can tell me everything?"

Her blond hair swished back and forth. "I work on Saturdays."

"You were at Lou's on Tuesday, so you obviously take a break to eat at some point. But maybe Saturdays are too busy for breaks. Good news is that I'm an early riser." Always had been.

His mother used to say the sun wouldn't rise if he didn't make so much racket to awaken it. For a second, her image popped into his mind, and there she smiled at him. In reality, he hadn't seen her smile in years. Certainly not the last few times he'd gone home. Instead, sadness and tears filled her eyes when she looked at him.

"How about we meet for breakfast before you go to work?"

Isabelle's gaze narrowed. "You don't even know what time I have to be at work."

"Bodie told me that you and your sister run the quilt shop on the square. Thanks to Sarah, I've developed a deeper appreciation for those old quilts my grandmother made and how much work went into them."

Hopefully, his mother still had the one his granny had made him. He'd been thinking about it more and more lately, wishing he had it.

"You talked about me with Bodie? Why?"

Of everything he'd said, that was what she'd focused in on?

"Because…" Zach hesitated. "He witnessed my crash and burn at Lou's the other day. He said I didn't have a chance with you."

"He's right. You don't."

"Because I'm military?" He refused to say former. Once a soldier, always a soldier.

She hesitated long enough that Zach knew the wheels were turning in that intelligent mind of hers.

"Because you're you," she finally answered.

Same difference.

"Then, breakfast it is?" he asked, knowing that despite her protests, she needed him to find her father.

Her mouth opened, no doubt to shoot him down, but before anything came out, the bubbly brunette joined them.

"Carrie loved your suggestion for the Petdanas and wants to implement that change to our online marketing immediately." She turned to Zach and flashed a smile so bright he almost shielded his eyes. "Hi, I'm Sophie. Nice to meet you."

Although at first glance their features seemed opposite, Zach could see a strong resemblance. The big eyes, even though Sophie's were brown. But mostly it was that their facial structure was similar, with high cheekbones and full, wide mouths. Mouths that were curved in opposite directions.

"Zach Dawson." He shook her hand, unable to keep from comparing the kind warmth of Sophie's gesture with the electric bolts that had shot through him when he'd grabbed Isabelle's hand. As different as night and day. Zach always had preferred the night.

"You're a guest at Hamilton House?" Sophie's eyes were as sparkly as her blingy Rudolph sweater with its flashing red nose.

"I'm a friend of Bodie's. And Sarah's," he added, knowing it was true. "I'm visiting while on vacation."

"That's wonderful. Welcome to Pine Hill." Sophie's smile radiated her sincerity. "Any friend of theirs is a friend of ours, right, Izzy?"

"I, uh…" Isabelle stammered, her fingers tangled in her sweater hem.

"Izzy?" Zach teased, causing her eyes to jerk to his with more death daggers shining in their depths.

"Don't you even start with—"

Zach laughed, loving her fire. "No worries. I prefer Blondie."

ISABELLE CRINGED AT the nickname. Or maybe it was how Sophie's expression had upped its wattage at Zach's teasing.

"Blondie?" Her sister's curious gaze bounced back and forth between them. "You two have met before tonight?"

"I rescued her earlier this week," Zach bragged, hooking his thumbs into his jeans pocket and looking as proud as if he'd single-handedly saved Christmas.

Sophie blinked. "Izzy had to be rescued?"

"Yeah." Isabelle snorted at Zach. "You were a regular white knight in shining armor."

His lopsided grin dug a dimple into his left cheek. "Glad you noticed."

Isabelle's heart hiccupped at the twinkle in his eyes. Oh, Saint Nick, he was gorgeo—annoying.

"Hard to miss that ego of yours." She turned to Sophie. "No, I did not need to be rescued."

"Don't let her fool you. She needed my help," he assured Sophie, then winked at Isabelle. "Not sure there will be much left of my ego by the time you're finished with me, Blondie. You pack a punch."

Isabelle rolled her eyes. "I think you'll survive, soldier boy."

Eyes huge, Sophie's jaw dropped. "You have nicknames for each other?"

"No." Why had she called him soldier boy?

"Yes," Zach said at the same time with another dimpled grin.

"That is so sweet. I don't think she has ever had a nick-name other than Izzy." Sophie's glee was so palpable Isabelle could feel it coating her skin.

She needed to get her sister away from Zach. Pronto. Glancing around, she spotted the Butterflies.

"Oh! There's Maybelle. I think she wants to talk to you."

Sophie gave her a dubious look. "I was just talking to her before I came over here."

Okay, dumb comment, but could Isabelle help it if her neurons didn't fire when Zach was nearby? Or more like every nerve cell in her body was firing, only not in any way that made logical sense.

"Isabelle is trying to politely make an exit without breaking my heart by refusing my breakfast invitation." Zach sighed, sounding as if he was disappointed.

"Breakfast invitation?" Sophie's palms slapped together with giddiness.

Isabelle's were itching to throttle Zach. He might have just met Sophie, but he'd immediately recognized her as an ally to getting his way.

"I asked her to have lunch with me tomorrow, but she has to work." Zach made a production of shrugging his broad shoulders. "I offered breakfast, instead."

"You didn't need to tell Zach no because of the shop. I can manage while you're at lunch." Sophie's hand flattened against her chest while she talked. "It would feel good to do something for you for once. You're always covering for me when I zip out for one reason or another. Please go, Izzy. I insist."

Could Isabelle just slide behind the foyer's big Christmas tree and hide? Ugh.

Taking a deep breath, she told her sister, "You're missing the point. I don't want to go to lunch with Zach."

"Yes, you do. I can tell," Sophie assured. "Oh, Izzy, this is exciting."

Isabelle rubbed her temple. "No, it really isn't."

"Lunch it is, then." Zach's eyes twinkled. "Shall I pick you up at eleven?"

"One," she shot back, then realized what she'd done. She'd just agreed to go to lunch with Zach.

"One it is."

"No, I'll meet you at—" Not at Lou's because there would be a crowd on a Saturday afternoon. She didn't want anyone to see her having lunch with Zach. The Butterflies would go into a matchmaking frenzy. "How about I pack sandwiches and we walk to the park? There are picnic tables by the river where we can eat."

"A picnic by the river?" His gaze reflected that he knew exactly why she'd made her suggestion. "Sounds romantic. Good idea."

"That does sound romantic." Sophie's smile was so big it had to be hurting her face. It hurt Isabelle's face.

She shot Zach a cool-it look but wasn't surprised that he ignored it.

"Should I borrow a blanket from Sarah in case it's chilly?" he asked, lips twitching.

Sophie looked as if she was going to start bouncing around like a kid on Christmas morning.

"I work at a quilt shop," Isabelle reminded through gritted teeth. "If we need a blanket, I've got us covered."

He grinned. "Pun intended."

"Pun not intended." Darn that lip twitch of his that made her want to touch it.

"A romantic Christmas picnic." Sophie almost floated off the shiny hardwood floor as she happily sighed. "That is the most perfect lunch idea. I can help you pack that lovely basket Cole bought when he took me out for my birthday this summer. It's just the right touch for a romantic picnic. You should definitely bring a blanket and spread it close to the river. The scenery is lovely, even this time of year when the only green is the pines and firs."

Not a bad idea since if they were down by the bank, they could pick a more secluded area and not be as readily seen by anyone walking the greenway. Sophie wouldn't let the picnic idea drop, not when she thought something was happening that totally wasn't happening. Happily in love with Cole, Sophie was forever trying to get Isabelle to go out with this guy or that one. She'd even scooted over so Trevor Reeves could sit next to Isabelle during bible study on Wednesday evening. Her sister had been hanging out with the Butterflies too long.

"I, um, okay. A picnic by the river." She couldn't bring herself to say romantic.

Their picnic was nothing more than a business meeting. She really did need to talk to Zach if he was going to find her father and perhaps doing so would cool Sophie's encouraging Trevor. He was too nice to lead on when he just didn't excite her. Her gaze touched on Zach. That wasn't excitement running through her. It was annoyance that he was right about them needing a business meeting.

Only, no business meeting had ever tied her nerve endings into bow ties.

Chapter Four

"I REALLY LIKED Zach," Sophie announced as they walked into their house later that evening.

The night air hadn't been too chilly during their drive home, but Isabelle welcomed the comforting low hum of the heating unit and its warmth greeting them.

"Did you see how sweet he was holding Jeannie when Sarah went to get another package of ornament hangers?" Sophie continued as Isabelle took off her jacket. "How great were all those cute ornaments everyone brought for her first Christmas tree?"

Yes. Isabelle had noticed. How could she not when she'd felt a ping deep in her belly at the sight of the big muscular man holding the baby, who stared up at him with complete adoration? He'd had Jeannie cooing at him when, smiling, he'd leaned closer to say something just for her little ears. What had he been saying that she found so mesmerizing? Baby-whisperer, she mentally added to Zach's growing list. The ones she'd jotted on her real list read: ANNOYING. AGGRAVATING. PAIN IN MY SIDE. MOST IRRITATING MAN I'VE EVER MET.

"I loved the angel one you made with her name embroidered on it." Isabelle hung her coat on a rack just inside the doorway, then reached for Sophie's, hoping to distract her sister.

Sophie had talked about Zach the entire drive home, wanting to know everything about him. What could Isabelle say if she'd wanted to? That she hadn't liked how his gaze kept meeting hers while they'd decorated the tree cookies or how he'd seemed more interested in her than the game they'd played after decorating Jeannie's tree with their ornament gifts? Not that Zach's seemingly not paying attention had kept him from being brilliant at the game. Thanks to his quick answers, his team had beaten hers, which sure hadn't added any stars in his crown as far as she was concerned, but had won him more points with Sophie, who'd been his teammate. Isabelle wasn't a sore loser, but she preferred to win. Yeah, those weren't things she wanted to tell hearts-in-her-eyes Sophie.

"The ornament you gave of the dog who looked like Harry was my absolute favorite." Sophie peeled off her jacket and handed it over. "That was so perfect. Bodie and Sarah both commented on how much they loved it. Even Harry seemed impressed. Did you see how he kept turning his head one way, then the other, as he stared at it?"

"Harry is a great dog, but not nearly as awesome as you, right, Bobbin?" Isabelle bent to pick up the orangey-yellow cat that had followed them into the house. She ran her hand from his head to tail, stroking the feline's soft fur.

"And to think I once thought you'd disapprove if you knew I was feeding a stray." Sophie smiled at how the cat purred at Isabelle's affection.

"I always knew," Isabelle reminded. "It was hard to miss

that box and bedding on the front porch." She took a step toward the hallway. Maybe, just maybe, she'd be able to sneak into her bedroom without more grilling about Zach. "Not that Bobbin used it much once you started letting him into the house."

"It took me long enough to lure him in." Sophie followed behind Isabelle as she entered her room. "Speaking of luring in, tell me about when you met Zach."

"I didn't lure him," she denied, sitting on her bed and eyeing where Sophie crawled up to sit facing her. *You're going to miss this*, she reminded herself, even as the thought of talking about Zach made her stomach hurt.

"You met Tuesday?" Sophie prompted.

"More like the wind blew us together the day I delivered the choir sashes. Your wedding checklist escaped from my notebook." She still hadn't figured that one out because she knew she'd had it tucked safely inside the journal Aunt Claudia had given her last Christmas. She should have transferred the loose checklist over to the book with the dozens of other lists jotted there, but how could she have known? "Zach caught it before the wind could blow it away, then acted as if he'd slain a dragon for me or something."

"He looks as if he could slay a few dragons." Leaning forward to pet Bobbin, Sophie waggled her brows. "I think you should let him."

"What?" Isabelle frowned and gasped simultaneously. "I don't need him, or anyone, to slay dragons for me."

Did Sophie think Isabelle needed someone to slay dragons? That she hadn't done a great job taking care of their family since their dad had left? Had she missed something?

"I didn't say you needed him to. I said you should let him." Sophie giggled as Bobbin licked her hand. "Zach sure acted as if he wanted to impress you."

Isabelle rolled her eyes. "The only way he's impressed me is with how annoying he is." *Liar. There's that something in his eyes when he looks at you and what about when he'd grabbed your hand? What had all that razzle-dazzle sparking to life inside her been about?* "Even if I was interested, which I'm not, his having a military background would nip that."

Sophie's chin lifted. "Cole has a military background and he's the best man I know."

"Cole is the exception." Hopefully, she'd still believe that fifty years down the road.

"On that, he really isn't." Sophie picked up a throw pillow, toying with the tassels. "Take Bodie, for instance. He's a great man, too. Just look at what a protective, loving husband and father he is. I've never seen Sarah happier."

Isabelle couldn't argue. Their friend had always been a happy, positive person, but Bodie had brought a whole new level of joy to her life.

"Besides," Sophie continued, hugging the pillow. "You really need to stop judging every person who's been in the military by what Dad did. Dad was the exception, Isabelle. Not Cole or Bodie, and probably not Zach, either."

Ouch. She and Sophie rarely discussed their father and hadn't mentioned him since the dress fitting. That she was trying to track the man down for her sister didn't mean she wanted to talk about him. She didn't.

"I know that not every person who has been in the military suffers with transitioning back into civilian life the way that Dad did." She shrugged. "I know that most don't. Thank goodness. Maybe they try harder than Dad did."

Sophie's face was aghast. "You think Dad didn't try to fit into our lives? Just because he was the exception doesn't mean he didn't want to fit in. He did."

Isabelle's skin prickled to where she suspected whelps were popping out. She stroked Bobbin's length again, letting her fingers curl around his long tail, hoping it would calm her. "Let's not have this conversation."

"I think we should," Sophie surprised her by saying. "I know I was younger when Dad left, but I don't think his leaving was an easy decision."

"Like you said, you were younger." And because she'd rather discuss anything other than their father, she asked something that would redirect Sophie. "What do you think I should pack for my picnic with Zach? I don't know what he likes."

Sophie eyed her for a moment, then made a decision. The right one. "He likes Christmas cookies because I saw him munching on several tonight."

"And Ruby's Christmas sausage balls." Isabelle sighed with relief that Sophie had let her get away with the subject change. "I thought he and Bodie were going to fight over who got them when Ruby started packing up and wanted to know if anyone wanted the leftovers."

"Well, there you go. Cookies and sausage balls." Sophie smiled. "My thoughts are that he doesn't care what y'all eat, Izzy. It's your company he's after."

Her pulse pounded. "I'm not sure why. We don't get along."

"I've always heard opposites attract."

"Maybe." Isabelle picked up Bobbin, stroking the cat's fur. "Why am I stressing over this? I told him I'd pack sandwiches and that's what I'll do. I'll slice an apple and bring some yogurt. It'll be fine." If it wasn't, too bad. He shouldn't have put her on the spot that way in front of her sister. Hugging Bobbin close, she leaned over and kissed Sophie's cheek. "Thanks for the pep talk, sis. It's been a long day and I'm tired."

Sophie said good night.

Then, as she reached the door, Isabelle stopped her. "Hey, Sophie? Don't make a big deal out of lunch with Zach, okay? Because it's really not."

It wasn't, but that didn't keep Isabelle from seeing his grinning face when, after getting ready for bed, she crawled between her sheets. Bobbin leapt up beside her, deciding sleeping by her head was where he deigned to be. Once he settled down, his long tail plopped across her face.

Brushing away his tail, Isabelle rolled toward the cat, who yawned, then closed his eyes, leaving Isabelle a little envious of his easy slumber.

"I don't like Zach, Bobbin. I really, really don't."

A PLEASANT BLEND of cinnamon and pine hit Zach the moment he stepped into The Threaded Needle. Although the walls were white, color splashed everywhere. Christmas was prominent, but there were themed areas featuring other holidays, colors, babies, kids, sports teams, and military. His gaze lingered on the military section with its intricate red, white, and blue quilt proudly displayed. Stars with perfectly angled points ran across the quilt diagonally and arrows bordered the edges. Immediately, he was drawn to that display, taking in the patriotic fabrics, surrounding supplies, and the quilt's intricate stitching.

"If you touch that quilt, you have to buy it," Isabelle scolded from where she'd walked up behind him.

Even over the shop's merry fragrance, he could smell her apple pie lotion and fought the urge to deeply inhale as he turned toward her. She wore a fuzzy, green, long-sleeved sweater. Her hair fell straight, framing her face. Her blue gaze stared at the army star on his chest. Sarah had suggested he change. He'd declined. He liked keeping his wardrobe simple and had packed accordingly, bringing only a handful of T-shirts, jeans, and a few workout items.

"Buying such a beauty wouldn't be a bad thing." Not that he believed her warning, but if so, it would be a nice addition to his rather barren DC condominium and would give him something to mimic if he ever ventured beyond making blocks. "How much do I owe you?"

"Actually, you're in luck, as that particular quilt isn't available." She almost sounded disappointed that he'd acquiesced so readily. "Sophie plans to donate it to Quilts of Valor."

"The organization Sarah sews for?" That he also sewed for, but he wasn't ready to share that with Isabelle.

She nodded. "Sophie heads up the local chapter and Sarah is an active member."

Studying her, he asked, "You're not a member?"

"No." She didn't elaborate, and she didn't need to.

Her annoyed expression was answer enough. Yeah, he'd just keep his own active membership to himself.

"What they do is important. Sarah's quilt and generous heart pulled Bodie from a dark place." And had indirectly done the same for Zach.

He wasn't sure how to explain how Bodie telling him about Sarah and her quilt had reached inside him at his darkest point when he'd been wrestling with demons too many of his brothers and sisters in arms lost their battle with. His wise occupational therapist had used his fascination to help him focus on rehabbing his hand and his inner psyche.

He was quite proud of the squares he'd made for the group's annual block drive. "I'd like to buy something for Sarah. She's the kindest person I've ever met. Will you help me choose something she'd like?"

If Isabelle had looked surprised before, she now looked floored. "You want to buy Sarah a gift? I … of course, I'll help. That's my job. What's your price range?"

"Whatever you think." Money didn't mean much to Zach. He'd inherited a hefty sum from his grandmother, had lived minimally, and invested wisely. He had his military check and Lukas paid him a small fortune. Financially, he didn't have to work. But mentally and emotionally, Zach needed to be serving in ways that made the world a safer, better place.

"I'm not sure telling a business owner whatever she thinks is a good idea when she's trying to sell you something," Isabelle pointed out, still eyeing him with an odd expression.

His gaze met hers, and for once she didn't immediately look away. "I'll buy Sarah whatever you suggest, Blondie. I trust you."

Odd since she professed to not like him, but Zach did trust her. His every instinct said Isabelle Davis was a woman of her word—except when it came to her claims of not liking him. On that, her eyes contradicted her words of dislike.

"I, uh, okay," she stammered, then tucked her hair behind her ear. "Lucky for you, I won't march you over to our longarm machines."

The fancy sewing machines must be the most expensive item in the shop.

"Does Sarah need a longarm?"

Eyes wide, Isabelle shrugged. "Sophie would say every woman needs a longarm quilting machine, but your wallet is safe. Sarah prefers to sew on her Aunt Jean's old Singer."

Zach knew the machine Isabelle referred to. It was the one Sarah had been using that morning when she'd grilled him on his picnic with Isabelle and had offered advice as if he planned to woo and date her friend. He wasn't going to be in town that long, so dating Isabelle wasn't why they were going to lunch. But she fascinated him, and he wanted to help her.

"Sarah has been eyeing some of the quilt kits that Sophie recently put together. Maybe you could get her one of those?" Isabelle gestured to the red, white, and blue quilt he'd touched.

"What's in a quilt kit?"

"The items you need to make your own quilt already gathered together. Sophie organizes everything and does a fantastic job meeting our customers' needs. There are various kits. Some just have patterns. Others have everything you need to complete the quilt top. Others include batting, backing, thread, the whole works from start to finish. Essentially, we offer something for everyone."

"I'll take that one." At Isabelle's questioning look, he clarified. "The one with everything."

She named a price as if that might scare him off.

"That's all? Make it two, then." Maybe he'd give making a quilt from start to finish a try, especially if he ended up staying as Sarah was insisting he do.

"Two?" Isabelle's forehead scrunched, then, seeming uncomfortable, she pulled a couple of bulky packages from the shelf. Her lower lip disappeared between her teeth and her fingers tugged at the plastic wrapping. "Can I ask why you're buying Sarah a gift?"

He arched his brow. "Isn't it customary to give a house gift when a guest, or did you expect me to be such a heathen that I wouldn't know that?"

"Definitely the latter," she said, still picking at the plastic. "Do you want me to ring these up now or after lunch?"

He had nowhere to store them since he'd had Bodie drop him off. "I'll pay now and grab them after lunch."

Isabelle headed toward the cashier counter. She rang up his items and told him the total. "I'll get our lunch from the back and then we can get this over with."

"Don't sound so excited," he teased, handing her his debit card. "By the way, I feel guilty. When I invited you to lunch, I didn't mean for you to prepare our food."

"It wasn't a big deal." She slid his card into the machine.

He started to say it was, but she stayed him. "Really, it wasn't. I didn't do a single thing. I got up this morning planning to make sandwiches to find Sophie already in the kitchen with a basket and cooler bag packed with who knows what?"

"You didn't look?"

She shook her head. "She wasn't finished and said she would bring them to the shop. I was busy when she got here and never took the time."

"No worries. Your lunch is perfect," Sophie called, obviously listening in to their conversation, as she came through a door behind the counter. Wearing a bright red shirt covered with tiny Santa faces with fuzzy white balls on top of each hat, she carried a large cloth bag with the shop's logo on it, identical to the one Isabelle had been carrying on the day they'd met. A Christmas quilt overflowed from the top. "Zach, I love that you're buying Sarah a hostess gift. That's so sweet, isn't it, Izzy?"

Isabelle grimaced. "Sugary so."

"Here. You're going to need this." Sophie handed Zach the bag. "Sarah called a little while ago and said you were interested in signing up for my sewing class."

He hadn't even known Sophie had a sewing class, but that the shop would offer them made sense. He suspected Sarah had her reasons for telling Sophie he was interested, reasons that involved the woman frowning at her sister.

"Why would Sarah think that?" Isabelle handed Zach's debit card back to him.

"Zach's been helping her cut and pin pieces and has even sewn a few pieces with her." Sophie smiled big, even as

Isabelle's jaw dropped. "She's not getting to sew as much as she'd like since Jeannie's been born and says you've been a great help on her current quilt."

Heat flooded Zach's face. "Sarah's a good teacher."

"Isabelle is, too," Sophie assured. "Our Grandma Belle taught us when we were little, but since Mom doesn't sew, it was Isabelle who helped me fine-tune my sewing skills. She's a perfectionist and, although not necessary, that trait comes in handy when quilting and wanting your seams to line up properly."

Shoving his packages toward him, Isabelle shook her head. "I'm not the one who teaches sewing classes."

"Not usually, but you have when needed." Sophie smiled sweetly at Zach. "She's promised to cover any of this session's classes that I need a night to prepare for the wedding. It's the week before Christmas, you know."

Color splashed into Isabelle's cheeks. Zach gave Sophie credit. She knew how to play her sister, but Isabelle wasn't going down without a fight.

"Ben may not like you recruiting competition." She turned to Zach. "He's one of Cole's best friends and a fellow firefighter. He only signed up because Sophie assured him most of her other students were single women under thirty."

Sophie's laugh was sparkly. "Ben may not be back. The women in the class were more interested in him than he was in them or sewing, unfortunately." Concern flitted across her face. "With Andrew being married, and now Cole about to be, I do worry about him. He's the one who's always wanted a wife and children, but just hasn't met the one yet." Sophie's gaze pinned Zach. "What about you? Are you looking for the one?"

"No, ma'am." He coughed to clear his throat. "Marriage isn't for me. I'm a bachelor for life."

He'd never wanted married life, never even considered it as an option. He'd only wanted to be a soldier. Now, he couldn't do his first love, but still couldn't picture himself living a white-picket-fence life. He'd likely die working at iSecure or someplace like it where he still tasted remnants of the life-on-the-edge he'd once lived.

Giggling, Sophie waved her hand dismissively. "I've heard that before. Be warned. Pine Hill has a way of claiming hearts."

"Okay, Soph, you can leave Zach alone now," Isabelle advised, obviously embarrassed by her sister's blatant matchmaking. "I'm not going to have time for lunch if we don't get on the move."

Unfazed, Sophie ignored Isabelle and kept smiling. "You really should sign up for my class. You've missed the first two, but from what Sarah says, you didn't need those bare minimum basics, anyway. But if you did, Isabelle can catch you up."

"I'll think on it," Zach said, doubting he'd agree.

"I'm starved." Isabelle scooped up the basket and gestured toward the cooler bag. "Zach, grab that, please. You can carry it and the blanket bag. We need to be on our way to the park so I can get back to work."

"Great to see you again, Zach," Sophie called from behind them. "Come back real soon. My next class is Monday evening at six. Hope to see you there."

ISABELLE HAD BEGUN to wonder if they were ever going to leave the shop.

The sunny November day greeted her when she stepped out onto the sidewalk, causing her to wish she'd grabbed her sunglasses. The soft breeze carried the scent of Mom and Pop's Pizzeria, making her stomach growl. She'd been in such a rush to get away from Sophie's picnic planning that morning that she'd not eaten breakfast.

"I like your sister."

Isabelle squinted at Zach. "Everyone does."

"Does that bother you?"

"No. The sun was in my eyes." However, that he'd moved into step beside her to where he shaded her face from the sun did bother her. Not that she didn't appreciate his instantaneous chivalry, but it was easier not to think of him as considerate.

As they walked along the sidewalk, Carrie stepped out of Paw Parties and waved. Isabelle smiled, waved back, but didn't pause to talk to the shop's owner.

"Besides," she mused, walking faster, "why would everyone liking Sophie bother me?"

She couldn't imagine the person who wouldn't like her sunshiny, life-is-a-bowl-of-Christmas-candy sister.

"You tell me. You're the one whose voice went up an octave or two."

"*Humph*. That had nothing to do with Sophie and everything to do with you," she assured, marveling at how he stayed perfectly in step with her increased speed, keeping her face shadowed. Once they crossed the street, heading down Main, she abruptly slowed, just to see if he'd match suit. Without missing a step, he did.

His lips twitched. "Why is that?"

"Because you're so annoying. Surely someone has pointed out that to you in the past?"

He snorted. "Only my brother."

"You have a brother?" The serious, almost sad way he answered had Isabelle wishing she could take her question back.

She didn't want to think of him as human, either. Then again, he wasn't human. Humans didn't anticipate pace changes the way he had.

"Hard to believe I didn't just crawl from the fiery recesses of the earth, eh?"

That his demeanor had instantly gone back to teasing relieved her in ways she would tear apart later, when she wasn't with him. She needed all her brain cells to stay on task for the here and now.

"Well, I didn't quite buy that a stork dropped you off at your parents' doorstep."

"No stork," he assured, chuckling. "Although, in this town, you probably believe that it's flying reindeer who drop off babies."

Isabelle bit back a smile. "There are those in town who could be convinced of that."

"But you're not one of them?"

"I'm a realist," she admitted, suspecting he was the same. "Do you have other siblings?"

Zach shook his head. "No, Brett and I are it."

"Are you close?"

He shrugged. "Not particularly. He never understood my career choice."

"He didn't want you to join the military?" Why was she asking personal questions?

She didn't need to know any of this for him to find her father. The less she knew about Zach, the better.

"That was just the start." Zach shrugged. "Even before my military career ended, he thought I'd made a mess of my life and should have followed in his and my dad's footsteps."

Curiosity almost got the better of her, but Isabelle forced herself not to pry. Possibly because of how his shoulders had lifted, almost defensively. Zach seemed so together on the surface, so easygoing, but maybe that wasn't really the case.

"I can't imagine not being close to Sophie," she admitted as they made their way along the sidewalk toward the city park.

Why would his brother think he'd made a mess of his life? If he had, was that why he was staying at Hamilton House? Had Bodie and Sarah put him in the Beds for Vets suite for reasons other than that the room had been open? Sarah had mentioned injuries. Was there something wrong with Zach? Something that couldn't be seen? *Not your business, Isabelle.*

"Do you think that closeness will change after she and Cole get married?" Zach stayed in step beside her, even though they'd made it beyond the storefronts and were heading down a shady street that led to the park entrance.

"Even when I lived in Nashville, we talked most days." Plus, she and Sophie would still see each other frequently between the shop and church. "I've no doubt we'll always be close."

"You lived in Nashville?"

She cut her eyes toward him. "Why sound so surprised?"

"I got the impression no one ever left Pine Hill."

She gave a low laugh that really didn't have much humor to it. "Shocking that some of us do, isn't it? No worries, though. We always seem to find our way back."

His expression grew thoughtful. "Is Sophie why you came back?"

Glad to see the park wasn't that busy, Isabelle headed toward the concrete greenway that began on the opposite end of the parking lot and ran along the river.

"Although she was three years younger, Sophie and I both worked at the quilt shop during my high school years. I left for college. Sophie stayed, finished school, and started working full-time. After I graduated, I stayed in Nashville and worked for an accounting firm until the shop came up for sale and Sophie needed me as her partner to pull off buying it."

"Any regrets?"

"None." She'd always known she'd come back to be near her family. It was why she'd not allowed herself to be too devastated when Greg had dumped her after they'd dated for three years. He'd been a workaholic, too, and sometimes she thought they'd just enjoyed having someone to go to dinner with after their long workdays. Still, his telling her he no longer wanted them to be a couple had stung.

"You sound as if you enjoyed your job in Nashville."

"I did," she admitted. "But I enjoy the business side of

the quilt shop, too, watching it grow and become more successful. Sophie is why the shop looks so fabulous."

"And you're the brains behind the scenes?"

"Sophie does more than her share and has pulled long hours over the years since we bought the shop. She's the creative genius of the business and I'm happiest in the office, crunching numbers." She smiled. "I like numbers."

"Me, too."

Stepping onto to the greenway, Isabelle gave him a questioning look.

"Numbers make sense." He stayed next to her beneath the large oak tree-lined path as they headed past a playground with a few families there. "Numbers are black and white and mean what they mean." He shrugged. "They just make sense."

"Exactly."

A girl Isabelle had gone to high school with sat on the bench near the playground, watching her kids play and, spotting Isabelle, waved. As she'd done with Carrie, Isabelle waved back, but didn't stop to chat. There were times living in a friendly small town were problematic. She'd hoped no one would see her and Zach. She supposed she should be grateful it had only been the few so far and fortunately no Butterflies. *Yet.*

"Numbers are constant and unchanging," he continued. "Finite. You know what you're getting. You—"

Isabelle came to a quick stop to gawk at him. "No. No. No."

"What?"

"Just..." The gentle November breeze messed with her

hair and, tightly gripping the bag she carried, she blew the stray strands from her face. "I don't want to have anything in common with you."

He laughed. "Afraid I'll win you over?"

"You can't win me over." Not really, but he'd been surprising her from the moment he walked into the quilt shop.

A big, buff soldier who bought his hostess a thoughtful gift? Yeah, she'd liked that. That he helped Sarah? Yep, she liked that, too. That his take on numbers echoed hers? Well, she didn't want to think of him as an intelligent being.

Sighing, she glanced around, decided the sooner they got started, the sooner they'd finish, so their current location was as good as any. She stepped onto the grassy park lawn and walked past a couple of concrete picnic tables located near some trees along the bank that would provide a cover from anyone walking the greenway.

"I can't?" He fell into step beside her. "You should know that I've never backed down from a challenge, even missions deemed impossible."

Shifting the picnic basket, she eyed him. "Is that what I am to you? A challenge because you're bored during your visit to our little Christmasy town?"

"I'm not bored, Blondie."

He didn't look bored. He looked amused. At her expense. She could blame no one but herself. She needed to quit giving him entertainment fodder.

"You didn't answer my question," she reminded. "Do you see me as a challenge? Is that what this is about?"

He studied her, then shrugged a shoulder. "If I say yes, you're a challenge, that's going to upset you. If I say, no, you're not a challenge, you're going to set out to prove me wrong so that you can be upset. Either way I can't win and, as much as I enjoy sparring with you, I'd rather enjoy this semi-nice weather and your company without upsetting you."

Was that why she'd persisted? Because she'd purposely set him up to fail? She wanted him to fail. Needed him to fail because she didn't want to like him. Fine. She'd talk about something else. Anything else.

"The weather is more than semi-nice. For November, it's wonderful. The high temperature was supposed to be in the low sixties, but it feels warmer. Great, even, for the time of year. If you're cold, you should wear a coat." She wished he was wearing a coat. Anything that covered up those muscled arms and that blasted T-shirt had her vote.

"I'm not cold."

A hair tickled her face again, and she swiped her forearm across her cheek, hoping to fix the disarray. "Then why say semi-nice?"

"Because that breeze keeps blowing your hair in your face. I want to tuck it behind your ear, but figured I'd be facing an arctic chill if I did."

Her stomach launched into gold medal-worthy somersaults. Ugh. She was too smart to be taken in by this man's charms. He was a here-today, gone-tomorrow military man. Could there possibly be a worse choice for her to be attracted to? Not that she was attracted to him, but if she were, he'd be a terrible choice.

"I should have worn a scarf," she murmured. Putting the basket down on a mostly shielded from the greenway picnic table, she then tucked her hair behind her ears in hopes it stayed. No reason to tempt fate. Not fate. Zach. No reason to tempt Zach. *He was not her fate.*

He gestured to a grassy area thirty or so yards away. "Let's do as your sister suggested last night and eat by the riverbank. I'm sure that's why she sent the blanket."

Isabelle had no doubt. Sophie had learned from the best. "There's no telling what she packed in her Christmas picnic basket."

"Or in this giant bag." He gestured to the one with the shop's logo. "It's heavy at the bottom."

When she stopped ten feet or so from where the bank sloped down to a rocky area along the river, Zach pulled the quilt from the bag. "Yep. Lots more here than just a quilt."

Eyeing the red and green holly-patterned pillow Zac held, along with the matching holly Christmas quilt, Isabelle glanced in the bag and shook her head. "You'll have to excuse my sister. She's getting married in a month and has bride brain. Hopefully, she'll learn to pack lighter prior to her honeymoon."

"I don't mind a tiny Christmas tree, Christmas mugs and"—he gestured to the thermos she pulled from the bag— "based upon the bag of marshmallows, I'm guessing this is hot chocolate."

"I'd rather have water," Isabelle mumbled, placing the bottle on the ground, then helping him smooth out the quilt over the grass. "And be at work."

"Than to be outside? Breathing in fresh air? Hearing the rippling of the water? I like numbers, but it's a rare day I'd rather be indoors than outside. Relax." He popped one of the tiny marshmallows into his mouth. "It's only lunch."

Lunch her sister had packed. Lunch with a man who rattled her insides. Lunch that was a picnic by the river, but okay, it was only lunch. A romantic Christmas picnic kind of only lunch.

Shaking her head at Sophie's whimsicalness, she picked up the plastic tree to place it on one corner of the quilt and noticed the bottom. "I think we're supposed to listen to Christmas songs while we eat. This thing winds up."

"Cool. Wind 'er up, then let's see what's in the basket. I'm hungry and these marshmallows aren't cutting it."

"Hey, stay out of those," she scolded when he scooped a few more out of the bag. "They're for the hot chocolate."

With "Rocking Around the Christmas Tree" mingling with the river's gurgling, they pulled item after item from the basket and cooler bag.

Pausing to look at the spread, Zach whistled. "She's good."

"Yep." And not just her, because there was no way her sister had put this together by herself.

She'd had help. Butterfly help. Isabelle should have suspected when she'd glanced up at the shop's security monitor and seen Ruby coming into the shop. And not thirty minutes later, Aunt Claudia and Rosie had. Eyeing the foil-covered loaf, Isabelle frowned. That had better not be what she thought it was. Kneeling on the quilt, she picked up the loaf and began unwrapping the foil. Even before she could see the contents, cinnamon wafted on the air.

"I'm telling Santa on all of them. Nothing but coal for the whole lot," she grumbled, wondering if Zach would think her crazy if she tossed the bread into the river.

He'd been unpacking plates with candy canes on them, red cloth napkins, red utensils, and two wrapped Christmas presents.

Leaning over to see what she held, his brows knitted together. "You have something against cinnamon bread?"

"I have something major against this particular bread." Sophie was in so much trouble when Isabelle got back to the shop. Those presents better be handwritten apologies. "This is Rosie's cinnamon bread."

"The blue-haired lady with a lot of spunk?"

Isabelle nodded.

"It smells good." Before she realized what he was doing, Zach pinched off a generous piece and took a bite. "*Mmm. That's good.*"

"No! Spit it out." Panicked, she grabbed for the remaining bread in his hand.

"Too late." Confusion distorted his face. "Have I been poisoned?"

"Same as." She sighed. "Rumor has it that Rosie's cinnamon bread has special powers to make a man fall for the first woman he sees after taking a bite."

Chapter Five

*T*OO LATE. SWEAT beaded on Zach's skin. No, he hadn't fallen for Isabelle. But he did like his self-proclaimed realist who was in a panic over hocus-pocus, love-potion cinnamon bread.

Snatching the piece back that she'd wrangled from him, he stuck it in his mouth, enjoying the sweetness and the look of horror on her face. Realist, his foot.

"I think it's happening." He clutched at his chest and carried on as if something major was developing within his ribcage. "Quick, give me more bread."

"You shouldn't eat that, Zach." She moved the bread behind her, trying to keep the loaf out of his reach. "You don't know what you're messing with. The Butterflies … they don't play fair when it comes to matchmaking."

Laughing, Zach reached behind her, easily breaking off a chunk. They both knew the bread's supposed power was as fake as the plastic Christmas tree chiming another merry tune.

"Are my pupils heart-shaped yet?" Grinning, he batted his lashes.

Sighing, she rolled her eyes. "Don't say you weren't warned."

"Aw, come on, Blondie." He held the morsel toward her. "Take a bite. It's good."

Forehead crinkled, her lips parted, probably to reprimand him some more, but Zach took full advantage by popping the treat into her mouth.

"Now, let's see if that sweetens your disposition."

He'd expected her to close her eyes and savor the baked goodie as he had. Instead, she froze, a cringe on her otherwise lovely face. When she just sat there staring at him, he reached around and took the loaf from her lax fingers.

"It's bread, Blondie. Nothing more. Unless… Does the bread work both ways? Is that it?" he teased, loving the rising color in her cheeks. "One bite and you're going to succumb to my lackluster smarm, after all? Here, have another piece. The entire loaf, even."

"This isn't funny," she stammered in a muffled voice.

Reaching for one of the napkins, she covered her mouth. Had she just spat out the bread? Surely, she didn't believe the bread was anything more than a tasty combo of flour, sugar, butter, and cinnamon?

"Are realists superstitious?" She could claim whatever she wanted, but a dreamer lurked within her, waiting to be let out and given free rein.

She gave him one of her loaded glares. The one that said she'd really like him to hitch a ride to the North Pole and stay there. "Did I mention that I'm a cautious realist and don't take unnecessary chances?"

"If it's only the guy who falls, you have nothing to fear. I'll sacrifice myself by disposing of the entire loaf to keep you safe." He waggled his brows. "White knight material all the way."

Eating the delicious bread would be no chore. He didn't believe such tomfoolery as love-potion sweets. Even if he did believe and fell, he'd never let Isabelle know. To do that would be too complicated. He was too complicated.

"Because you could never fall for someone like me?"

He'd expected some wisecrack. Instead, the vulnerability was back in her softly asked question and in the big blue eyes studying him. The urge to take her into his arms and hold her until every self-doubt she'd ever had melted away hit, shocking him yet again that he wanted to hug her. She was so tough and ready to fight, and yet, her question revealed a fragility that had him ready to armor up in her defense.

"Any man could fall for you, Isabelle. No hocus-pocus, love-potion bread needed." His gaze locked with hers. Who had hurt her? What kind of idiot tore down a woman of her caliber? "You're smart, sassy, quick-witted, and beautiful."

He kept all teasing from his tone, wanting to build her up for whomever would come down the road and could be the kind of man she deserved.

"I … thank you." Pink tinged her cheeks and rather than say anything further, she began popping open the containers of their food. "I hope you like chicken salad, but if not, there's some of Ruby's sausage balls you liked so much at Jeannie's tree-decorating party." She opened a plastic Christmas tree-shaped container. "Oh, and what Christmas picnic would be complete without a cheeseboard?"

Sure enough, the plastic tree container was filled with slices of cheese, rolled up pieces of turkey and ham as garland, plus a variety of fruits and vegetables as ornaments.

"There's more fruit," she continued, opening a small container. "Strawberries made into tiny Santa heads with whipped cream."

Zach's stomach rumbled in appreciation. He'd gone on a few picnics with his parents and brother growing up, but his memories were of businessmen in their golfing garb, women in their finery, and overdressed kids who were expected to sit quietly in the sweltering sun while eating dainty snack foods that weren't that appetizing. Nothing like what Isabelle's sister and the Butterflies had prepared.

"Christmas picnics are officially my favorite type of picnics. Let's eat."

"There's an elderly woman in a camo hoodie watching us from eleven o'clock."

Belly full from eating too much, Isabelle twisted in the direction Zach mentioned.

A couple sat at one of the concrete picnic tables. The white-haired man was shaking his floppy hat-covered head and saying something to the hoodie-pulled-tight-around-her-face, dark sunglass-wearing woman, who when she spotted that Isabelle was looking her way, dropped her binoculars, picked up a book, said something to the man, then pointed up into a nearby tree as if its branches weren't bare.

That was no bird watcher.

Poor John. Maybelle had dragged the man who'd crushed on her from afar since their teens into a Butterfly spying expedition. Maybelle feigned fascination with something in a large oak, said something to John, and the older man glanced toward where Isabelle and Zach could be seen through the trees and nodded. Maybelle must have asked if Isabelle was still looking their way.

Isabelle couldn't resist waving. The older couple were too far away to be sure John's face had just gone bright pink, but his hand had definitely slapped against his forehead, knocking off his hat.

"Interesting friends you have," Zach said from where he sat near her. Too near, but since the blanket was only so big, she couldn't really tell him to scoot over, or he'd be in the grass.

"They're good cooks, though." She gestured toward their mini feast. "You may have recognized that some of this was leftovers from Jeannie's party. Without the Butterflies, Sophie wouldn't have pulled off something so elaborate on such short notice."

"Then I love me some Butterflies."

"Me, too. Each one of them has played an intricate role in my life. Our resident bird watcher was my Sunday school teacher several years running. No doubt the Butterflies relished getting involved with our Christmas picnic." Isabelle eyed the man licking meat sauce off his fingers. Even in Isabelle's tight, wondering-what-was-she-doing-on-a-picnic-with-Zach state, she hadn't been oblivious to how good the food was and how thoughtful her family and friends had been in their unwanted matchmaking. As far as why she was there with Zach … the only reason she was with him… Her stomach contents threatened to rebel.

"Do you really think you can find my father for Sophie's

wedding?" Why did she feel as if she were nine years old and standing with her heart in her hand? Cliff Davis had no power over her. She was only doing this for Sophie.

"If he can be found."

She eyed where Zach had lain back, propped his head on the Christmas pillow, and looked out toward the river. There didn't appear to be a tense muscle in his stretched-out body.

"You're that sure of yourself?"

"I've found people a lot slipperier than a runaway father."

A runaway father. That was what Cliff was, but hearing Zach say it out loud stung.

"I can't pay what Bodie says iSecure charges," she admitted, then embarrassment hit. "I mean, I could, but not easily, not with Sophie's wedding, and still making payments on the shop's mortgage, and—"

"You don't have to pay me," he interrupted, not seeming concerned.

With as calmly as he was lying back on the pillow, she was beginning to wonder if he was planning a nap. Did he remember that she was only on a lunch break?

"I don't want your charity," she insisted, glad that he hadn't closed his eyes, but had looked her way with his thickly fringed hazel eyes.

"But you can't afford the company I work for?" His expression became thoughtful. "How about we make a trade?"

"A trade?" she asked suspiciously.

He flexed his arms, placing his hands behind his head, the muscles beneath his T-shirt crunching into the perfect abdominal snowman pose. "I'll find your father and in exchange, you teach me to quilt."

Her jaw dropped. "What? I can't teach you to quilt."

"Sure, you can. Sophie said you fill in teaching her class."

"That's different," she insisted.

His brow lifted. "How?"

Because those students weren't good-looking soldiers who threw me so off-kilter that I'd likely stitch my fingers together. Nope. Couldn't tell him that. He'd tease her mercilessly if he knew she thought he was attractive.

"Why do you want to learn to quilt?" She changed tactics.

"From the first time Bodie told me about the Quilts of Valor Foundation, my interest was piqued. I've been helping Sarah with her current quilt and want to learn more, but I feel guilty taking up any of her free time." He rolled his upper half into an upright position, picked up his Christmas mug, took a sip, then pinned her with his gaze. "Teach me to quilt, and in exchange, I'll find your father."

What he said about not taking up Sarah's limited time made sense and once again painted him in a considerate light. Ugh. Fine. She'd sign him up for Sophie's class to teach him the basics and she'd feel in the gaps. That way she wouldn't have to spend that much time with him.

"If I do this, you'd better find him."

Zach's left dimple dug deep with his lopsided grin. "You doubt my ability to do so?"

No, she didn't. Zach's self-assurance didn't come across as vanity. Just his acknowledgement of his capabilities. If her father could be found, Zach would find him. Her stomach convulsed around her chicken salad and a wave of nausea hit.

Nausea and uncertainty. What had she done?

Because she wasn't sure she wanted Cliff Davis found after all this time. Some things, some people, were probably better left in the past.

NOT SURPRISING TO Isabelle, three Butterflies fluttered around The Threaded Needle and were all eyes and ears when she and Zach returned from their business-meeting picnic. Maybelle and John had disappeared not long after Zach had pointed them out, but Maybelle wasn't with the ladies so it wouldn't surprise Isabelle to learn that they'd just changed spy position and made better use of their binoculars.

"Back so soon?" Rosie looked all innocent. "We weren't expecting you for hours and hours."

"You sent enough food for days." Isabelle waged a battle between gratitude at their generous love and frustration at their matchmaking. "Thank you. It was delicious, but Sophie shouldn't have asked y'all to do that. I'll be useless this afternoon after eating so much midday."

"Nonsense." Aunt Claudia dismissed her claim, giving Zach a smile that said he had her approval. "We're always up for stocking a Christmas picnic basket."

"Especially for someone who enjoyed my Christmas sausage balls so much." Ruby beamed at Zach, giving her stamp of approval, too.

"Now…" Rosie fluttered her fake lashes. "What did you think of your Christmas presents?"

Heat washed over Isabelle's face. "We, uh, we got in a

rush to leave because there was this odd, nosy couple with binoculars who kept spying on us, and we forgot to open them."

There. That let them know she was onto them.

Three Butterflies giggled and looked back and forth at each other.

"Spying on you?" Aunt Claudia shook her head. "Dear, when not making lists, you've quite the imagination. They were probably just bird watching."

If Isabelle hadn't already known the women were in on the spying, that her aunt mentioned exactly the cover that Maybelle and John had used would have given them away.

"Ah, bird watching. I bet you're right." She pulled the corner of the quilt from the bag Zach carried and tapped the pattern. "These birds are so lifelike, aren't they?"

Next to her, Zach chuckled.

Aunt Claudia focused on him. "Zach, you must go with Isabelle out to Harvey Farm for their Christmas kickoff."

To give him credit, he didn't leap at the nugget they'd delivered, which should make Isabelle happy because she didn't want him encouraging them. That so wasn't disappointment she was feeling instead.

"Christmas picnics and kickoffs? It's not Thanksgiving yet."

Every female in the room burst into laughter, including Isabelle.

"You can tell he's not from around here, bless his heart." Rosie patted Zach's arm. "No worries, though, hon. We'll have you celebrating Christmas three hundred and sixty-five days a year, like the rest of us, soon enough."

"Speaking of Harvey Farm, you're invited to a couple's shower for Sophie and Cole tomorrow afternoon." Ruby beamed, obviously proud that she'd been the one to invite Zach. "We're not serving my sausage balls, but your tongue will still smack against the roof of your mouth in gratitude of how good everything tastes."

"Tempting," Zach said, looking as if he really was tempted. *What was he doing? And would a swift kick to the shins knock some sense into him?*

"And Thanksgiving, Zach." Aunt Claudia practically fell over herself as she smiled up at him. "You should come to Thanksgiving dinner. Our whole family will be there, plus quite a few friends. The more the merrier. We'd love you to join us."

Zach started to say something, but Isabelle could contain herself no longer and knocked her elbow against his arm, letting him know she had this.

"Aunt Claudia, I appreciate that you asked Zach to dinner. That's so thoughtful of you, of all of you, to include him." She forced a smile that hopefully didn't convey how much doing so hurt with her teeth gritted. "But Zach's only in Pine Hill a short time." Exactly how long was he there? She hadn't thought to ask. If he hadn't found her father by the time for him to leave, would he continue looking? "He will be spending Thanksgiving with his own family."

After all, he'd mentioned parents and a brother.

"I won't be going to Atlanta for the holidays."

Ignoring the curious Butterflies, Isabelle frowned. "You're not going home for the holidays?"

His expression pinched for the first time since they'd entered the shop. "Nope."

"Not even for Christmas?" Aunt Claudia looked aghast.

He shrugged. "I'd meant to go to the Keys when I left here next week."

Next week? He was leaving that soon? Why did that make Isabelle's chest hurt?

"Sarah insisted I spend the holidays in Pine Hill. I hadn't planned to." He glanced toward Isabelle, his gaze meeting hers. "But now, I've reason to stick around for a while."

Three Butterflies and her sister collectively sighed and lit up like they were fireflies. Isabelle, on the other hand, was about to convulse like one of those popping bugs. Enough was enough. If she hadn't known better, she'd have been sighing, too. Zach looked at her as if he truly thought her the most interesting, beautiful woman he'd ever met. Even knowing his visual caress was nothing more than his perpetual teasing, she found herself retracting lackluster from adjectives she could use to describe anything about him. Wowzers.

Panic hit that he could mess with her head so readily. Why had he insisted upon coming inside the shop? She'd told him there was no need and that she could carry their picnic items, but he'd insisted. Plus, there had been his need to retrieve Sarah's gift.

"Oh, Isabelle," Sophie practically cooed, clasping her hands as she glanced back and forth between her and Zach. "This makes me so happy."

Ruby was all smiles. "A Christmas miracle."

"She fed him my cinnamon bread!" Rosie stage-whispered to her friends, then, facing Isabelle, said, "We're so happy for you both."

Aunt Claudia nodded. "It's about time some young man saw through your all-work-and-no-play façade to realize how wonderful you are."

Moisture prickled Isabelle's skin, making her palms clammy. Did they think her so hopeless that they got this excited over a first date? Their assumptions about her and Zach were misplaced. And would they please stop acting as if she and Zach were some smitten at first sight lovebirds?

Determined to set them straight, Isabelle put the picnic basket on the checkout counter.

"You have this all wrong. Zach and I aren't—" she began, but completely lost her ability to vocalize when he leaned down and kissed her cheek fairly close to the corner of her mouth. Stunned, completely unable to vocalize, she gawked at him.

"I've got to go." He winked at the women, causing another collective sigh, before his go-with-me-on-this eyes met Isabelle's. "Walk me outside, Blondie."

She'd walk him outside alright. Once there she was going to give him a piece of her mind. Walking behind the counter to grab the bag she'd put his quilt kits in, it was all she could do to keep her tongue in check. How dare he kiss her in front of the Butterflies and Sophie? How dare he kiss her at all? How dare he turn her to complete jelly at that simple gesture? How dare he look so calm when she was *so* not calm? How dare—just how dare he?

"Zach, it was lovely seeing you again." Sophie's face radiated sunshine. "You really should consider that sewing class. I'd love to have you join us."

"Thanks, but I'm going to pass. Isabelle's giving me private lessons."

Every female jaw dropped, including Isabelle's. Her stomach had taken a dive, too. Shoving the bag at him, she grabbed his other hand and dragged him toward the front door.

"Bye, ladies," he called, amusement heavy in his voice.

"Bye, Zach," chorused from the counter in a he's-so-dreamy singsong.

Once the shop door had closed, she turned her back to the display window so any spying Butterflies couldn't read her lips. Or her expression because she was going to blast Zach.

"Do you have any idea what you just did?" she hissed. Then deciding they were still too visible to the eyes glued their way, she pulled him down the street until they rounded the corner.

"I know exactly what I did." He had the gall to sound proud of it, too.

"By the time I get back in there, they'll be planning my wedding instead of Sophie's!" Realizing she was still holding his hand, his big warm hand, Isabelle let go, watching almost as if in slow motion as their skin parted ways. Instantly, she felt the loss of his touch. Had he felt that?

"You can thank me now or when I stop by later."

"Oh, no, you aren't stopping by later." It was all she could do to keep from wagging her finger at him. If she knew Maybelle and John's whereabouts, she'd be waving her hands with animation for sure. As it was, she shoved them into her pants pockets. "The last thing I want is to see you again today."

Her brain and emotions were already a tangled mess that would take her hours to sort.

Eyes twinkling, he rocked back on his heels. "Then I guess you better thank me now."

His calmness was infuriating. When her insides were raging, from his cheek kiss, from his lackadaisical attitude over flirting with her in front of the Butterflies, from having held his hand as she'd dragged him down Main Street, from everything about him, how could he act as if it were all no big deal? Then again, to him, it wasn't. Soon enough, he'd be gone.

"Thank you for what?" she demanded. "If anything, you owe me an apology for the mess I'll be facing when I walk back into the shop. The Butterflies are going to be all over that sappy look and awful kiss. Sophie, too."

"Saving you from blowing our cover on why we'll be spending so much time together over the next few weeks," he drawled, as if she shouldn't have had to ask.

"Unless you're a really slow learner"—she cleared her throat as if she thought that a distinct possibility—"teaching you to sew is not going to take more than a few days, tops."

"I want to learn to quilt, Isabelle, not hem my pants. It's safe to say that's going to take more than a few days, but that wasn't what I was referring to." He gave a thumbs-up. "Good point, though, as we'll be spending time together sewing, too."

"Then what were you referring to?"

"You inviting me into your home, showing me photos of your father, talking about him in front of your family and friends so I can pick up on clues on where he might have gone when he left Pine Hill."

Isabelle's stomach clenched. He thought she was going to do all that? Wrong again.

"Sophie was four when Dad left. She has no idea where he's at." If her sister had, no doubt Sophie would have already found him. "My mother doesn't know where he went, either."

At least, if Darlene knew, she'd never said. Her poor mother had just thrown herself into her work and cried herself to sleep night after night. Not that Isabelle was supposed to know the latter, but she'd heard those devastated sobs and been so thankful when they'd happened less and less frequently. If Zach did find Cliff, Isabelle would make sure her mother was okay with him showing up at Sophie's wedding. If she didn't want him there, then Isabelle would just never tell Sophie she'd found him.

"Maybe not, but your mom knows things about him. Things he liked, things he disliked, hobbies and interests, places he wanted to see, things she might not have mentioned to her daughters. People he knew outside of Pine Hill that he might have told her about," he continued, his expression serious. "Your mother knows things I need to know."

A spasm fired at the corner of Isabelle's eye as panic rose. "You can't question my family, Zach. They'll know something is up. Sophie can't know that I'm trying to find him for her wedding until we know we're not delivering bad news. I won't have her wedding ruined because of something I did, even if that something was meant to be what she wanted. And I won't have Mom hurt by this."

"You're right. I can't ask without raising suspicion."

Relief filled her. She'd not expected him to give in so quickly. Unfortunately, her reprieve was short-lived.

"Not as your hired help," he clarified. "But as the new man in your life, it's only natural that I'd be curious about your family, including your father. No one will think anything of your boyfriend asking about your dad."

"No." She did not want him prying into her life. Nor did she want him as her pretend boyfriend. "Couldn't you just do some computer magic and find him that way?"

"The more information I have, the more likely I am to find him in time." What he said made sense. Unfortunately. "You know your family better than I do. Can you think of another scenario in which they are going to openly discuss your father with me, other than if they believe we're a couple?"

Everything he said was logical and yet the emotions pumping through her left no room for reason. Zach hanging out with her family as her pretend boyfriend—"There has to be another way."

"A way that doesn't risk Sophie discovering that we're searching for your father?"

She cringed. "I'll think of something."

"You do that, Blondie." He touched her cheek, just a quick brush of his thumb in what was probably for show since he was sure to have spotted Maybelle and John peering out of John's truck that was parked down the street. They must have been parked across from the shop and relocated when she and Zach had rounded the corner. "In the meantime, we'll do this my way. I'll call you later to set up my first lesson."

Knowing she was being watched didn't give her the ability to drag her gaze from him as, carrying his purchases, he took off walking, turning onto Main and leaving her a bundle of crazy emotions.

Argh! she internally screamed. Then, taking a deep breath, she spun, looked straight at Maybelle and John, and turned up her palms as if to ask what they were doing. John slid down in the driver's seat, but Maybelle acted as if she'd just noticed Isabelle and waved, all cheery-like. That alone would have given her away. Maybelle didn't do cheery. Rolling her eyes, Isabelle headed back to the shop to face the repercussions of what may have been the worst decision of her life.

But she couldn't think of a single other reason why Zach would pry into her family's darkest moment without raising suspicion.

As far as the world was concerned, she was dating Zach Dawson.

Chapter Six

"A BSOLUTELY NO PUBLIC displays of affection. No prying into anything you don't absolutely have to know. Do not take unfair advantage of my friends or family. Find out what you need to know without making anyone suspicious and don't you dare do anything that will hurt any of my friends or family."

Zach eyed a Christmas-red-dress-and-boot-wearing Isabelle sitting in the driver's seat of her sedan. She was barely in the car before she'd started ticking off items as if reading them from one of her lists. The scent of freshly baked apple pies filled the car.

This was the most fun he'd had in … forever. Spending the next few weeks with Isabelle almost made being on vacation okay. Almost.

"Let's shut this charade down. The faster, the better," she continued, glancing both ways before pulling the car out of Hamilton House's driveway.

"Quit rushing me, Blondie," he teased. "Our relationship is new and I'm not that kind of guy."

Her cheeks lit up to match her dress. "You're infuriating. You know that, right?"

He knew, but his smile stayed in place despite the flash-back of the last time someone had pointed out his failings with those exact words. He hadn't needed his brother's insights to know that his family didn't think much of him.

"Just like you know you're beautiful when you blush, right?" His compliment seemed to throw her off-kilter. Hard to imagine that she wasn't used to being complimented, but that she wasn't was apparent. He'd correct that for however long he was in Pine Hill.

She paused, frowned, then sucked in a deep breath. "Don't flatter me with your smarm."

"Lackluster smarm," he reminded, eyeing how her knuckles white-gripped the steering wheel.

"Yes, that." She stared straight ahead at the road cutting its way through the rolling hills dotted with cattle, horses, and the occasional farmhouse. "Lackluster. Totally and completely. Lackluster. That's you."

The corner of his mouth hiked up. "Keep telling yourself that, Blondie, but we both know I'm growing on you."

"Like a fungus."

He chuckled, loving her quick wit. "Fungi serve their purpose. Let's talk about mine. Prepare me for what to expect when we get to Harvey Farm. What exactly is a couple's shower?"

The car rolled to a stop at a four-way, and she twisted toward him. "First, I have a question."

"Fire away."

Her blue eyes pinned him. "Why did you ask me to pick you up from Hamilton House when Bodie and Sarah will be attending the shower?"

He'd known she'd eventually ask. She was too sharp not

to.

"They meant to swing by to pick me up after church before driving to Harvey Farms to assist with decorations. They got hung up at church with something Sarah's father asked her to help him with." He shrugged. "When they were already running behind, swinging by for me was going to put them in more of a time crunch, so I offered to have you pick me up."

She considered him for a few moments. "What if I'd said no?"

"You didn't." He gestured to her rearview mirror, pointing out the pickup truck that was barreling their way. "We should get to moving."

Putting on her signal, she turned the car left. Once they were moving along the paved two-lane road, she asked, "How did you get to Hamilton House?"

"Bodie picked me up at the airport. He assured me that it didn't make sense to rent a car while I was staying with him and Sarah." *Since Zach wasn't supposed to be driving.*

"Oh," she mused. "That does make sense."

His answers were all true, but guilt riddled him that he kept the biggest truth from Isabelle. He had to go thirty days without a *spell* before his neurologist would clear him to drive. Then it would be basic vehicles only and no planes, helicopters, or heavy equipment until he'd gone a full six months.

"Now it's your turn." He redirected their conversation to his earlier question. "Brief me. Who is going to be at this shower, and what do I need to know?"

Her nose curled at his *brief me.* "It's a wedding shower

for Cole and Sophie being given by the Butterflies to where everyone is invited, men and women. As far as what to expect? With those ladies, your guess is as good as mine. They know no limits. If you'd been here last Christmas for Rosie and Lou's wedding, you'd understand what I mean." She sighed. "I love them, but that doesn't mean I'm not upset over their matchmaking after we got back from our business meeting."

"Romantic Christmas picnic," he corrected. "Remember that you're supposed to be welcoming their matchmaking as you're incapable of resisting me."

She rolled her eyes. "Just so long as you remember to keep your hands to yourself."

"Yes, ma'am." He held up his hands.

"And your lips. Don't think that I'm letting you off the hook for that icky stunt you pulled in the quilt shop yesterday."

"I never dreamed that you would." Awful and now icky? He'd never had his kisses called that before. At least, not to his face. Not that his peck on her cheek had been much of a kiss, but no guy wanted his affections classified as *awful* and *icky*.

"What was that, anyway?" She tapped her fingers against the steering wheel.

"A lethal silencer." As simple as the peck had been, he'd replayed it in his mind dozens of times. He'd acted on instinct and usually trusted his instinct implicitly. With Isabelle, he was in unknown territory.

Her gaze cut toward him.

"You needed to get quiet, fast," he clarified. It was what

he'd concluded had been his reason for the impromptu kiss. He was a man used to doing whatever a job required to achieve success. "I silenced you."

"Lucky for you that it was on my cheek, or I'd have silenced you." She raised her knee for emphasis.

Even as he chuckled, Zach's stomach clenched. "Yeah, lucky for me."

PLEASE LET TODAY go okay. Isabelle silently prayed as she parked her car at Harvey Farm. She'd wanted to help hostess Sophie and Cole's shower, but the Butterflies had insisted that she was doing enough and to let them handle the party. The reality was she'd marked off everything that could be marked off her list until closer to the wedding, and until others completed their tasks, such as Zach finding the bride's wayward father to walk her down the aisle and the Butterflies finishing Sophie's wedding dress.

Although the sun shined, the air held a crispness that it hadn't the day before and Isabelle grabbed her jacket from the backseat prior to locking the car's doors.

His shoes crunching through the grass, Zach joined her. "Smile, Blondie."

"I can't." Pulling her gaze from the event barn in the distance, she crinkled her nose at him. "I'm too worried about what you're going to do to embarrass me today."

Rather than come back with some smart comment, he took her hand and turned her toward him. "I enjoy our sparring, Blondie. You're a worthy opponent. But I'm not going to intentionally embarrass you at your sister's wedding shower. I'm not all a bad guy."

"Just mostly," she mumbled, buying herself a moment to let what he said sink in. To take in the warm comfort of his hand holding hers. His hand should not be comforting.

The gold flecks in his eyes glistened. "Exactly. It's what makes me good at my job."

"Yeah, well, just don't forget that your job is the only reason you're here today."

"I won't. It's you forgetting that concerns me."

"No worries there," she assured. "I would never really date a military man, so you have nothing to be concerned about on that front."

He gave her a curious look. "I meant you forgetting to pretend to be affectionate toward me, so no one sees through our ruse."

Heat flooded her cheeks. She should have known he hadn't thought…

"I'll stomach my way through it," she managed, moving around him to head toward the event barn. A breeze whipped at her dress, flapping the long skirt about her knee boots.

"There's my girl." He kept pace beside her.

"But only until you find my father."

"And you teach me to quilt," he countered.

That he wanted to learn seemed so strange. Not that the quilt shop didn't have numerous male customers. Just that Zach seemed too larger than life to spend hours at the machine.

"A Quilts of Valor quilt," he clarified, taking her hand

back when she stumbled in an uneven spot hidden by the grass right before they reached the gravel road that led to the event barn. There were a few cars coming up the main drive, so Isabelle didn't pull her hand free.

"You'd be better off taking Sophie's class." Her sister's enthusiasm for the organization was admirable. "You only refused to be ornery."

Stepping across the small ditch that separated the grass and gravel, Zach held out both hands and lifted her across the divide.

Oh! He'd picked her up as if she weighed nothing and, surprised, she stared up at him, taking in the angles of his face, the strong line of his nose, the cleft in his chin.

"I refused your offer of signing me up for Sophie's class because that wasn't our deal." He clasped his fingers with hers. "You're supposed to teach me."

Standing next to him made her feel dainty and feminine. She bit into her lower lip. "I'm a teacher who knows how to delegate."

He laughed. "Odd, when I get the impression you have great difficulty delegating most things."

Isabelle couldn't argue. She was used to being in charge. Things went smoother that way.

"You're a bit of a control freak, aren't you, Blondie?" he asked as they began walking toward the barn.

"I am not," she defended, despite her previous thoughts, taking care not to scuff her boots or trip in the gravel.

"What's with all the lists, then?"

"You've seen one list, Zach. One." Not that she didn't have lots of others, including the one with his name at the top. In bold letters she'd written, DO NOT FALL FOR THIS ANNOYING MAN.

"Is that it? Your only list? I don't think so. Your aunt commented on your list-making yesterday. My guess is that you have a list for everything." Grinning, he glanced her way. "I bet you have a list in your purse that says, ATTEND SOPHIE AND COLE'S SHOWER, that you'll mark off later today."

She clutched her purse close.

Laughing, he gave her hand a gentle squeeze. "I'm right."

"Aren't you always?" she retorted. She tightened her hold on her purse. "In your mind, if nowhere else."

"Say what you will, Blondie, but that list is there." He grinned. "What I want is to know what you have written there for when you drive me home? Take the long way home so I get to spend more time with Zach?" he teased in a mimic tone. "Walk Zach to the front door? Kiss Zach good night?"

Frowning, she gestured toward his shoes. "You better hope those are comfortable because I seem to recall it saying, make Zach walk home. Or maybe you could call Santa to see if he will give you a ride home in his sleigh?"

Laughing, he lifted her hand to his lips and pressed a kiss there. "Thanks for making my visit to Pine Hill entertaining, Blondie. Also, smile. We're being watched."

Isabelle fought the urge to look around to see who watched and forced a smile instead.

"Perfect," he praised, his hazel eyes twinkling. "Now, let's go be a couple."

"We still have a bit before the shower," she reminded, searching for onlookers without moving her head away from his direction. Maybe the Peeping Toms were behind her. It was definitely a possibility since a couple of cars had come up the drive and were now parked near where they had. "We're early so that we can offer to help."

His brow lifted. "Afraid they didn't get something right?"

"No," she denied, frowning when he laughed. She didn't pull her hand free, just walked silently beside him as they made their way to the event barn's entrance. Fresh garland wreaths with red bows adorned the double wooden doors and an ornate tripod sign read, DAVIS & AARON SHOWER.

Inside the barn, Isabelle was pleased that at first glance everything appeared in order. Red tablecloths covered the numerous round tables. Holly-encircled candles flickered as centerpieces and gold plate settings added a splash of elegance. A spicy Christmas cranberry scent wafted through the large open room.

"Doesn't it look perfect?" Sarah came up and brandished a smile at them both. "Maybelle hired that new catering company and they're on point. The Butterflies are helping with the food, of course, because they can't resist showing off their culinary skills. But I'm so impressed with how wonderful everything looks."

"Me, too," Isabelle admitted, feeling a bit useless. She'd wanted everything to be perfect, but now she had idle time.

"Hello, lovelies," Rosie greeted, entering the room with a basket full of pens and paper.

Maybelle followed closely, Jeannie in her arms.

"There has to be something we can help do." Isabelle gave the ladies a hopeful look.

"If you insist. Place a pen and paper in each seat, please." Rosie handed the basket to Zach. "Isabelle, darlin', you come with me to grab the other basket."

"Yes, ma'am." Zach took the basket and went to the first table. Sarah followed, talking animatedly to him, but low enough Isabelle couldn't make out what her friend said.

With one last look toward where Zach smiled at whatever Sarah was saying, Isabelle followed Rosie, even though she knew she wasn't needed to carry the other basket.

"Y'all did a great job," she praised.

"Of course we did." Rosie waved her hand dismissively. "We've had decades of experience." Her expression became thoughtful, and she relented. "Well, the other Butterflies have had decades. I'm still in my prime, just a young, fluttery thing."

Isabelle smothered a smile. "That's what I thought. Now, are you going to tell me why you wanted me to go with you away from the others?"

Rosie giggled. "Not away from the others, silly girl. Just away from that hunky man of yours."

Isabelle started to correct her but held her tongue. For the moment, she had to go with the idea that Zach was hers. For Sophie.

"I got the impression yesterday that you Butterflies wanted me with Zach, not away from him."

"Oh, we do," Rosie assured. "But I'm not buying it. Hence the need to talk away from the others."

Uh-oh. Rosie saw right through them. Isabelle wasn't really surprised. She and Zach were so antagonistic.

"Not only did you look all twitterpated yesterday ... today, too, actually," Rosie continued, leaning against the wall, "but you looked happy."

Had she? Isabelle didn't recall feeling happy. She recalled being upset with how they were playing matchmaker and making comments that had made her feel as if she were an old maid.

"But Zach is military."

"Not active." Isabelle stunned herself as much as Rosie, whose eyes had widened at the defensive comment.

"Active, not active. That's never mattered. So, last night I was telling Lou that something was up."

Isabelle winced. They were barely started and already had been figured out.

"Then I realized the truth on why you're rushing into a relationship with a man who you usually wouldn't give the time of day. Not that he's not gorgeous, mind you, because he is, but I'm worried about you."

Wavering back and forth on just how much Rosie had figured out, Isabelle chose her words carefully. "I'm fine, Rosie. I promise. Sure, it's going to be different, but I'm happy for Sophie."

"Oh, I don't doubt that," Rosie assured. "You've always wanted what's best for your sister and been willing to sacrifice yourself to make that happen. But what I want to know is if that's why Zach is really in the picture?"

"Is that why you think he's in the picture?"

"To convince Sophie that you're happy and going to be just fine when she moves out?" Rosie gave her a pointed look. "It wouldn't shock me."

Rosie's tone set Isabelle's brain into motion. "What has

Sophie said to you?"

The older woman's face flushed. "Nothing."

"Something," Isabelle corrected, chest tightening. Sophie was worried about her? That wasn't the way of their world and shouldn't be now. Isabelle was the one who did the worrying, not the other way around. "You let my sister know that I am ecstatic over her marriage to Cole and that she has nothing to worry about where I'm concerned. I'm good. Better than good. I'm great."

Rosie's drawn on brow lifted. "Then you're not using Zach?"

"Using him?" Her jaw dropped. "Did you seriously just accuse me of using Zach?"

"I saw how that young man looked at you yesterday. He's falling hard, probably because you plied him with my cinnamon bread, even though we both know that you'd never give your heart to someone with a military background. The poor man doesn't realize you'd never trust enough to let that happen." Rosie sighed. "My bread has him blinded."

Isabelle rubbed her temple. "Let me get this straight ... you're warning me not to break Zach's heart?"

The irony of it made her want to burst out laughing.

"Well, of course, I don't want you to break his heart." Rosie fluttered her lashes. "Although he says the right things and smiles freely, there's something haunted in his gaze that tells me there's more than what meets the eye."

"I'm sure you're right, Rosie." There was a lot more to Zach than what met the eye.

Hysteria bubbled inside her, threatening to tumble free.

As if a small-town someone like her could hurt a seasoned soldier like Zach. How did that even work that Rosie was worried about him? The Butterflies were her friends. She was the hometown girl and Zach, the stranger. Shouldn't they be worried that he'd hurt her? Did they think her so emotionally invincible that she couldn't fall for someone?

She could fall. She had fallen and look where that had gotten her? Realizing she'd just admitted that Greg's ending things with her had hurt more than she'd ever let herself acknowledge, Isabelle winced, then forced a smile at the woman watching her closely.

"You have nothing to worry about, Rosie. I'm not going to hurt Zach." He'd have to really care for that to happen. Their relationship wasn't real.

SO MANY PEOPLE filled the Harvey Farm event barn that Zach wondered if the entire town had shut down for the shower. If so, they'd done so happily. Laughter rang out, breaking above the constant conversation hum. The food was good enough to make everyone smile. Ruby hadn't been kidding when she'd bragged about it.

Sitting next to him at an upfront table, Isabelle stretched to lean close, as if she was telling him something private. "What were you and Sophie talking about earlier?"

Her breath tickled his ear, causing goosebumps to prickle his skin. He'd stuck close, watching her fret, trying to meet her sister's needs before Sophie had even realized there was a need. This was their first semi-alone moment, and she hadn't hesitated to seize it.

"Things." Tossing a wedding bell shaped mint into his mouth, Zach savored the flavored chocolate candy.

"Zach!" Realizing she was louder than she should have been, she grimaced. "Ugh, at being the center of attention. Don't they know they're supposed to be paying attention to Cole and Sophie?"

As many eyes were on them as on the engaged couple. To give credit, they kept their stares subtle. Well, except for the older ladies, and they didn't mind making eye contact when he'd look their way. Rosie had even winked conspiratorially, and Isabelle's Aunt Claudia had given him a thumbs-up.

He eyed the remaining goodies on his plate. He'd foregone cake in favor of fruit, nuts, and the mints, but might make another trip through the buffet line for a second helping of everything. He'd be lucky if he hadn't gained ten pounds by the time he left Pine Hill. He should probably up his workout.

"What do I have in common with your sister to talk to her about?"

Isabelle stared expectantly at him. "Me?"

Nodding, he pushed his chair back, then headed toward the buffet, not surprised when Isabelle followed and pulled him over to a long table that had been set up with photos of Cole and Sophie. He let his gaze run over the pictures. Cole wore various expressions, but Sophie's face was joyous in each one. Did the woman ever not smile? Then again, she had Isabelle running interference for her, trying to make every day seem like Christmas.

For the sake of their audience, she pointed out a photo of Sophie and Cole horseback riding. "My sister is the kindest-hearted person to ever walk the face of the earth. She sees the positive in everyone. There's nothing I wouldn't do for her."

The love in Isabelle's voice was humbling. Not that Zach didn't feel the same for his family. Or maybe he didn't, because he hadn't been able to give up his military career when they'd insisted he do so. He sure hadn't been able to stand the pity in their eyes when he'd returned home a broken man. Nor had he agreed to work for his father's company. They'd probably breathed a sigh of relief when he'd gone back to the rehab facility to finish recuperating. Going home when he hated life probably hadn't been great timing.

"Sophie is lucky to have you. Not many would go to the lengths you do to insure her happiness."

Isabelle's gaze lifted, full of questions.

"You're pretending to date someone you profess to not like so that he will find the father that you don't want found," he clarified.

"That about sums it up, but for the record, I more than profess not to like you." Her chin lifted and she gave him that annoyed look she loved to flash his way. "I really don't."

Glad her spunk was back and distracting himself from his family thoughts, Zach grinned. "Keep trying to convince yourself of that, Blondie, but I'm not buying it. I'm fully aware that you waylaid my trip to the buffet so you could walk me straight over to stand beneath the mistletoe. All you had to do was ask and I'd have been happy to oblige you."

Isabelle glanced up, gasping that there really were green

twigs hanging above them. "Don't you dare."

"Oh, I'd dare," he assured, wondering why the thought of kissing Isabelle had danger warnings surging the same as if he were in a combat zone. "But you wouldn't be able to contain your excitement if I kissed you, so I won't. We already have too much of the spotlight on us."

"Kind of you." She snorted, seeming relieved that he wasn't upholding the tradition.

"I'm a good, decent guy that way."

"Ha, you keep telling yourself that, but we both know better," she tossed back, then with one last squinted glare, she walked over to get another cup of Christmas punch.

Knowing they had an avid audience, Zach kept his broad grin on his face as he watched her pick up a pre-filled cup and toss it back as if it contained liquid courage rather than a Christmas cranberry concoction. Once done, she refilled and headed to their table.

How could he feel so protective of someone that he also loved to rattle so much?

Making his way to the buffet, he gathered additional helpings of the meats and vegetables, then rejoined Isabelle.

Along with the others at the table, she was answering the questions on the "Bride or Groom?" papers Zach had distributed earlier.

Rather than scribble answers on his sheet, he took a bite of the holiday-shaped cracker he'd placed a slice of cheese on. "Since I just met the bride and groom this week, I'll pass."

"Just guess. Fifty-fifty odds aren't too bad. It's in fun, anyway." She wrote BRIDE next to WHO MADE THE FIRST MOVE? Then wrote, AND THE SECOND AND THIRD AND…

out to the side of her answer. With the way Cole looked at Sophie, it was difficult to imagine that sweet Sophie had had to do much chasing.

Cleaning his plate, Zach watched Isabelle answer the next couple of questions. "Maybe I'll just have fun and write MAID OF HONOR in each spot."

Looking up, she frowned. "Have you read the questions?"

"Who planned the honeymoon?" he read out loud. "I'd get that one right with my answer."

Isabelle's cheeks pinkened. "Only because Cole asked for help. He wanted to know if Sophie had ever mentioned somewhere she'd want to travel to. Every time he'd ask, she'd just say that where he was is where she wanted to be and where that was didn't matter."

He could hear Sophie saying that.

"You told him Paris?"

Jaw dropping, Isabelle shushed him. "I can't believe Cole told you. I thought he didn't want anyone other than Andrew and I knowing where they were going in case the Butterflies decided to do a French Flutter."

"A French Flutter?" Zach chuckled. "I'm right about where they're going, then?"

Her color heightened as she realized she'd been played. "That was a lucky guess."

"Not really. Paris is considered the most romantic city in the world. Your sister has probably been dreaming of strolling along Avenue des Champs-Élysées, putting a lock on Pont Des Arts Bridge with her true love, and eating crepes to her heart's content since she was a kid."

Isabelle's eyes widened. "Better be careful. You're sounding a little romantic yourself."

"I'm the least romantic guy you'll ever meet." Romance had never been a priority. Or even a consideration. When it came to ladies, he was a gentleman—his parents had raised him that way—but romance? Nope. Not his style. Nor theirs, really. "I just saw that scenario happen over and over when I was in Paris."

"You've been to Paris?" There was a light in her eyes that made him think that Sophie wasn't the only Davis girl who'd dreamed of visiting the city of love.

"I've been all over the world." He'd seen fabulous locales and some that had made him wonder if hell was a place on earth. "For the record, I never stepped foot on that bridge, even when it was legal to put locks on it. Never wanted to."

"I'm suddenly feeling very small town and uncultured." She gave a nervous laugh, then bragged, "I went to Florida once."

The truth hit him. "You went to some magical kingdom because Sophie wanted to go?"

Her expression said he'd hit the nail on the head. "You make it sound as if it was torturous. That's far from the truth. We had a great time. It's one of my favorite memories."

Eyeing her, listening to her wistful, yet defensive tone, he asked, "How old were you?"

"Twenty-one."

The depths that Isabelle had gone to, to give Sophie a good life, shouldn't shock him, but his realization about the trip still had him staring at her with renewed appreciation.

"You brought your sister?"

"The trip was my gift for her high school graduation. Academia wasn't as easy for her as I found it. She'd worked hard, made good grades, and deserved a getaway to somewhere completely magical."

Isabelle set the bar high on sibling standards.

"Where did you go on your high school trip, Isabelle?" That he'd called her by her name instead of Blondie should have told him that the question was too personal.

"I worked at the quilt shop all summer, saving as much as I could, so I guess you could say that my senior trip was to Nashville. It's a great city."

Where she'd likely found a job, worked while going to school, and pinched pennies to where she'd been able to take Sophie on her dream senior trip. She'd been looking out for her sister her whole life, but who'd looked out for Isabelle? Battling the protective emotions assailing him, he leaned over and wrote MAID OF HONOR next to WHO WOULD MAKE THE BETTER CHRISTMAS TREE ANGEL TOPPER?

Glancing at the question, Isabelle snorted. "I'm no angel."

Zach disagreed. She was Sophie's guardian angel.

"COLE WILL BE here in a few minutes to pick Mom and I up to take us to dinner." Sophie put her purse and jacket on a chair's armrest. "Are you sure you and Zach don't want to go with us? We'd love to spend time with Zach."

Isabelle had no doubts. Her sister had been talking about

Zach nonstop since the shower, going on and on about how much she liked him.

"Not tonight, but thanks." At Sophie's disappointed look, she added, "He really wants to learn to sew. I thought teaching him on Grandma Belle's old Singer would be a great place to start. No bells or whistles, just high-quality basic stitches."

"I'd wondered why you weren't meeting him at the shop."

Because Zach wanted to look at old photo albums of their father. To do that he had to be at their house, and she'd needed an excuse as to why he'd be there. As much as she hated to admit it, his dating ruse had been brilliant in that regard.

It had been so long since she'd dated that maybe this was good practice in case she ever decided to do so for real again. She doubted many men would find sharing her life exciting. Definitely, a man who'd lived on the edge and traveled around the world, such as Zach had, wouldn't find her routine, small-town existence appealing.

Where had that come from? She liked her life. Who cared what Zach thought of it?

After Cole picked up her mother and Sophie, Isabelle took out the bag she'd packed supplies into at the shop before leaving that day. She'd pulled a basic sewing kit that had needles, thread, thimble, ruler, scissors, pins, and pincushion, along with a few pieces of fabric remnants.

She'd bypassed several patriotic pieces and chosen pink cupcakes, unicorns, and kittens leftover scraps instead. Eyeing the colorful cartoon print, she suppressed a giggle. If she had to do this with Zach, she might as well have fun with it.

A knock sounded. When she opened the front door, her breath halted at Zach holding and sweet-talking Bobbin. The yellow tabby cat didn't usually warm to strangers, but he was purring and rubbing his head against Zach's arm as if he was dipped in catnip. Figured that her cat would like him.

"Okay to bring him in?"

She stepped aside so he could enter. "Bobbin was a stray who adopted our family. We let him come and go as he pleases. He's happiest that way."

Once inside, Bobbin happily cradled in his arms, Zach moved from one embarrassing captured moment hanging on the living room wall to the next, studying each one as if he was putting it to memory.

"I'm not very photogenic," she explained when he paused at her cap and gown senior photo, displayed next to Sophie's gorgeous smiled one.

"You're beautiful, Blondie. A photo is always going to pale in comparison to the real deal, but never doubt how attractive you are on the outside, but even better, on the inside. That's a rare combo."

"I, um, thank you." Warm and fuzzy heat fluttered in her belly. "I wasn't fishing for a compliment, but I do appreciate your kind words."

"Nothing kind about telling the truth." He moved on to a collection of framed snapshots.

Cheeks warm, she moved closer to where he looked and couldn't keep from smiling at the full of love pictures proudly displayed. "Sophie got a kiddie camera from Santa when she was seven. That morning and every year since, she takes a Christmas morning photo."

He gestured toward where clearer photos started. "Looks as if she upgraded her camera."

"Very observant. I gave her a camera for her sixteenth birthday."

He turned, met her gaze, and his hazel gaze had her stomach flip-flopping. Why was he looking at her that way? As if he could see right inside her to her very being?

Breaking eye contact, she took Bobbin from him. The cat gave her a what-are-you-doing look, slapping her hand with his paw once before wanting down. Isabelle put him down.

Watching the cat head to Sophie's room, she sighed. "We should get started with your lesson."

"Aren't we going to look at the photo albums that have photos of your father first?"

"I suppose we should." Her flip-floppity stomach contracted into a tight ball. He was right. They should find the pictures first. Her family would likely return within an hour.

"You don't like sharing personal things, do you?"

Not meeting his gaze, she shook her head. "Not with strangers."

"We're not strangers."

Because he really could read her thoughts and knew her better than anyone?

"Under normal circumstances you wouldn't be in my house, about to look through my life," she reminded, walking over to the end table cabinet where her mother kept old photo albums.

"Afraid I'll learn all your secrets?"

"You already know my worst one."

His tone had been teasing, but her embarrassment burned deep. Feeling his gaze boring into her, she bent to pull out a stack of albums.

"If your father leaving is your worst secret, then you're luckier than you think."

His tone implied that he had secrets far darker. Part of her wanted to ask, but to do so implied an intimacy she didn't want to encourage. They were business partners. Nothing more.

She placed the photo albums on the coffee table, then sat on the sofa. "Let's get this over with."

Chapter Seven

ZACH POINTED TO a photo of Isabelle wearing her mother's high heels and a pink feather boa. "I see you've always had a great sense of fashion."

"Sophie and I were playing dress-up in Mom's things." She smiled at the memory. "You don't have to look at every photo. The purpose of this is to figure out where my father is, not to gawk at my childhood."

"Ah, now, Blondie. Nothing wrong with proving that you're a natural blond."

"I wish I weren't." How many times had she considered coloring her hair to erase the reminder? Hundreds? Thousands?

Zach's gaze shifted to her. "Why is that?"

"The women in my family resemble my Grandma Belle. Sophie is a younger version of her with her dark eyes and hair." A resigned expression came over her face. "Then you have me."

"You look like your father?" he guessed.

She nodded.

"He must have been a handsome man."

Isabelle shrugged. "My mother must have thought so."

"There aren't any photos of him hanging on the walls."

"Of course not." Had he thought there would be?

His expression unreadable, he studied her. "But there are photos of him in these albums?"

"We just haven't gotten to them." Years ago, she'd wanted to toss every photo of Cliff Davis, but Sophie had made her promise she'd leave them alone. As it had been years since she'd looked at the albums, that they were still there hadn't mattered.

"You chose an album full of fun photos of you and yet you complain that I'm looking at every photo?" He shook his head and flipped to the next page. "It's never dull with you around, Blondie."

"Yeah, yeah. I'm just a barrel of monkeys." Biting her lip, she eyed the stack of photo albums, her gaze lingering on a faded burgundy one in the middle. Her stomach felt as if it were a barrel full of caffeinated monkeys.

"We don't have to do this if you don't want to."

His gentle offer had her turning, surprised at how much empathy shined in his gaze.

Not liking his pity, she straightened her shoulders. "If we didn't have to do this, you wouldn't be here." Reaching for the album, she pulled it free and handed it to him. "Here, you look at this. I'm going to get a drink. Do you want something?"

"Me, a drink, and photo albums?" He shook his head. "Nope. Thanks, though."

He made a good point. As shaky as she felt, she shouldn't have liquids anywhere near the photos. Then again, if she damaged certain ones, maybe she'd never have to see them again.

Because deep in her gut, she dreaded what opening that binder was going to reveal.

Outside of her mind, she'd not seen Cliff Davis in years. Not in person or in photographs. She'd purposely kept it that way.

In the kitchen, she poured a glass of water, planned to stall for several minutes, but cringed when she heard the front door. What were her sister, mother, and Cole doing back so soon?

Isabelle rubbed her temple, wondering how best to explain that they'd walked in with Zach looking through the family albums. Or maybe she wasn't going to have to, she thought moments later as Sophie's exclamation sounded loud from the living room.

"Oh, look at this one of Izzy winning her fourth-grade spelling bee!" No doubt her sister had cozied up on the sofa next to Zach. "She's always been so smart. She was valedictorian of her senior class and had a full scholarship to an Ivy League school in Nashville."

"I've always been so proud of her," her mom added. "She's my rock."

Heat flooded Isabelle's face. Guilt plagued her for eavesdropping, but she couldn't bring herself to return to the living room quite yet, either.

"Mine, too," Sophie assured. "No one has a better sister, or best friend, because she's that, as well. My sister, best friend, business partner." Emotion cracked Sophie's voice. "She's the most selfless person I know."

Her guilt blossomed. She and Sophie had never kept secrets from each other. Would her sister understand that

Isabelle hadn't told her about looking for their father for her own good? That pretending to like Zach had been a necessary evil to give her the wedding she dreamed of?

"I agree. She's brilliant and her eyes are as blue as the Mediterranean. So beautiful. Now, tell me more," Zach encouraged. "What about boyfriends? Any past relationships I should be worried about?"

Zach was going along with their cover, but his praise made her breathy, made her wonder if he believed what he said or if it was all just part of his getting her family to open up to him in hopes of gleaning information about where her father might be.

"There was this music exec in Nashville for a few years. They met while in school. We thought they'd marry, but that ended several years ago. These days, she rarely dates."

Good grief. Any moment Sophie would be telling him that Isabelle's first kiss had been when she was sixteen and that the guy had broken up with her the next day, making her forever wonder if she'd been that horrible.

"But don't think that it's from a lack of interested men," Sophie assured. "The high school's music director has been trying to get her attention since he moved to Pine Hill. Trevor's a sweetheart, kind, stable, and wants a wife and kids. I kept encouraging him to not give up, but as always, Izzy knew best. She's been waiting for you."

Isabelle groaned. All along, she'd thought the man had a thing for Sophie, but instead her sister had been encouraging him to like her? No wonder he had made googly eyes when she'd dropped off the Christmas sashes for Annabelle's choir concert. For that matter, her sister insisting Isabelle be the one to drop them off made more sense, too.

She'd met Zach that windy day. Who would have thought that the handsome man who'd rescued her list would end up pretending to be her boyfriend so he could find her father? What a whirlwind that meeting had ended up being!

"Be sure to let him know that she's taken." The possessiveness in Zach's voice made Isabelle's head spin. What would it feel like for a man to truly feel that way about her? To want her to the exclusion of all others? What would it feel like for Zach to really feel that way about her?

"I'll let him know her heart beats to the melody of yours."

At her sister's music-teacher pun, Isabelle rolled her eyes and fought putting her hands on her hips as she made her presence known. "Seriously, Sophie? Zach and I barely know each other and you're talking as if we're madly in love. We're"—her gaze met his and the warning reminder there about undid her as she mumbled—"we're taking things slow."

How could her sister think she'd have fallen for him? She'd worried her sister wouldn't buy their charade, and instead, Sophie was all hearts and flowers. Part of her was disappointed that her sister hadn't picked up on just how much Isabelle didn't like him.

He was the epitome of what she wouldn't want in a man. Not true, a nagging voice pointed out. He was intelligent, brave, strong, confident, had a wicked sense of humor, and was honest almost to a fault, except for their fake relationship, and that was forgivable, since it was for a good cause.

Inherently, she recognized those things about him. He was also military. She'd never trust that a switch wouldn't flip and he'd disappear.

Good thing theirs wasn't a real relationship.

"Mom, do something with your love-sick-so-the-rest-of-the-world-must-be-too daughter."

"Being in love is the most wonderful feeling in the world," her mother surprised her by saying from where she perched on the sofa's armrest, apparently having been peering at the photo album. "Sophie, I think we're embarrassing your sister. Perhaps tossing your wedding bouquet her way would be a little more subtle."

And her family wondered why she didn't date?

"Thanks, Mom. That was helpful." Isabelle smacked her forehead. "Run while you still can, Zach."

From where he sat next to her sister, Zach was taking in the exchange. Isabelle wouldn't blame him if he called off their deal. If Zach had been a real boyfriend, he'd have already been out the door.

"I'm not going anywhere," Zach said, earning a look of approval from Cole, Sophie, and her mother.

"Because my family behaving as if I'm a desperate old maid is way too entertaining to miss out on experiencing again?" she guessed.

"Something like that." His gaze was more serious than she would have expected, given the circumstances. That light in his eyes made her think she'd rather see amusement than whatever that look was.

"Smart man," Cole said, putting his arm around Sophie's shoulders as she scooted closer.

"He knows when he's met the most amazing woman in the world." Sophie patted the place she'd vacated between her and Zach. "Come sit, Izzy. We got our food order to go and brought extras in case you and Zach were hungry. We came home early because we decided to decorate the Christmas tree Cole and I bought at Harvey Farm this morning. Originally, we'd planned to do it tomorrow, but I couldn't wait." Sophie's enthusiasm for Christmas rivaled Santa's. "But I've not looked at these in ages and needed to pull a few more for the wedding. What better way to set the tone for putting up our Christmas tree than sweet memories?"

Glancing at the album Zach held, she realized it was the book they'd been looking at prior to her shoving the burgundy one at him. She'd only been in the kitchen a few minutes before her family had returned. Was it possible that he'd continued looking at the original album after she'd left?

What started out as awkward torture ended up as smiles and belly laughs at some of the crazy photos she and Sophie had taken over the years. That they only made it through the top few albums prior to moving on to decorating helped. Although it was why Zach was there, that burgundy album would have been a certain mood killer.

"Is the star even?" Isabelle asked from where she stood on the seat of a kitchen chair.

"Looks good to me." Next to her, Zach had his hand on the chair back in a steadying hold.

Glancing down, she realized he was looking at her and not the tree. She narrowed her gaze, but he only grinned.

From across the room, Sophie eyed the tree. "Maybe just a little to the left."

Isabelle stretched to straighten the star but couldn't quite reach it.

"Be careful."

Her gaze shifted to Zach. "You'd catch me if I fell, though, right?"

"Every single time."

Staring into his eyes, it would be so easy to believe him.

"I SHOULD HAVE asked to leave earlier but I didn't want to pull you away from the tree decorating. I'm sorry that you're having to drive me back to Sarah and Bodie's so late." Since squeezing himself into the passenger seat of her sedan, watching Isabelle had fascinated Zach much more than watching Pine Hill's nonexistent nightlife out the window. He felt quite useless sitting there, twiddling his thumbs. God, he hated being a burden. Always had.

"I can pull over and let you drive."

As independent as she was, he was surprised she'd offered. He was also frustrated that he couldn't say yes if he wanted to. Just a couple of more weeks without a spell and his driving restrictions would be lifted. Hopefully, permanently this time.

"From what I've seen, you're a great driver, Blondie." No rolling through stop signs for Isabelle. Unlike his lead-footed hostess, Isabelle abided by the speed limits, too. "I was referring to inconveniencing you."

In the glow of the dashboard partially illuminating the car's interior, she huffed. "Of all the ways you've inconvenienced me, this is the one that bothers you?"

"How else have I inconvenienced you?" He studied her profile, taking in her no-nonsense straight haircut, the light makeup highlighting her cheeks and pretty eyes, her twisted with annoyance lips.

His gaze lingered there, wondering what it would feel like to have Isabelle Davis curve her mouth in a smile toward him. A real smile, one full of happiness and … and what? Friendship? More?

When she stopped the car at a traffic light and turned to him, her gaze connecting with his, Zach's heart rate bypassed every speed sign between her place and Hamilton House, making him glad Bodie wasn't around with his radar gun, as no way could the thundering in his chest not register.

"I—well." Her chest rose and fell with a deep breath. "From the moment we met you've been completely irritating."

He arched a brow. "By rescuing your list?"

"By not immediately returning my list and by laughing at me chasing it." Giving him another annoyed look, she broke eye contact and sighed with relief when the light changed to green.

"I was laughing with you, Blondie. Not at you." Zach smiled when she glanced both ways twice before letting her foot off the brake to turn the car to drive them through town.

"I wasn't laughing." Her gaze stayed on the road.

Garland wreaths with twinkling lights hung from each lamppost and most shops were already decorated to Christmas card perfection.

"Life is short." Oh, how he knew this one. Everyone, him included, had thought his would be much shorter. At one point, he'd wanted it to be. "You should have been laughing."

Instead, she carried too much of a load to let herself go often. Seeing her laugh to the point she had to hold her belly, that she had to wipe tears of joy from her lovely face—as she had while Sophie had been ribbing her about some of the photos, or how the two sisters had giggled at various points when they'd shared looks, at how they'd teased each other when they'd been stringing popcorn to hang on the tree—convinced him that Isabelle's happiness mattered more than it should to a man who was just passing through. Way more.

"I'll keep that in mind the next time I go chasing after my blown-away list."

Ah, Isabelle and her lists. Wonder what she'd say if he snatched one of her lists and wrote, LAUGH OUT LOUD?

"How's that going?"

She glanced his way. "My list?"

He nodded and, gaze back to the road, she shrugged.

"You tell me. After our embarrassing walk down memory lane and wasting a bunch of the popcorn while joining in on my family Christmas tree decorating, are you any closer to finding my father?"

"The popcorn looked better on you than the tree." Shifting in the seat, he repositioned his cramped legs.

Isabelle's cheeks pinkened. "You made a mess by throwing it at me."

"I wasn't the one who dumped out the whole bowl," he

pointed out.

"You deserved it," she countered.

"Maybe," he agreed, laughing.

"Definitely. As far as the album, did you look at it before they got back?"

He shook his head.

"And after they did, Sophie was so excited showing you those awful photos of me that we never got to them."

None of the photos had been awful. Far from it. What they'd been was a record of a girl who'd taken on too much responsibility too early in life. Straight-A student, winner of this award and that award. From what he could tell, the only time Isabelle cut loose and had fun was when it involved Sophie.

"Which means you still want to look at them. Tell me again how looking at old photos is going to find someone who left two decades ago."

"Just like how you and Sophie were bringing up memories tonight, photos trigger things forgotten." Wasn't that what the therapists had told him during the months after his injuries when they'd been working with him? Not that it had worked. That blow to his head had obviously done too much damage for some things to be remembered. If he ever did, well, what he might recall scared him more than he wanted to admit.

"I know you're right. I'll even admit that tonight wasn't as awful as I've let on, but as far as the photos triggering memories of Dad—" Isabelle tightened her grip on the steering wheel as she stared at the road. "I really hate to do that to Mom. She doesn't need that burden, and Sophie and

I were so small when he left that our memories aren't going to help. I know I have to talk to her about this, to make sure she's okay with his being there, prior to telling Sophie, but I don't want her hurt by any of this."

"Yeah, you definitely need to talk to her."

"I will if you find him."

"I will find him." He wouldn't rest until he did. "We need to look at the albums. I need photos to run through age simulators."

"Because we need to know what he looks like now." She sighed. "Fine. We'll go through that album." She sounded as excited about doing so as he felt about going to any of his many specialists. "But not at my house. I'll … I'll put it in my car, and we'll go through it soon."

"Why not at your house?"

"You know why not." She took a deep breath. "Sophie means well with all her matchmaking, but without thinking things through, she assumes everything will work out all Christmas morning jolly. Even if all this were real, you and I have nothing in common. She should recognize that with our histories, we aren't a good match."

Isabelle was right. They weren't. She was way too good of a person for the likes of him. She was a good girl rule follower, and he was a rebel with a past so bad his brain refused to remember it.

"Besides, I don't know who Sophie thinks is going to take care of Mom if I ever did meet someone," Isabelle continued, more to herself than to him, revealing private thoughts that exposed another layer of that protective, responsible-for-everyone depth that she bound herself by.

"I imagine she recognizes that your mother is a grown woman and can take care of herself."

Isabelle's sharp intake of breath cut deep to his core because that was how intense her reaction was.

"You don't really know my family."

"I know that you feel responsible for your mother and Sophie. Not that there is anything wrong with wanting to take care of one's family, but you take it beyond what's normal. Why is that?"

"You think I'm abnormal because I want to take care of my family?" She gripped the steering wheel so tightly that he wondered if she was imagining throttling him rather than the car. "Of course, I'm responsible for them. I have been since my father left."

Bingo. When Cliff Davis left, Isabelle had made sure her family didn't fall apart. Only problem was, she'd been a child and shouldn't have had to carry that responsibility. From what he could gather, Darlene had been overwhelmed with grief and wondering how she was going to support her two daughters after her husband's disappearance. Isabelle's mother had thrown herself into working long hours six days a week, leaving her girls in their Aunt Claudia's care until Isabelle got old enough to watch over Sophie. A role that years later she'd not relinquished.

"Maybe it's time for you to recognize that your sister is grown and about to be married, that your mother seems to be doing fine, and they don't need you taking care of them anymore."

Her jaw clenched. "You're in no position to be giving me advice on taking care of my family."

Zach winced. She was right. He wasn't. Look at his own family. If anything, he'd always been the one to rely on Brett to be the responsible one, leaving his brother to step into the family business and deal with their parents while Zach went off to chase his military dreams.

Looking at the tense set of Isabelle's jaw, memories of his last row with his brother hit. Was that how Brett felt about him? Was that why he had been so disappointed when Zach had come home a broken man, feeling obligated to put him back together again in ways Zach hadn't wanted or welcomed? His deepest wounds couldn't heal because they were locked inside his head. Zach knew that, even if his brother hadn't recognized anything beyond the surface.

Isabelle pulled the car into Hamilton House's drive. There were a few cars Zach didn't recognize, indicating that new guests had arrived. She didn't look toward him, just sat in the driver's seat, waiting on him to get out of the car.

"Thanks for bringing me home."

She nodded and he got out of the car and watched her drive away.

Rather than go into the house, he sat down in one of the front-porch rocking chairs, breathing in the crisp November air and musing over the night with Harry's company since the dog had wanted to be let out.

Scratching the dog's scruff, he admitted that Isabelle was right. He did understand and saw what he was positive she didn't see herself. Sophie wanted her father to walk her down the aisle, but Isabelle needed him there so she could step back from the self-imposed responsibility for her family's well-being that she'd taken on when he'd left. For whatever reason, Isabelle had felt she had to fill her father's shoes and had been doing her best to do so ever since.

Zach was going to find Cliff Davis.

Not just for Sophie, but for Isabelle, in hopes it set the little girl inside her free.

"LAST NIGHT WAS so much fun." Sophie leaned against Isabelle's office doorframe. "Mom, Cole and me, and you and Zach. He seems completely smitten, Izzy, and fits right in with us, doesn't he?"

Because he was faking it. Isabelle really didn't want to talk about Zach, so she pretended to be absorbed in printing out the shipping labels for the online items they'd sold so she could drop them by the post office on her way home.

"I love that he helped Cole carry in the tree and how he loves to tease you." Giddiness oozed from Sophie's voice, making Isabelle guilty that she continued to stare at the computer screen even when Sophie came into the small room and pulled a stackable chair next to Isabelle's desk.

"You light up when he does that, you know?" *From internal combustion where he drove her crazy.* "I like him. Cole likes him. Mom likes him. Even Bobbin likes him, and you know how finnicky our cat is." *Traitorous cat.* "It makes me happy that you like him, too, Izzy."

Isabelle winced. She did like him. Only she didn't. And yet, she did. Was it possible to really truly dislike someone and like them at the same time?

"I have a surprise for you." Sophie's voice held its usual

cheer as she tapped her fingernails to a Christmas tune.

A sinking feeling in her gut, Isabelle glanced toward her sister's hand. Sophie's nails were painted blue, and she had a sparkly white snowflake on her thumbnail. Smiling snowmen covered her other nails. Dragging her gaze from those blasted, happy snowmen, she forced a smile to her face, despite the unease wreaking havoc in her belly.

"What kind of surprise and please tell me that it doesn't involve Zach?"

"Of course it involves Zach." Sophie's exuberant smile said it all, and Isabelle's sinking feeling Titanicked. "Since y'all never made it to his sewing lesson last night, I've rescheduled his lesson."

Isabelle swallowed, hoping the tightness in her throat eased. "At your class?"

"No, silly. Why would he do that when he has you to give private lessons?" Sophie clasped her hands together. "He'll be by at six for his first one."

"We close at six," she automatically responded, fighting her rising panic.

"Which is why he's coming by then," Sophie explained, all smiles. "Mom has a meeting at church regarding the Christmas festival booth. She's so excited to be helping this year." Sophie's expression grew dreamy. "Cole wants me to come out to the farm to make sure I like the paint color for my new sewing room. He's such a thoughtful man to suggest that we turn one of the spare bedrooms into a sewing room. Isn't he just the best?"

Isabelle nodded, her mind still processing that Zach was going to be there in—she glanced at her watch—thirty minutes. "Call Zach and cancel." She gestured to her computer. "I've got a ton to do tonight."

"There's nothing that can't wait." Frowning, Sophie eyed her more closely. "I've seen how you are when you're with him, Isabelle. I know you like him, and he likes you."

Frustrated, Isabelle glanced toward the computer screen. Sophie was the person she shared everything with. Only, with Zach, she couldn't share. Why was it the one time she needed to vent to her sister, that she wanted Sophie's thoughts, she had to hold everything inside?

"My relationship with Zach is complicated," she admitted, thinking truer words had never been spoken.

"Because he's military?" Sophie leaned forward, as if being closer would make Isabelle understand better. "You can't let that get in the way of what's happening between you two."

What was happening between them wasn't real.

"Sarah says he's wonderful."

Sophie had discussed Zach with Sarah?

"She barely knows him," Isabelle pointed out, although that wasn't how Sarah had told it when she'd called that morning.

She'd gone on about how great Zach was with Jeannie, how helpful he was around Hamilton House, how sweet he'd been to buy her the quilt kits, and how much she loved getting to know Bodie's friend. She couldn't say enough kind words about her houseguest. Someone should award her sister and friend future Butterfly badges. *Ugh.*

"Bodie has known him for years." Sophie remained unfazed. "He'd never let someone he didn't trust spend so much time alone with Sarah and Jeannie."

Isabelle couldn't argue that. Bodie was relaxed with Zach in ways that she'd never seen him be with other veterans who'd stayed in their Beds for Vets suite. But that was probably because all the other veterans had been strangers prior to their arrival, just individuals sent to Hamilton House by Lukas for Sarah and Bodie to help them find their way again.

Was Zach really just there visiting his friend or had Lukas sent him for the same reason? If so, why? Zach seemed so together, a charmer who didn't take life too seriously. At least, not on the surface. Appearances could be deceiving, though.

Meeting Sophie's expectant gaze, Isabelle sighed. "I know you're so happy in love with Cole that you want me to be just as happily in love, but you can't force that to happen, Sophie. Throwing Zach and I together, saying the things you said last night, well, they make me feel panicked. I know you mean well, but, just … just don't, okay?"

Sophie's eyes widened. "I went overboard in my excitement, didn't I?"

Isabelle nodded.

"Oh, Izzy, I'm sorry. Please tell me that I haven't ruined this. I'd never forgive myself."

Guilt hit. Why had she said all that to her sister about a relationship that was only fake? She didn't want Sophie worried or thinking she'd been the cause of the demise of something that had never existed.

"You haven't ruined anything, because regardless of how I feel, or don't feel," she added for emphasis, "we both know

Zach is only here for a short time and I'm tied to Pine Hill."

Sophie considered her a moment. "You do realize that if you want to leave, you can?"

"Why would I want to leave?" Isabelle frowned. Was that how her comment had come across? Leaning back, she tucked her hair behind her ear. "I'm happy here. Pine Hill is my home."

"I feel the same," Sophie agreed, but didn't relent. "You may not talk about it, but I know you were happy in Nashville, too."

"I've never regretted coming home and buying the shop with you. Please don't let whatever is happening between Zach and me make you think otherwise."

Especially when nothing was happening. Nothing but a business deal.

"Good, because I don't want you to regret that." Sophie's smile was genuine, and she seemed back to her joyous self as she said, "Getting to work with you is one of the best parts of my life."

"Agreed." She hugged her sister. "For the record, I was happy in Nashville, but I'd always meant to come home. After graduation, my job offer was so good I didn't think I should turn it down." She didn't say that she'd worried how she'd help her sister with college expenses if Sophie decided to pursue that avenue. She'd been tucking every penny away. Her frugalness had paid off when the quilt shop had gone up for sale and, full of dreams, Sophie had asked Isabelle what she thought about their trying to make a go of purchasing it. "I missed you, Mom, and Pine Hill," she admitted truthfully.

"We are pretty awesome." Sophie studied her. "Now, let's get you tidied up before Zach arrives."

"The shop is still open," she reminded. "Shouldn't you be out front?"

"Annabelle and Gwen have things under control." Sophie grabbed her purse from a filing cabinet. "Here. I know it's not a color you'd usually wear, but Rosie gave me this for my birthday and says a girl can never go wrong with Christmas red lipstick."

Isabelle eyed the tube. "Zach's coming for a sewing lesson, Sophie. I don't need lipstick."

Eyes sparkling with mischief, Sophie waggled her brows. "If you're wearing the right lipstick, you might."

Chapter Eight

SARAH HAD TO be at church at five to work on snowflake ornaments for the upcoming Christmas festival, so Zach rode with her into town. The church sat right off the square, and she'd tried to convince him to hang out with her and Jeannie until his lesson at six, but he'd been too on edge to hang out with a bunch of church ladies making snowflakes.

Restless, he wandered around the square, browsing through one shop and then another before landing on the same courthouse bench he'd been standing near on the day he'd met Isabelle. Unlike that day, the air was still, and the flag hung silently above him.

Reading the monument's inscription, he sighed.

Why had he jumped at Sophie's invitation to come to the shop? Better yet, why were his fingers clutching the Paw Parties, Inc. paper bag? Isabelle was not going to like what he'd bought and that was exactly why he'd bought it. Was he trying to antagonize her?

Hearing someone approach, he glanced up and saw Cole. Sophie's fiancé glanced toward the flag, his expression one of pride and honor. Then the Marine-turned-firefighter sat down next to Zach.

"Humbling to look at this monument and know it could

easily be referring to us, isn't it?"

"Sometimes I think it should have been." Probably not something he should admit to Isabelle's future brother-in-law, but the words slipped out.

"Those of us who saw action, lost friends, all suffer some degree of survivor's guilt. It's something Bodie and I have discussed. Our conversations have helped me more than any of my therapy sessions."

Zach had done the mandatory sessions. He'd undergone all sorts of sessions in an attempt to uncover what his brain had hidden away. His body had been reopened on numerous counts, and they'd supposedly gotten the last of the shrapnel with his last surgery. But the mental wounds? How could those ever truly heal when he couldn't remember the details?

"I don't recall much of what happened during the worst action I saw," he admitted, surprised, as the explosion wasn't something he talked about. "One minute I was there, fighting, hoping to take out as many of the enemy as I could to help some of our team make it out. Then I was waking up in a hospital, busted up, full of shrapnel, and had zero recall of the previous few months."

And one hundred percent guilt that some of his brothers and sisters had died that day.

"That's tough. Glad you made it." Cole's gaze dropped to the bag Zach held. "You planning to get a pet?"

Zach shook his head. "It's for Bobbin."

Cole laughed. "That cat has a way of growing on you. I'm not sure they've officially discussed who gets him after the wedding. Although I wouldn't mind having a good mouser for the barn and she sure loves that cat, I suspect

Sophie will leave him with Isabelle."

"If Sophie wanted the cat, Isabelle would tie a bow around his neck and insist she take him."

Cole nodded. "She would, but Sophie is no pushover. When she makes up her mind on something, she's as stubborn as they get." Cole grinned as if a particular memory of that stubbornness was hitting. "Most tenacious woman I've ever met."

"Obviously runs in the family."

"Yup. Thanks for helping me carry in the tree last night. The ladies and I could have gotten it in, but since Sophie wanted the tallest one that would still fit in the house, it sure was nice having you there." Cole glanced at his watch. "I'm taking her to Lou's for dinner and then to the farm to decorate our tree. She insisted we get one for both places. You and Isabelle want to join us? No tree carrying required as Ben helped me lug ours into the house yesterday morning."

Was this what normal people did in small towns? Talk and go visit with each other? Dinners with his family had always had an agenda and been more about future business deals and social status than comradery.

"We got distracted with looking at the photo albums last night and then with the tree decorating. We never got to my lesson. I'm meeting her at the shop at six. I thought I'd order pizza."

Not that he was positive Isabelle knew about his pending arrival or would agree to dinner during his lesson.

"Better watch or Sophie will have you joining her quilting group. She hasn't gotten me to sewing, but I help with her events. You must have really impressed Isabelle for her to have shared family photos."

"She was going to show me a photo of her father, but we never made it to the older albums." He glanced toward Cole, wondering if he knew anything of Cliff Davis's whereabouts. "Does Sophie mention him?"

"Occasionally. More lately than in the past." He shrugged. "With the wedding, it's normal for her to bring him up more frequently."

"What does she say?"

"That she wishes she could tell him how much she misses him and wants him to come home." Cole glanced toward him, his pale-blue eyes piercing in a way that made Zach wonder if the man knew there was more to his questions than idle curiosity. Or maybe the look was because of his next comment. "That's not how Isabelle feels. I thought she and Sophie were going to fall out because of my military background when we first got together."

"She's very protective of Sophie."

"So am I." Cole's gaze held a warning. "Of Sophie and Isabelle. I'd never allow anyone to hurt them."

"I understand," Zach assured, not sure if Cole referred specifically to him or to Cliff Davis. "I feel the same."

Cole's expression remained serious a moment. Then he gestured to the Paw Parties, Inc. bag. "It's going to take a lot more than whatever is in that bag to win over Isabelle."

"Got any advice on what might?"

Cole shook his head. "What worked for me isn't going to do a thing for you."

"Which was?" Zach asked, curious.

Cole grinned. "Fall head over heels in love with her sister."

"Yeah, I'll leave that one to you. Falling in love isn't for me."

"No?" Cole eyed him a moment, then laughed. "Good luck with that. The Davis women have a way of getting to you."

That they did.

"HEY, BLONDIE, READY to teach me all you know?"

From where she stood at the counter with Sophie, Isabelle turned to face the man she had such mixed emotions on seeing. Standing next to her future brother-in-law, Zach wore well-worn jeans and a plain white T-shirt rather than his usual army one. Did the man not own a coat? Not that it was that chilly outside with the lows only dropping to the mid-fifties, but still, couldn't he cover those biceps? When their gazes met, he grinned. Oh, heavens, how his crooked smile and that dimple in his left cheek sent her stomach into quivers.

He held a Paw Parties bag, so he must have picked up treats for Harry. Had Sarah asked him to, or had he just been being thoughtful? Ugh. Why did he have to be so … so … everything? She did not want to like Zach Dawson any more than she wanted to be wearing this bright red lipstick.

"Too bad your brain isn't as big as your ego," she retorted, hoping said lipstick hadn't smudged onto her teeth, "or it might could hold all I know."

Cole snorted and gave Zach a look that hinted the two men had bonded. Great. One by one, Zach was winning over her friends and family. Why did that have her feeling betrayed?

"Izzy!" Sophie elbowed her.

Oh, yeah, she and Zach were supposed to like each other.

"No worries. Nothing I say fazes him," she assured her sister, then smiled pretty as you please at Zach with her painted lips.

His twitched as he stood there, tall, proud, and completely filling the quilt shop with his masculine presence. That the patriotic section was behind him, giving him a red, white, and blue background fit and yet served as a reminder of just why she should not let herself like him. *You do like him*, an inner voice mocked. *That's the problem.*

Probably the same stupid voice that had said Sophie could apply the lipstick.

Sophie moved from behind the counter to kiss Cole's cheek. "Love you," she told him.

Zach tilted his head ever so slightly. He knew better. It would serve him right if she marched over, plopped a wet kiss on his cheek, and left a crimson stain there.

He held out the Paw Parties bag. "This is for Bobbin."

Isabelle's gaze dropped to the bag. "You bought something for my cat?"

He nodded and tilted his chin toward her again. "You going to thank me properly?"

"Absolutely." Trying to file away whatever feeling that was floating in her chest because he'd bought something for her cat, she gave him another smile. "Thank you, Zach. I'm sure Bobbin will appreciate the gift. He may not express it or show you any affection for doing so, but deep down, he'll be appreciative. Then again, with the way he acted around you last night, he might meow his gratitude."

Zach laughed. Cole and Sophie, holding hands, exchanged looks. Tired of being the entertainment, Isabelle took the bag and put it onto the countertop without peeking inside to see what he'd bought.

"Zach, buying Bobbin a gift was so sweet of you." Sophie's lashes fluttered. "I can't wait to see what it is."

"Catnip."

"He'll like that," Sophie assured.

Isabelle didn't say anything. The bag held more than catnip from the feel of it when she'd put it on the counter.

"Let's get started." She glanced at her watch. "Time is ticking away and I've several things to do after finishing your lesson." There, that let him know that as soon as they were finished, he needed to leave. "Are you ready to do everything I tell you exactly the way I tell you?"

"Yes, ma'am." His eyes danced with merriment. "I can do that."

"We'll see," Isabelle mused, wondering if she'd made a huge mistake in agreeing to teach him. Still, how else would she have been able to find her father? She needed his help, so a few sewing lessons were a small price to pay.

It was the whole pretending-to-be-a-couple thing that was the problem.

"Oh, before we go…" Sophie beamed at them. "I know you've been busy with online orders, so I set up a machine and everything you'll need for Zach's lesson."

Isabelle blinked. "You did?"

Looking quite pleased with herself, Sophie nodded. "I've been working on some of the most adorable table placemat kits for Christmas and thought using one of them would be perfect for Zach's lessons."

Christmas table placemats. Not too big, so easy to maneuver. Depending upon the pattern Sophie had chosen, Isabelle should be able to teach him the basics of sewing, sandwiching, quilting, and binding. She could guide him through the first one, then supervise the next three, so he built his skills.

"That sounds perfect, Sophie. Thank you," Isabelle agreed. "I'd meant to just teach him the basics with remnants, but his working on and completing a project is better."

"Exactly. That way when he's finished, he'll have something wonderful that you two made together that he can treasure always." Sophie's smile almost blinded them. "I'll grab my bag, then we're off. Y'all have fun."

"Yeah, y'all have fun making Christmas placemats." Cole appeared amused as he and Zach exchanged looks again, making Isabelle wonder what the two men had been up to prior to coming into the shop.

Had they just bumped into each other and their arrival together been a coincidence? Or had they bonded over tree-carrying and popcorn-tossing?

After Sophie had gotten her bag, Isabelle followed her sister and her fiancé to the front of the shop, then locked the door behind them.

"Making sure I can't escape?" Zach asked, his eyes twinkling.

"You're the one who said yes when Sophie called and invited you here after hours," she reminded, walking toward the sewing machine area.

"She asked so nicely. I didn't have the heart to say no, even though her sister is quite scary."

He was the one who was scary.

"Sophie wouldn't have taken no for an answer, even if you had."

"Because she thinks I desperately need to learn to quilt?"

"Sophie believes everyone needs to quilt." She motioned toward where they had several different sewing machines, a cutting machine, and a longarm set up. "Ready?"

"I was born ready."

She glanced his way, trying to picture him as a newborn and couldn't.

"I was a cute baby, the cutest, in case you were wondering."

"What happened?" she couldn't resist asking, even as she wondered if the military had taught him mindreading along with whatever other skills he'd acquired.

Grinning, he snorted. "Sophie sure upped my entertainment for the night when she called. Nice lipstick, by the way."

Her cheeks no doubt matching her lips, Isabelle ignored his comment. "Sarah's at the church meeting?"

His gaze lingering at her mouth, he nodded. "She and Jeannie are there. Bodie's working. He's pulling extra shifts so he can take vacation over Christmas."

"Sarah loves Christmas as much as Sophie does."

"We're going to have to do something to up your love of the holidays."

"I like the holidays. They're really good for the shop. Our biggest day of the year is this coming Friday." So true and she hadn't been lying when she'd said she had several things to do after they finished his lesson. She did. "I should be getting things ready for our black Friday and shop local Saturday sales rather than giving a sewing lesson."

"The lesson can wait. What do you need to do? I'll help."

"Oh, no, you don't." She pointed her finger at him. "We're doing your lesson tonight and then you're leaving."

"Yes, ma'am." He walked over to the table and picked up a piece of fabric. "Snowmen?"

Isabelle closed her eyes and took a deep breath. Why would her sister have chosen that material? The one with the jolly snowmen that she'd hidden away on the night of Sophie's dress fitting.

"Do you want me to find something else?" Please say yes. "She has other kits."

Ones that didn't make Isabelle think of abdominal snowmen.

He shook his head. "Your sister picked this one. Let's impress her with how well we do."

Rather than answer, she pulled an extra chair over to one of the smaller sewing machines. "Let's get this over with. I want to be home for dinner by eight."

"Hungry? We could order pizza."

"Dinner is not included in our deal." She shook her head. "Besides, I wouldn't risk getting sauce on the fabric."

"We could take a break, sit outside on one of the benches," he suggested. "How do you like your pizza? I'm an everything kind of guy."

"Makes sense. I'm starved"—she'd worked through lunch—"but am a cheese-only kind of woman. We're complete opposites."

He laughed, almost as if that was what he'd been expecting her to say. He slid his hand into his front pocket, pulled out his cell phone, and punched in a number. Had he already researched the number?

When he hung up, he met her gaze and grinned. "We can carry it to the park and have another picnic to keep from getting anything on the fabric. See how easy it was to find a solution?"

"By ordering half a pizza one way and half another?"

"By meeting me in the middle."

"The only reason we're meeting at all is because we have a business deal," she reminded, giving him a pointed look. "Which did not include dinner."

"Let's get started before dinner arrives. Show me what I'm making."

She handed him the kit instructions. "Sophie comes up with the design, picks the fabrics, cuts the pieces, and puts everything together. We sell them online and in the shop."

"Her instructions are very thorough." Looking impressed, he glanced over the sheet, then back up at her. "You wrote them, didn't you?"

How had he known that often Sophie scribbled notes and Isabelle translated them into the simple, concise steps that included photos? "We help each other. It's what families do."

Zach's gaze shifted from hers, and Isabelle found herself wondering about his family. He'd mentioned them a few times—his parents and a brother.

"Why aren't you planning to go home for Thanksgiving this week?"

Tension stiffened his shoulders. "Because I'm here."

"Here is a long way from there?"

"Long enough."

Leave it alone, Isabelle. Zach's family is none of your business.

"It might help to talk about it," she suggested, anyway.

His gaze cut to hers. "It?"

"Whatever keeps you from wanting to go home for the holidays."

His brow arched. "Trying to get rid of me, Blondie?"

"Just wondering why you'd choose to be in Pine Hill over being with your family."

"Because my new girlfriend is here, of course."

Part of her glad that his tension seemed to ease, she rolled her eyes. "It's just you and me, so you can cut the act."

"Is it really just us? I noticed the security cameras the first time I walked in here. How do you know Sophie isn't logged in on her phone, watching and listening to everything we say?"

"It's video only and she's not." Even as Isabelle said it, she wondered if Sophie was indeed logged into their system. Her sister had hung out with the Butterflies long enough that Sophie might do a few brief check-ins to see how things were progressing.

"No? You should smile and play nice, just in case." He

waggled his brows. "Come over here and give me a welcome kiss. It would be a shame to waste that lipstick."

Shaking her head, she glared at him. "I really don't like you."

"That's okay, Blondie. Most days, I don't like me, either."

She was used to his jesting, but his comment threw her. He almost sounded serious, but he couldn't be. His self-assurance oozed from every handsome pore, and he was always teasing and smiling. She'd just mistaken his tone for something more than it was.

"Sit down," she ordered, not liking the unsettled feeling that if he had been serious, then ... then, nothing. Zach Dawson was none of her business other than business.

Zach sat. "Yes, ma'am."

"First rule is to make sure you keep your fingers out from under the needle."

He gave her an odd look, then shrugged. "Good rule."

"Second rule is to double-check everything before you cut or sew. It'll save you a lot of time."

"Makes sense," he agreed.

"Third rule is, go slow."

His lips twitched. "Slow as Christmas morning's arrival."

Unable to resist, she asked, "Did you anxiously await Christmas morning each year?"

"Maybe," he admitted. "It was a long time ago."

"Meaning you don't look forward to Christmas morning now?" she pressed, eyeing him as he examined the machine, probably figuring out every knob and button before she gave the first explanation of what each one did. Then again, Sarah had probably already explained all that.

"Meaning Christmas morning has been just another day on the calendar for more than a decade. The holidays aren't a big deal."

"Did you never get leave to spend the holidays with your family?"

His face pinched. "Once."

"It wasn't pleasant?"

"Nope."

Don't ask, Isabelle. It doesn't pertain to you. Leave it alone. Don't do it.

"Did something happen?"

"Something always happens when I go there." He leaned back in the cushy black chair and flexed his neck from one side to the other, making a popping sound as he did so. "My brother and I don't mesh the way you and your sister do."

Hurt hung in the air and darned if she didn't want to hug him. No, she did not want to hug him. She wanted to give his sewing lesson and be done before the pizza arrived so they could eat and he could leave.

Only, she placed her hand on his shoulder. The warmth of his skin radiated through his cotton shirt and her heart raced. "I'm sorry, Zach."

"Don't be. It's not a big deal."

But it was. Her heart felt for him. She knew what it was like to have family issues better off not discussed. Sensing his discomfort and knowing she'd had no right to pry to begin with, or to touch him, Isabelle pointed to the instructions. "That's good. Now, read the kit's instructions. What do they say to do first?"

"DID SHE PURPOSELY just bump against him?" Ruby and the other Butterflies gathered at Lou's Diner huddled around Sophie's phone.

Maybelle tapped her manicured nail against the tabletop. "Her hand definitely lingered on his as she was guiding the material."

"Do you see how he is looking at her?" Aunt Claudia sighed happily.

Rosie puckered her lips, then made a smacking noise. "That lipstick is fabulous. Why hasn't he kissed her yet?"

Cole shook his head at Sophie and the Butterflies. "We only stopped by Lou's to pick up dinner and should already be at the farm. Isabelle would not want you watching her lesson with Zach."

"A lesson in romance." Rosie snickered. "How is he resisting her *Rosie* red lips?"

"It's not as if she didn't watch us when you'd come into the shop," Sophie reminded Cole, her cheeks pinkening.

"That was a little different, since it was during business hours, and she was at her desk facing the monitor screens rather than after hours logging in on a phone while at Lou's surrounded by nosy Butterflies." Cole slid his hands into his jeans pocket and gave the women a pointed look.

"There is that," Sophie agreed, then giggled. "Maybe she'll look at the camera and stick her tongue out at me."

"Isabelle?" Cole snorted. "I wouldn't count on it."

"Stranger things have happened."

"Like us grabbing our dinner and heading to the farm

where we're supposed to be?" Cole asked, glancing at his watch.

"You can't leave now. It's just getting interesting," Ruby said, gesturing to the phone. "This is good stuff. Do you see her laughing?"

"Yep." Cole nodded. "At him. Poor guy."

"But she's laughing, and, if it is at him, he doesn't look as if he minds," Sophie assured. "Besides, his goof-ups are intentional. Sarah says he sews like a dream. I just adore that he has my sister smiling."

"Your fiancé would be smiling if we'd eaten our dinner on time."

"You're not going to starve if you stay just a few more minutes." Maybelle gave a look that said he and Sophie weren't leaving until she said they could.

Cole's stomach grumbled. "I might."

"If you don't want to wait, you can go ahead. We don't have to do takeout. Either way, I'll make our delay up to you with some of my sugar cookies," Sophie promised, not lifting her gaze from the phone screen as Zach did something that had Isabelle laughing again.

Eyeing the women around the phone, Cole leaned his head against the booth's back. "If Zach made it through Ranger training, I guess he can handle a few nosy Butterflies and their beautiful accomplice."

"If he can't, he's not the right man for our Isabelle." Aunt Claudia patted Cole's shoulder, then became distracted by the screen. "Now, go ahead and eat, so you'll quit talking about leaving. Oh, what's in that bag Isabelle just picked up off the counter?"

"Zach bought Bobbin a present."

Rosie snorted. "He should have brought Isabelle a present."

Cole shook his head. "Isabelle is more impressed by things being done for those she loves than by someone doing something for her."

"Very observant," Maybelle praised. "Zach made the right choice, which is a good thing, since he has major points against him where Isabelle is concerned."

There was another collective Butterfly sigh. They watched Isabelle open the bag, glance inside, then glance up at Zach with a horrified expression.

"What did he give her?" Maybelle wanted to know.

"He said it was catnip, but I don't think that's what it is," Sophie said.

Ruby scratched her head. "Does Carrie sell anything that warrants that look?"

"Whatever it is, Zach thinks it's funny," Aunt Claudia pointed out. "Do you see the smirk on his face?"

"I do. What a cutie." Rosie fanned herself. "That dimple is just like Christmas morning twenty-four seven."

"Shh, Lou might hear you," Aunt Claudia warned.

Waving her hand dismissively, Rosie giggled. "Wouldn't matter. He knows my eyes are perfectly fine, but that my heart belongs to him. That man is the best."

"He must be to put up with you," Maybelle said, causing Ruby and Claudia to snicker.

Rosie gave her a tight smile. "Hmm, that's what I was thinking about John."

"John and I are just friends," Maybelle insisted.

"You looked quite cozy during your bird-watching adventures."

"You mean Zach and Isabelle-spying adventures?" Cole shook his head again. "You ladies have no limits."

"Our limitlessness worked out quite well for you, didn't it?"

Cole glanced toward Sophie, meeting her happy gaze. "Not sure about Butterfly limitlessness, but meeting Sophie worked out better than fine,"

Four Butterflies sighed, their gazes on him rather than the phone, until Sophie called their attention back to it. "Oh no."

"Well, isn't that just the cutest thing ever?" Ruby said.

Maybelle frowned. "Is the boy daft? He knew better than to buy something like that for Bobbin."

"Does he want her to fall for him or not?" Rosie looked around the booth as if she expected one of them to give her an answer.

Aunt Claudia sighed with disappointment. "There went those points in his favor."

Chapter Nine

NOSE CURLED, SOPHIE held up the pet-sized outfit. "You don't seriously think Bobbin is going to wear this? Or that I'd let him?"

"I didn't think you wore that shade of lipstick but was pleasantly surprised. You will be, too, when you see how dashing Bobbin is in camo." Zach had known the kitty uniform would push Isabelle's buttons.

That had been why he'd bought it. Yet, when she'd gone to open the bag, he'd wanted to stop her so as not to end the lightness they'd shared during his lesson.

"Besides, didn't your mother teach you to say thank you when someone gives you a gift?"

"She taught me to be leery of gift-bearing men," Isabelle shot back, then relented. "Thank you, though. It was very thoughtful of you, but Bobbin is not the kind of cat to wear clothes."

She left her *thank God* off, but Zach heard it.

"You're welcome, and you think he isn't? I hate to break it to you, but during all that rubbing against my leg last night, he assured me he'd make a *purrrfect* soldier."

Isabelle rolled her eyes. "Not that I'd put this on him, but if I tried, he'd either claw me to bits or poison my morning coffee."

Zach grinned. "Surely he wouldn't claw the hand that feeds him?"

"It's bite the hand that feeds him, and if I put that on him, he'd never forgive me."

"You've misjudged that poor cat. All this time, he's been hoping for something camo. Can he help it if no one heeded his meowed pleas until he met me?"

Isabelle snorted. "Fine, O great cat whisperer, sign a release waiver, and I'll let you try to put this on him."

"Okay." Because it meant spending more time with her and he wasn't ready for their evening to end. "When we're finished with my lesson, we'll go by your place and enlist Bobbin. I need to see those photos of your dad, anyway."

Isabelle's face tightened. "You're not enlisting my cat. Besides, Mom will be home."

"It's okay. She won't think anything of us looking at the rest of the albums. She likes me."

Isabelle placed the outfit on the counter, then gave him a skeptical look. "What makes you think that?"

"She told me. A dozen or so times when Cole and I helped her carry your Christmas totes in from the storage building out back." He leaned against the counter, grinning at Isabelle's head shake. Good. Maybe they could get back to relaxed. "Cole was a little jealous of how many times she said it, actually."

"Cole knows Mom adores him. She tells him over and over, too, so don't go thinking you're something special. You're not. She's just not used to me bringing men home."

Which made Zach feel special, even if he knew the real

reasons why he'd been there.

"Why is that?"

Isabelle shrugged. "Mainly the shop and that I've not met anyone worth bringing home."

"Then I'm glad you think I am."

"You. Are. Pretend." She tapped her finger against his chest with each word. "Remember?"

He placed his hand over hers, flattening her palm against his sternum and marveling at how her warm touch energized his pulse. "I don't feel real? You're sure about that?"

She jerked away, shaking her hand as if something clung to it. "You knew what I meant. We are pretend. You and me, not real. Fake news."

"That's right. How could I forget with you reminding me so often?"

"Well, you behave as if you keep forgetting."

Because it was easy to forget that he wasn't himself when Isabelle was around. Maybe he even wanted to forget. Too bad he couldn't pick and choose what his mind retained. If he could, if he could be someone different, he'd point out that she once again stood beneath mistletoe. No doubt Sophie had hung it over the register counter because it didn't seem something Isabelle would do.

"Be grateful I'm so immersed in the part I'm playing as your boyfriend."

Wiping her hand on her jeans, she eyed him. "Yeah, well, hate to break it to you, but there's no Emmy for this role, so it's okay if you tone it down."

She was right. He knew she was right. But for a while during his lesson, when they were laughing, when she was smiling at him, he'd not been thinking about anything except enjoying the moment.

"Yes, ma'am. Now, what I really want to know is how impressed were you with my sewing skills?"

Relief that he'd changed the subject brightened her face. "I'd rather not say."

"I know I did good," he teased. He'd had enough practice that he should do well.

"Then why ask? We both know you've been working with Sarah."

Now was the perfect time to tell her that he already sewed, just had never quilted. But that opened a topic he'd rather not get into. He didn't want Isabelle's pity regarding why he'd had so much time to learn. That might undo him. So, instead, he said, "She's extremely patient, but very busy."

Relaxing more, Isabelle nodded. "She volunteers with the church all year, but especially at the holidays."

"And Sophie does. How about you?"

"I volunteer." Her chin lifted. "As a matter of fact, I'm volunteering this Saturday."

"You're closing the store on Shop Local Saturday?"

She laughed. "Don't sound so incredulous. We do close from time to time. But, in this case, no, I'll be working that morning until noon during our sale. After that, I'm helping with the kids' activities at the Pine Hill On-the-Square Christmas Festival."

"Sounds fun."

"Then you should volunteer," she challenged, giving him a pointed look.

"Okay."

She frowned. "That was a rhetorical comment. Not a real invitation."

"So, it was a fake invitation to your fake boyfriend? What's with you and all these fake situations?" he teased.

"Odd how they all involve you."

He chuckled. "Isn't it, though? However, I was serious about volunteering. As long as I'm working with you, sign me up for wherever you think I'll be most useful."

"Remember you asked for this."

Noting the gleam in her eyes, suspicion grew. "Did I just sign up for the pie-in-the-face booth or something?"

Zach didn't know if Pine Hill had such a booth, but Isabelle's laughter was worth ten pies in the face.

"You wish it was pies in the face." She practically doubled over.

"Okay, spill it, Blondie. What torturous volunteer work are you enlisting me for?"

"Oh, nothing too strenuous. I mean, you only have to stand there with your eyes closed."

"While you shoot sugar plums off my head with a bow and arrow?"

"Don't tempt me, but that's not it." She drew out telling him another few seconds, obviously relishing every moment. "I'm in charge of this year's kissing booth."

Isabelle teasing him seemed so unlikely that even though his gut said that was what she was doing, Zach wasn't sure. "Pine Hill has a kissing booth?"

"Oh, yes. We set it up down by the assisted living center." She batted her lashes, then blew him a kiss. "I think this year's is going to be extra successful. Don't you?"

Zach gulped. Did she mean that she was signing him up to be kissed? Or that she was, possibly while wearing her new red lipstick that he kept having to drag his gaze from?

Either way, if she was serious, he'd prepurchase both of their entire time slots, because there was no way he was going to stand there while other men kissed her. That would be torture.

And the only person he wanted to kiss was Isabelle.

HANDS LADEN WITH the numerous dishes Sarah had made to bring with them, Zach followed a similarly loaded down Bodie up the front steps of a well-kept, white-frame two-story home. Although he and Isabelle hadn't directly discussed his coming to her Aunt Claudia's for Thanksgiving dinner, the woman had invited him and called Sarah to insist that she not let Zach say no. Who was he to turn down what promised to be another amazing home-cooked meal?

"You're going to regret not taking my advice to wear something with an elastic waistband." Bodie pushed the front door open, letting Harry go in first. "Because you're about to have the best meal of your life."

His friend's comment and the delicious aromas from the containers they held had Zach's stomach growling.

"From now until Christmas"—Bodie made an *mmm* sound—"this town likes to show off. My guess is that the New Year's resolution to start a diet originated in Pine Hill, thanks to the pounds packed on during the holidays."

Bodie's fit figure didn't seem to be suffering too much

from all the extra calories. His morning runs with Harry kept him fit. Glad for the physical release and determined to not lose the strength he'd worked so hard to regain after his extended hospital stay, Zach joined them. It wasn't as if he didn't wake before the sun, anyway. Old habits died hard.

"Hope you're hungry." Sarah came over to them with Jeannie in her arms. "Aunt Claudia will expect you to have at least two helpings."

"As much as I taste-tested yesterday and today, I'm not sure about a second plate, especially since I'm wearing Bodie's shirt. It's already a little snug, but I'm looking forward to the first plate."

Having suggested he dress up a little from his usual T-shirt, Sarah had loaned him another of Bodie's dress shirts. He'd only planned to stay in Pine Hill a week and then to go to the beach. Dress clothes hadn't been on the agenda, but he should probably buy a few things since his plans had changed.

"Thanks for helping Bodie and me." Sarah smiled. "You make a great assistant baker."

"It was the least I could do after you put my fears about Pine Hill having a kissing booth to rest." Plus, he enjoyed hanging with his friends and seeing how normal their lives were. Zach hadn't felt normal or seen it in years. Pine Hill was broadening his horizon. "Hopefully, I didn't demolish too many of those chocolate no-bakes you made."

"Isabelle teasing you like that was great." Sarah's eyes twinkled. "And between you and Bodie enjoying them so much, I decided to leave what was left of the cookies at home. They're in the Santa jar on the kitchen counter."

Zach would have high-fived his friend if they weren't carrying the containers.

"Sarah, Bodie, Zach," Isabelle's Aunt Claudia greeted them. With her salt-and-pepper hair pulled into a bun, red dress and ruffled white apron, she looked exactly how Zach imagined Mrs. Claus would. "It's good to see you, but this little sweetie is who I want to love on before that baby-hogger Maybelle realizes y'all are here."

Sarah handed Jeannie to the woman, who immediately showered the baby with kisses and sweet talk. "Let's go brag to the others that I got to hold you first."

"Don't you go stirring up Butterfly trouble on Thanksgiving," Bodie warned in his sheriff's deputy tone.

Claudia giggled. "Well, you and I both know it's those other Butterflies that you have to watch out for. I'm the innocent one who gets dragged along on their shenanigans whenever George and I are home from one of our trips. Have I mentioned that we're going to the Amalfi Coast this spring? I sure do love to travel."

Smiling, Sarah and Bodie exchanged looks.

"Come on, Zach." Bodie gestured toward their right. "Let's put these in the kitchen."

"Tell the girls I'll be there in a minute. Everything's mostly done, but they're keeping an eye on the rolls while they finish." Claudia pressed more kisses to Jeannie's chubby cheek. "I'm going to relish holding this one a minute as I likely won't get another opportunity while Sarah and I talk about my trip."

Zach followed Bodie into the kitchen. Sophie stood at a kitchen island and was removing the lid from a dish. Seeing him, she smiled. Back to him, Isabelle peered into the oven.

"The rolls are almost done, Aunt Claudia." She turned, saw him, and took a deep breath. "You're not Aunt Claudia."

Zach found an open spot on the packed counter and set the containers down. "Nope. Happy Thanksgiving, Isabelle. You, too, Sophie."

"Aww, that's sweet. Thanks. You, too." Sophie took Bodie's containers and placed them on the counter. "Zach, would you mind keeping my sister company while I take Bodie to talk with Cole? We're thinking about knocking out a wall to make two small upstairs bedrooms into one larger room. Bodie is our go-to guy for handyman advice."

Not waiting for an answer, Sophie hooked her arm with Bodie's, then led him out of the kitchen, leaving Zach alone with Isabelle.

"Your sister is about as subtle as a locomotive."

With another glance into the oven first, Isabelle popped the tops on the containers he'd carried. "Sarah's been busy."

"She's cooked nonstop for the past two days." He glanced around at the island and kitchen countertops packed with a multitude of dishes and tried not to think about what his mother's kitchen counter looked like. Had she hired the same catering company she'd always used or had Brett's wife placed the order to make sure all the traditional dishes were covered? No matter the outlandish cost, the spread wouldn't compare to the one before him. A twinge hit that he wished they were there to share in this feast, that they'd be a part of the happy, noisy activities, rather than the sedate, formal meal. Then again, he couldn't imagine that they'd have the same appreciation for the mismatched made-with-love ensemble that he did.

Eyeing him, Isabelle leaned against the counter. "I figured you'd be here tonight."

"But had hoped I wouldn't?" he countered. Maybe he shouldn't be. Maybe he had no right to intrude on this happy affair. Not that he belonged with his family, either. He'd never fit there. He'd never fit anywhere other than in the army.

"I didn't say that."

"But thought it?"

She shrugged. "Not really."

"What?" He eyed her. "You calling a truce tonight?"

"It's Thanksgiving. I didn't want our star kissing booth volunteer left at Hamilton House alone."

Alone. Being alone had never bothered him, but rolling off Isabelle's tongue, the word felt heavy and something to be dreaded.

"Then I'll count my blessings that I'm here instead." He didn't consider himself a religious man, but being with Isabelle and her family was a blessing.

A small smile played on her lips. "It's the holiday for doing just that."

"Not wearing your lipstick tonight, Blondie?"

She looked sheepish. "I told you the other night that red lipstick was Sophie's."

"And I'm sticking to what I said," he reminded, his gaze dropping to her naturally pink lips. "That I don't believe Sophie wrestled you to the quilt shop floor and painted your lips the prettiest shade of red."

Isabelle put her palm to her forehead. "I knew better."

Dragging his gaze from her mouth, he arched his brow. "But did it, anyway? That doesn't sound like you."

"There're a lot of things that don't sound like me when I'm around you."

That she admitted as much didn't sound like her, either. Had she missed him as much as he'd missed seeing her the past few days?

"Has Bobbin worn his outfit yet?" Why he longed to hear her say that she'd put the tiny uniform on the cat made no sense, but he held his breath while he waited.

"No." She gave him a *duh* look. "It was no coincidence that he wasn't at the house when we got there that night."

Zach made his expression one of suspicion. "Unless you texted a warning, I'd say it was exactly a coincidence."

Her eyes twinkled. "He's a smart cat."

"He could be a fashionable cat if you'd just let him."

Isabelle's nose curled. "That's a matter of opinion. You're trying to make my cat dress like you."

Zach's lips twitched. "Are you saying that I have bad taste in clothes?"

She raked her gaze over his slightly tight through the shoulders shirt. "Let's just say that I don't think you should plan to take up fashion as a new career."

He rubbed his chin, then shrugged. "I guess I'm stuck with my fake boyfriend job."

Her forehead creased. "You plan to do this again?"

"Nope. You're my one and only." Realizing what he'd said, Zach added, "Fake girlfriend, that is."

Her gaze connected with his. "I'm glad."

Air lodged in Zach's throat. "Because?"

She hesitated long enough that whatever her response, it wasn't what originally popped into her head.

"I'd think it obvious," she finally said, crossing her arms across her chest. "If you have to trade out being a fake boyfriend for another sewing lesson, then it means I did a terrible job teaching you. I'm not much on being a failure. Speaking of failures, did the photos help?"

On the night of his lesson, afterward, when they'd gotten to her house, he'd stealthily snapped pictures of several photos of her dad while she'd kept her mother occupied in the kitchen under the guise of making hot cocoa.

"They will. I've run them through a few of iSecure's aging programs and uploaded the originals and aged ones into the company's face recognition program. It'll take a while, but the program will search out possibilities. Then, I'll follow up on those leads, along with the ones I got on his Social Security number."

She bit into her lower lip. "For Sophie's sake, I hope you come up with something soon."

For Isabelle's sake, Zach hoped so, too.

"Now, let's talk about my being the star of the kissing booth this weekend. As Sarah cleared up that there was no kissing booth, what I want to know is if you were planning to start a private one, just so you'd have an excuse to kiss me?"

Isabelle's face went as red as the lipstick he'd been teasing her about. "She shouldn't have told you."

He arched a brow. "And let me continue to think I would be kissing grannies for ten bucks a smackeroo?"

"For someone who claims to be great at figuring things out, you shouldn't have needed Sarah's clarification on that one." Her hands went to her hips. "Besides, you deserved to be taught a lesson about volunteering for things without knowing what you're getting into."

He shrugged. "I'm used to being given orders without knowing what I'm getting into. At least, I was."

Her expression became pensive, and she surprised him yet again by asking, "You miss being a soldier?"

"I'll be a soldier until I take my last breath, Blondie." His stomach grumbled and, determined not to fall down a dark hole, Zach picked up a piece of ham.

Isabelle slapped his hand. "Stop that. We haven't said prayers yet."

"Then someone better get to praying because I'm ready to eat."

"IS THAT A third helping of banana pudding?" Isabelle asked when Zach returned to the card table that was one of many scattered around her Aunt Claudia's house to accommodate the thirty-plus dinner guests. Family and friends filled every nook and cranny and laughter sounded frequently.

Zach grinned. "Will you tell me no more if I say yes?"

She shook her head. "I'm not your mother."

"No, but this reminds me of my grandmother's. I'd not thought of it in years, but this has the same topping." His lips wrapped around his spoon.

"Meringue," she said, clarifying further at his blank look.

"The topping. It's called meringue. It's how my Grandma Belle made hers, and none of us would ever dare make ours any other way."

Zach's gaze met hers. "You made this?"

Embarrassment warmed her face. "You don't have to sound so surprised. I can follow directions on a recipe card just as well as the next person."

The gold flecks in his eyes glittered with amusement. "Which is why we had to scrape a burnt layer off the rolls."

Isabelle grimaced. "Don't remind me. I blame you for distracting me."

"Based upon the teasing already doled out"—Zach ate a bite of the sweet pudding—"I have a feeling you're going to be reminded of our slipup for years to come."

"Thanks for that." She could feel his eyes on her, studying her.

"For the most part, you've looked relaxed tonight, Blondie. I like it."

Ha. Looks were deceiving because ever since he'd asked his *Because?* earlier, she'd been an internal mess. That pesky voice that got her into trouble where Zach was concerned had answered in her mind that it was because she couldn't stand the thought of him being someone else's boyfriend, fake or real. She couldn't explain that to herself, much less to him. Just as she couldn't explain why she'd teased him with the kissing booth threat. Where had that even come from? Probably because of Sophie having put kissing into her mind with the lipstick talk.

"I relax," she assured.

She'd certainly done so during his sewing lesson where

he'd come off with the goofiest comments about his skills, and again when they'd shared hot cocoa with her mother, and even when he'd searched the yard to try to find Bobbin to dress the poor cat.

"Prove it," he challenged. "Come to the On-the-Square Christmas Festival with me on Saturday night."

"I'm working and so are you, remember?" At his questioning look, she clarified. "If you were serious about volunteering, then you're helping me with kid activities."

"I think I prefer the kissing booth."

"You would," she accused, but couldn't help smiling.

"Our volunteer stint runs all afternoon and into the night?"

"No, but I'm also volunteering at the church booth. Mom and I are sharing a shift and we'll be selling baked goodies."

"Will there be any of this?" He took another bite and slowly pulled the spoon from his mouth. "If so, I'll take the whole lot. Name your price."

Pleased he liked the pudding, she shook her head. "No pudding, but there will be banana bread."

He looked thoughtful. "That you made?"

"No. Sorry." Why did she have the urge to offer to make pudding for him? "Sophie made the bread. She makes several varieties. They're all great, but my favorite is her chocolate chips and pecan. It's so good heated up with just a dab of butter."

"Sounds good and that's saying a lot with how full my belly is." He smiled and put his spoon in his empty dessert dish. "Sarah has me helping with an early shift at the Quilts of Valor booth, but if you'll save me one, I'll pay for it when I'm done."

Isabelle frowned. "You asked me to go with you to the festival after you'd already promised to help Sarah?"

"I wasn't going to bail on Sarah, if that's what you're thinking. She signed me up for an hour. If you'd said yes, you could have hung out with me at the booth until I finished. I'd make sure you had a good time."

A good time at the military-quilt booth? Not even Zach could pull that one off.

Isabelle picked up her glass of sweet tea and took a sip of the cool liquid. Placing the glass back on the table, she then wiped the condensation from her hands with her napkin. "No thank you, but you'll likely see Sophie. She oversees the booth and spends most of the festival there since Cole's tied up with being Santa in the parade."

"You could give her a break so she can watch him in the parade," he suggested.

"Not me, but someone will." She didn't like his expression and became even more annoyed when she felt the need to explain.

She wanted to scream for him to not look so judgmental that she wasn't more like her sister and Sarah. They did their thing, and she did hers. There was nothing wrong with that. She could be, and was, an upstanding community member in all sorts of other ways.

"I'm volunteering at the church bake sale with Mom, remember?"

"I remember." Apparently wanting another bite, he picked the spoon back up and scraped it around the bowl, managing to capture a little of the pudding clinging to the sides. "Will you get a break?"

"I … I'll stay as long as I'm needed."

"And will offer to stay all night if it serves as a way to avoid me because I just upset you by wanting you to come to the Quilts of Valor booth with me?"

"Maybe," she admitted, both annoyed and impressed by his sharp mind.

He leaned close, whispering as if he needed to tell her something for her ears only. "Don't look now, but we're being watched, so smile."

"Oh, goodie. I'm so thrilled." She bared her teeth in a grimace-like smile. "For the record, we've been watched from the moment we stepped out of the kitchen together."

His eyes twinkled. "I wasn't sure if you'd noticed, what with the smoke billowing around us from the burnt rolls."

"There wasn't smoke. Well, not much," she relented, fighting back a real smile. There had been smoke. Not tons, but enough that her eyes had watered when they'd rescued the rolls. "Besides, even if there had been enough to warrant Cole suiting up, it would have been difficult to miss Maybelle's eagle eyes when you grabbed my hand during prayer." His hand holding hers during that prayer had felt … nice. That had completely unsettled her to where she hadn't been able to focus on the words her Uncle George spoke, thanking the Lord for their meal and for those who had prepared it, for their health, for family and friends, old and new.

"The man with Maybelle seems besotted. He's who was with her the day at the park?"

"John?" Glad for the subject change, she nodded and looked at where John offered Maybelle his last bite of pie and, shaking her head, she patted his cheek. "He is. Apparently, she was the bee's knees back during their teens and he's crushed on her ever since."

"That would be the Butterfly's knees," he teased, tilting his head expectantly until Isabelle smiled.

"You'd like John. He served in the Korean War." Why was she telling him this? She liked John, liked that Maybelle had his company, but she never discussed his background, and yet, she was. "My cousin Morgan presented him with a Quilts of Valor quilt last year. She's a nurse. You've not met her yet as she lives in California. They were planning to surprise everyone tonight, but unfortunately, they won't arrive until late tomorrow night."

Zach's gaze flicked from Maybelle and John to Isabelle. "She's married to Ruby's grandson? The one who is Cole's friend?"

"Yes. Morgan, along with her son, moved out west with Andrew after they married this summer. She's working at a hospital not far from where they live. She and Greyson are happy."

"Another person who escaped this town."

"Morgan doesn't really count. She didn't grow up here, just visited for summers and holidays when we were younger. She grew up at whatever base her military parents were currently assigned to."

His brow lifted. "For someone so anti-military, you sure have a lot of military in your family, Blondie."

"I'm not anti-military. I'm very thankful for the military

and the freedom it affords me, and not just because it's the holiday to be grateful." She was also grateful for the interruption when her phone buzzed. A shop employee's name popped up.

"I'm so sorry, Isabelle," Gwen said, sounding miserable when Isabelle answered the call. "I have a stomach bug and won't be at work tomorrow. I'd have called earlier, but I kept thinking I had just overeaten and would be better. Instead, I just keep getting worse."

"No worries. Just get better. We'll make do." Somehow. Isabelle hung up and slid her phone into her back pocket.

"What's wrong?" Zach asked when he returned from tossing his paper bowl into the trash bin.

"Gwen called out of work tomorrow." She sighed. "She's not feeling well, so can't help it, but it'll make tomorrow more stressful. Black Friday is our busiest day of the year."

Zach eyed her a moment, then suggested, "Put me to work in her place."

"You?"

He nodded. "Why not?"

How was she supposed to focus if he was there? He'd be like a reindeer in an ornament shop. It would be total chaos.

"You don't know anything about working at a quilt shop, Zach. Just because you have a knack for making quarter-inch seams doesn't make you qualified to fill in at my shop."

His gaze boring into hers, he asked, "You'd rather be shorthanded than to have me help you? Seriously?"

Did it make her terrible if she said yes?

"What business turns down free labor?"

Isabelle shook her head. "I wouldn't let you work for free."

"Zach is offering to work for free?" Sophie came to the table with a slice of chocolate pie. "Quick. Sign him up before he changes his mind."

"What are you being signed up for?" Cole sat down next to Sophie. His plate held Maybelle's pumpkin pie with a generous dollop of whipped cream and a helping of banana pudding. "Another kissing booth?"

Isabelle's cheeks heated. "No. Gwen called out of work tomorrow—" she started, but Sophie interrupted, giving Zach one of her biggest smiles.

"And you offered to help us out? That is so sweet! Thank you, Zach. Our customers are going to love you."

"No, they aren't," Isabelle corrected, frowning at her sister. "I told him no."

Sophie gave her a confused look. "Why would you do that? Tomorrow is going to be crazy busy." She turned to Zach. "We'd love to have your help. I'm sure Isabelle only said no because she didn't want to take advantage of your relationship."

Zach's lips twitched as he glanced Isabelle's way. "She's worried I'll be too much of a distraction, but I promise to keep her focused on the job at hand. Afterward, I'm all hers."

Right. All hers. Isabelle sighed. Could a pretend girl-friend take advantage of her relationship with her pretend boyfriend? And if so, was that why her chest was all fluttery at the prospect of Zach being at the shop?

Chapter Ten

"OKAY, OUR FIRST activity is the Make-a-Candy-Cane game," Isabelle announced to the forty-plus kids bouncing around the church playground in a variety of winter garb from light jackets to fully decked out from head-to-toe outer layers.

The ones in the thick layers were rosy faced as the town couldn't have asked for better festival weather. Although temps were expected to drop into the low thirties that night, currently, the sunshine took the edge off the midafternoon sixty degrees and the fun Rudolph sweater Isabelle had borrowed from Sophie that morning was just right.

As promised, Zach had shown up to volunteer. Sarah must have told him he had to get into the Christmas spirit as he wore a long-sleeved, green T-shirt with a large, jolly snowman on the front and the back of the snowman on the back side. Isabelle suspected Sarah had gifted the item to her houseguest. Why had her friend chosen a snowman? It wasn't as if Isabelle didn't struggle enough with abdominal snowman thoughts when she saw Zach without actually seeing a happy snowman over his chest and stomach.

Catching her eye, he winked, and her heart hiccupped. Well, that was what it had felt like, anyway. Just as it had hiccupped repeatedly the day prior when he'd helped at the quilt shop. He'd been wonderful, only having to be told once how to do something to then just go with it. With his constant grin and friendliness, he'd had their customers eating out of his big hands. That he looked like a buff Hollywood superhero hadn't hurt. As wonderful as Gwen was, Zach had easily topped what her sales would have been.

Was there anything he wasn't good at?

"Ms. Isabelle and Mr. Zach are going to divide you into teams." Rosie clasped her bright-pink gloved hands together. She wore a matching pink scarf and boots over her Christmas-print green tights and thick sweater. Her pink hat had bells attached that jingled when she moved, and Rosie was rarely still, so there had been an almost constant jingle.

Wearing a simple red Christmas sweater with a single green wreath over her heart, Maybelle shook her head at her friend's bright outfit for the umpteenth time since she'd arrived at the church playground, then smiled at the kids. "Each team will have a package of red paper streamers and a roll of toilet paper."

"Your job is to use the materials to wrap around whomever you choose to create the most realistic looking candy cane." Isabelle focused on the words *candy cane*, so she didn't accidentally tell the kids to make snowmen. Relieved she'd gotten it right, she bowed her arms. "You want to choose someone who can stand really still with their arms bent to form the top of the candy cane."

Jasie Willis waved her hand. "Me, I can do it."

Isabelle smiled at the bouncing around redheaded girl, who she knew was a real firecracker from when she'd taught her in Sunday school at church, then continued, "You'll have five minutes from start to finish. Ms. Maybelle will say when to go and when to stop. So, pay close attention."

Maybelle gestured to where she'd had Zach set up an ornate Christmas hourglass on a table. "When the last grain of Christmas magic falls on the town below, it's candy cane judging time."

The kids whooped and hollered their excitement. With Zach's help, Isabelle divided the kids into small groups, smiling when Morgan's son, Greyson, and his friend Brianna ended up on the same team. Last Christmas, Greyson had told his mother he planned to marry the girl one day. Based upon the way the six-year-old smiled at the girl, he hadn't changed his mind.

"Start your Santa sleighs and off you go." Maybelle turned a handle that flipped the large hourglass.

One adult volunteer stood with each group, cheering them on. Zach got Greyson and Brianna's group and Isabelle's team was next to them. Her group took too long discussing who was going to be the candy cane, but finally agreed upon a grinning-ear-to-ear Jasie. Once decided, the kids began wrapping the red paper around her as she did her best to stand still, but got tickled, doubled over, ripping her team's efforts up to where the paper fell to her feet.

Eyes big, her hand covered her mouth. "Oops."

"It's okay. Just stay really still while they start again. Come on, y'all have got this," she peptalked, glad when they set back to work around a stiff Jasie.

Hearing Greyson's laughter, Isabelle glanced at her cousin's son and smiled. He'd been chosen as his team's candy cane and was being wrapped in the toilet paper by the other children, Brianna included. Catching Isabelle's eye, Zach gave her a thumbs-up, then returned to encouraging his team.

"Great job," he praised.

He was right. His team was doing a great job. Except for his sweet little face, Greyson was completely wrapped in white. Now Brianna was leading the other kids on, carefully wrapping him with the red streamers. He arched his back and held his arms out. It was going to take a lot to top Zach's group.

"Come on, team. Let's start over," she told her kids as another section of paper tore. "Jasie, you're going to have to hold still, or the paper is going to keep tearing."

"Yes, ma'am." But the girl couldn't contain her giggles as one of the kids wrapped paper across her face and continued around her head, leaving only her eyes showing, creating a mummy look rather than a candy cane pattern. Jasie must have thought so, too, because she made a haunted moaning sound. All Isabelle's team burst into giggles, obviously enjoying themselves as they enthusiastically began intention-ally mummy-wrapping the young girl.

Maybelle blew a whistle, then called, "Time! Boys and girls, turn off your sleighs."

A few of the kids snuck in an additional wrap, including Isabelle's giggling team.

The Butterfly judges moved from one group to the next. When they came to Isabelle's, Maybelle's brow arched. "I think you young ones had the wrong holiday in mind. This is an excellent mummy."

Isabelle couldn't argue, nor could she suppress her smile when Jasie moaned, and the kids all giggled.

"Great practice for next fall," Aunt Claudia praised, Ruby and Rosie nodding their heads in agreement.

Jasie moaned again and the rest of Isabelle's team joined in, causing the surrounding groups to laugh.

Smiling, Isabelle met Maybelle's gaze and let out a low moan of her own. "We're mummies of Christmas past."

"Ah." Maybelle and the other Butterflies made marks on their clipboards, then moved on to Zach's team.

Grinning from ear to ear, Greyson stood perfectly still with his shoulders and arms bowed. His team, including Zach, stood proudly next to him. The Butterflies made more clipboard marks, then finished judging the rest of the candy canes. No one was surprised when they announced Zach's team as the winner, who got the grand prize, but commented that all the entries were so good that they had prizes for everyone.

Morgan being off to visit her previous coworkers and patients at Pine Hill Assisted Living, Andrew had kept a hold on their dog, Andy's, leash and took photos of Greyson. Isabelle snapped a few, too, wondering at why she'd kept the angle wide enough to capture Zach. She'd edit him out later, she assured herself even as she snapped another photo.

"Yay!" Brianna wrapped her arms around a blushing Greyson. "We did it."

Trapped beneath the paper, Greyson just grinned, especially when Andrew winked and gave a thumbs-up with his free hand.

Zach came over to stand beside Isabelle. "Sorry that my

team won."

Watching Greyson and Brianna pose for a photo, she snorted. "No, you're not."

"You're right. I'm not." He grinned. "I just thought it the right thing to say, since I know you hate losing."

She smiled pretty-as-you-please at him. "I didn't lose."

He arched a dark brow.

"All of this is about the kids having fun. My team had a blast and still is." She gestured to where Jasie and a couple of other kids had tucked bunches of torn paper streamers into the tops of their jackets and were twirling and jumping around, the paper ends dancing about them. "That right there makes everyone here today winners."

"Spoken like a true loser," Zach teased, grinning at her eye roll. "Next thing you'll be telling me you wanted my team to win because of Greyson."

"Well," she began, causing him to laugh.

"But I'll grant you this one. The kids are having a fabulous time and I bet I'd feel like a winner even if I'd lost, too." He nudged her with his elbow. "Not that I'd know."

She snapped one last photo of Greyson and Brianna. "Yeah, yeah. Just be glad you got Greyson on your team. He was perfect."

"I've not had a lot of experience around kids, just Lukas's daughter on occasion, but Greyson seems great."

"He is. They just got here last night. I miss them living in Pine Hill."

His gaze went to where Andrew knelt next to Greyson praising him, while the dog grabbed at the paper and shook his head about. "Your family is close."

The way Zach said it had her glancing toward him. No, no, no, she did not want to wrap her arms around him. And, yet, she did want to, too. "I'm sorry that yours isn't."

His expression tightened and he averted his gaze, looking beyond the church playground down the street toward what could be seen of the busy square. "Actually, they are close."

"Just not with you?" she guessed, reaching out to touch his arm. Despite the nip to the air, warmth permeated through his long sleeve.

"It doesn't matter."

But his tone hinted that it did. His shirtsleeve being too much of a barrier, Isabelle took his hand in hers and gave a squeeze. "For whatever it's worth, I'm glad you stayed in Pine Hill for the holidays. I don't know what we would have done without you yesterday. Or today. Thank you for helping."

His gaze lowered to where she held his hand, making Isabelle self-conscious and yet, that vulnerability he'd shown kept her from letting go.

"I know how your brain works, Blondie. You're just happy you had free labor."

"I tried to pay you," she reminded, her whole body focused on where she held his hand. Big, strong, and yet capable of such gentleness.

"Don't worry. I remember and plan to collect."

She lifted her gaze to his. Happiness filled her at seeing the gold flecks back to their usual teasing twinkle. Zach's mood shouldn't have such an impact on her. And yet she fought smiling as she feigned disbelief. "You don't seriously want me to make a banana pudding just for you?"

His eyes stared into hers, almost daring her to look away. "Yep, and you're going to invite me for dinner when you make it."

Barely able to breathe, she swallowed. "Fine, but only because you're my pretend boyfriend."

Zach must have thought her whispered comment too loud, because he glanced around. "You'd never make it as a secret agent."

"Which you're an expert at?" she asked a bit flippantly, letting go of his hand.

He hesitated long enough that she realized that he likely was, which had her feeling a little intimidated that who he was in Pine Hill was only a shadow of who he was in his day-to-day life.

"Some might say that," he finally answered. "But that comment wasn't about me, other than my surprise you'd risk Sophie finding out what we're doing with Butterflies in the vicinity."

Isabelle glanced around, glad to see that the Butterflies were completely enamored with Greyson showing them Andy's tricks. "You're right. I need to keep quiet. It's just that when you're near, I—" She clamped her mouth shut before she said too much yet again.

"You what, Blondie?" he prompted.

"Get so aggravated that I forget to control my temper," she covered. "Speaking of aggravating," she mumbled. "It would serve you right if I called you soldier boy all the time."

"At least get it correct and call me soldier man."

More like soldier hunk.

"I HOPE MY sister told you how much we appreciated your help yesterday." Sophie placed a red, white, and blue quilt on a table, taking care to fold the material to showcase an embroidered label for all who visited their Quilts of Valor booth to see. "I told her we should permanently put you on the payroll and we'd have the mortgage paid off lickety-split. No one seemed able to tell you no when you asked them if there was anything else you could help them with."

Zach paused from where he was unloading brochures from a box. Did they owe a lot on their shop still? Their business seemed busy enough to be profitable, but what did he know about hidden costs and the like? His family ran a huge transport company based out of Atlanta, but Zach had never given thought to the details of what went into making the business successful.

"She expressed her appreciation," Zach told Sophie, continuing to unpack boxes onto the tables for her to arrange. "No permanent job offer, though, which is just as well, since she knows I'd decline."

"Because you work for Bodie's friend?" Her question made iSecure sound like some run-out-of-a-basement business rather than an international security firm that offered a variety of specialized services. "Maybe you'll fall in love with our little town and decide to stay."

It wasn't Pine Hill he worried about falling for.

"I won't stay, Sophie. I'll be back to work as soon as … after the holidays."

"Well, I'm sure you'll visit Isabelle as often as you can,

and you're welcome at the shop when you're in town."

Did Sophie really think he and Isabelle would continue their relationship once he left? Were they doing that good of a job in their pretend relationship? He didn't buy it and expected someone, everyone, to point out the obvious—that Isabelle would never really be in a relationship with someone like him unless it had something to do with the woman smiling at him.

"We all enjoyed having you at the shop," Sophie continued, as they arranged the booth for the evening's events.

"Not Isabelle." Although, to be fair, she'd been busy. They'd all been busy. But he couldn't say he hadn't enjoyed immersing himself in Isabelle's world.

"She was glad you were there. Just know that Izzy's a private person and doesn't like mixing business with personal. Other than working with me, of course."

"Of course." Little did Sophie know that he was business, and only business, as far as what Isabelle vocalized.

But he was no fool and saw how she looked at him. Although she didn't like it, they shared a connection. One that had them both off-kilter because her taking his hand earlier had the effect of shaking the ground beneath his booted feet. She'd thrown him off-balance from the moment they'd met.

"She also doesn't like that you're volunteering during my shift." Sophie gave an impish smile. "She was mumbling about it earlier. I think she's afraid of you being alone with me."

"Why's that?" Zach pulled more Quilts of Valor Foundation swag from a box he'd carried from the shop.

"I'm not sure what she thinks I'm going to say to you

that has her so worried." She laughed softly. "I offered to swap, to take her place at the church's bake sale and let her volunteer with you, but she refused." Sophie paused what she was doing to look at him. "Can you believe that?"

Zach could. "How is it that you're so involved with this organization and she's not?"

"She blames the military for our father abandoning us." She pulled another quilt from a box.

"But that's not the case?" Zach needed to know more.

For finding her father. No other reason. Definitely not that he wanted to know more about what made Isabelle tick.

Rather than put the quilt she held onto the table, Sophie hugged it to her. "Dad loved everything about being a soldier. I think he didn't know how to not be one and that's why he struggled so much when he came home. When he left, I always imagined that he'd reenlisted or found some other way to serve."

She could be describing him. Working at iSecure, often on military contracts, was as close as Zach could come to being a soldier without being directly on Uncle Sam's active-duty roster. He needed to get straight to the point. He hadn't considered that searching for Isabelle's father might dredge up his own shortcomings.

"Do you know where he went?"

She sighed. "I wish I did. I'd tell him to come home so we could wrap him in love."

"That's why you do this?" He gestured to the booth. "Because of your father?"

"Every time I wrap a Quilts of Valor quilt around a soldier, I imagine Dad also being wrapped in love and welcomed home." Sophie gave him a whimsical smile. "My sister thinks I'm a dreamer."

"Are you?"

"Oh yeah." Sophie laughed. "And so is she."

"I know."

Sophie studied him a moment. "Most people don't recognize that quality in Izzy."

"I'm not most people." Isabelle wanted the world to only see her tough, logical, list-making, control-freak, always-responsible exterior.

Thinking about how she'd laughed and carried on, moaning even, during the candy cane wrap, he had to wonder if that protective exterior wasn't unraveling. He longed to grab hold and spin her to freedom to laugh and embrace life, which seemed hypocritical since, until his vacation, he'd buried himself in work, rehab, and sewing blocks.

"Did you ever look for him?"

"More times than you'd believe over the years." Sophie surprised him by saying. "Obviously, I never found him." She shot a worried look his way. "You can't tell Izzy. She'd be upset if she knew I took off to find him and had to call Rosie to help me get back to Kentucky."

He put the pieces of what she was saying together in his mind. "How old were you?"

"Old enough to know better is what my sister would say. She's forever reminding me how my impulsiveness gets me into situations. I can't say she's wrong, but... Anyway, the last time I looked for Dad was right before Izzy's college graduation. I thought if I could find him, if he was there for her ceremony, that…" Sophie's arms clung tighter to the quilt. "You really can't tell her any of this. She wouldn't understand. I love her with all my heart and don't want her upset with me right before my wedding."

Interesting that Sophie had wanted to give Isabelle the gift of having their father at her graduation and Isabelle hoped to find him for Sophie's wedding.

"I won't tell her, but you should," he suggested, knowing it was true. "I don't believe she could ever be upset with you for long."

"Maybe not but knowing would upset her." Sophie gave him a shiny-eyed smile. "Especially as I've been looking for him again. For my wedding. I want to invite him and to ask him to walk me down the aisle." A tear slid down her cheek and she swiped it away. "Do you think I'm crazy for wanting him there when I've not seen him in so long?"

Yes. No. Maybe. How was Zach supposed to answer? He wanted to shake some sense into the guy at the pain he'd caused his daughters, but how could he judge the man when he knew, really knew, how one's mind could lead a person astray?

"It's understandable that you want your father at your wedding."

"Not according to Izzy."

"I imagine his leaving was hard on all of you."

Sophie nodded. "Especially Izzy. They were very close. She's never forgiven him. Mom and I have talked about it and, although the pain is real, we've both moved past that hurt. I'm not sure my sister ever will, but I want that peace for her so badly."

Zach winced at the pain Isabelle must have felt. Still felt. Sophie, too. Guilt punched him, reminding him that he'd left his own family, that he'd not been able to stand their pity and had arranged admission into a rehab facility. He'd had to escape the suffocation he felt within his parents' home, but he'd left a note. They'd known where he'd gone. Brett had even visited during a business trip to DC, mostly to chew him out, but his brother had come to the facility. Once, Zach had seen him. The second time, he'd sent him away unseen.

"Dad's why she's never let herself get close to anyone," Sophie continued, pulling Zach back to their conversation. "Not until you."

The irony of the closeness being because of her father wasn't lost on Zach. Him being the one who searched for a runaway family member was ironic, as well.

"Meeting you has been so good for Izzy. She likes you."

"Don't be fooled. It's just the aftereffects of Rosie's cinnamon bread. Eventually, its romance magic powers are going to wear off." More guilt hit.

Guilt that Isabelle did like him, despite her protests otherwise. Guilt that he was deceiving Sophie. Guilt that he hadn't found her father yet. A few of his leads were promising, but he couldn't be sure until he got there in person. Not going in person would risk Cliff taking off if he got wind someone was looking for him. Zach wouldn't risk that. Guilt that his own family wouldn't be unjustified to feel as abandoned as Cliff Davis's did.

"Ha. That's funny and maybe, but cinnamon bread or no bread, I know my sister. She likes you. A lot. She doesn't necessarily want to like you, though," Sophie added. "That's probably why you think she's just tolerating you. Just be patient. She's worth it."

"She is." The response slipped out of his mouth unbidden, stunning him and making Sophie's whole face light up with her smile.

"I knew it. I'm so glad you're here!" With that, she wrapped him in a hug, squishing the quilt between them and blasting Zach with guilt that what she thought she knew wasn't the truth.

But it wasn't just guilt engulfing him. Sophie's hug was so tight, so real, that it covered him in comfort as surely as if she'd wrapped one of her quilts around him. Not that he needed comforting, but her hug was humbling.

"WHO'S THE *HUNK* Grammy and Maybelle say you're in love with?"

Isabelle gawked at her cousin. She'd already been filled in on Isabelle's supposed love life? The Butterflies had wasted no time.

"I'm not in love with Zach." Face heating enough she could cut off the tent's heater, Isabelle straightened the baked goods with her gloved fingers.

Her mother had been there earlier, but had needed a bathroom break, and Morgan had volunteered to cover in the busy booth, with this being their first lull.

"Zach, yes, that's the name they said." Morgan emptied the last of the no-bake cookies onto the table. "So, you're not in love with him, but he is a hunk?"

"Zach is a great guy." As she said it, she admitted that he really was.

He'd been great at the kids' Christmas activities earlier, great at the shop, great at her Aunt Claudia's Thanksgiving, great at his sewing lessons, great … when was he not great? If she were looking for a relationship, if he weren't ex-military, maybe, just maybe, she'd give in to the allure of that lopsided grin of his. Doing so would be a mistake in the long run. "But it's not what you think."

Sliding the empty box beneath the table, Morgan shrugged. "I just got back in town. I don't think anything. I know all too well how the Butterflies can be. They are very excited for you, especially Grammy."

"Their excitement is premature. My relationship with Zach is complicated."

"Because of his military background?"

Isabelle nodded. "That and more. Zach's only here for a few weeks."

Her cousin regarded her, then smiled. "A lot can happen in a few weeks."

Isabelle rolled her eyes. "Not you, too."

"Loving and being loved is a wonderful feeling. When Trey died, I locked myself away because I was scared to feel again."

Morgan's first husband had been killed in a mountain-climbing accident. When budget cuts ended her nursing job in Georgia, she'd temporarily moved in with Aunt Claudia and gone to work at Pine Hill Assisted Living.

"Thank goodness Andrew freed my heart. Taking a

chance on our love is the best decision I ever made."

That didn't mean it would be a good decision for Isabelle. Not that she loved Zach. But something about him sure got under her skin. "Things are going well with married life, then?" she asked.

"It is. Andrew is a wonderful husband and father. Greyson adores him and still wants to grow up to be just like him. I miss him when he's called out and can't help but worry night after night that he's gone. How could I not when I know how dangerous his smokejumper job is? But he's happy, which makes me happy, and I'm getting better at focusing on the good instead of worrying about what-ifs." Morgan's happiness radiated from her smiling face, then her eyes widened. "Rosie wasn't kidding when she said he was tall, dark, and handsome."

Isabelle had to forcibly suck air in to fight off the anticipatory jitters taking over. "Zach's on his way over here, isn't he?"

Not taking her gaze off whomever had caught her eye, Morgan nodded. "Unless there's two new buff guys in town."

"Just the one."

"One's all you need."

"I don't need him. Or want him. He's super annoying and I—hey, Zach," she greeted when he stepped up to the booth. "This is Greyson's mom, Morgan," she prattled on, trying to cover her nervousness at seeing him and hoping her cousin didn't burst into laughter at how ridiculous she was acting. Why did she feel so self-conscious talking to Zach in front of Morgan?

"Nice to meet you." His hazel gaze turned toward Isabelle. "Hey, Blondie. Did you save me a banana bread?"

"Did you think I'd forget?"

He shook his head. "Nope. I knew you wouldn't. You have your lists to keep you from doing that. I was more concerned that you just wouldn't."

"Well, lucky for you, since we sold out, I did put one back."

"Good girl." He winked, and Isabelle's heart skipped a beat. "How much longer is your shift? Bodie tells me I have to try a bowl of Lou's chili. I thought you might want one, too."

"There's no need to wait on me. Go ahead."

"Grammy is who's taking the next shift, right? Her and Gramps? They've taken Greyson on a sleigh ride. He was so happy that Ralphie the Reindeer remembered him. I told them I'd be here when they finished, so why don't you go ahead? I'll man the booth until they arrive."

Zach grinned at her cousin. "I like you already."

"There's no need to do that, Morgan. I'm more than happy to wait on them." Isabelle gave her a cousin a pleading look.

A look Morgan ignored. "Nonsense. We're not busy now, and your mom will be back any moment. You two go, so you can properly introduce Zach to our On-the-Square Christmas Festival."

"What if you need help?" Isabelle tried one last time.

"Sarah and Bodie are on the other side of the booth selling snowflakes. If I need anything before Grammy gets back, I'll get Sarah. Besides"—Morgan gestured to the table—

"we've almost sold out since those guys from the firehall wiped us out."

Morgan refused to take no for an answer. Isabelle thanked her, then tightened her jacket.

"If I didn't know better, I'd think you didn't want to walk around with me," Zach said when they'd stepped out of hearing range of the booth. "Afraid people will think you actually like me?"

"Whatever gave you that idea?"

"Just a hunch." He grinned. "Hungry?"

Why did she feel so self-conscious walking around her hometown's square with Zach?

"I had a snack."

"Aw, so that's why your bake sale inventory dropped by a good seventy-five percent," he teased, looking way too handsome in his jeans, shirt, and light jacket.

"I ate one Christmas cookie," she defended.

"I'm teasing, Blondie. It wouldn't hurt if you had eaten your way across that table."

"Other than the sugar high and bellyache," she mused.

He grinned. "Yeah, other than those minor inconveniences."

Sirens blared off in the distance. "Sounds like the parade has started."

"You want to watch?"

She did, but... "I feel guilty watching when Morgan should be with Greyson and Andrew."

"Andrew planned to hop a ride on the fire truck and was taking Greyson with him once he finished with his sleigh ride. The kid was more excited about riding on the truck than he was being in the parade."

"He plans to be a firefighter when he grows up. Morgan met Andrew when he, Cole, and Ben talked to Greyson's classroom at school. The guys have missed Andrew, especially Cole."

"I gathered that they were close." He glanced her way again. "What about you? Who occupies your time?"

"Lately? You."

His gaze didn't waver from hers. "Before me."

She frowned. "I have friends, Zach."

"That you don't share blood with, go to church with, or work with?"

Isabelle snorted. "You just eliminated half of Pine Hill."

"Good point." He reached for her gloved hand. "Smile. We're faking it, remember?"

Isabelle wasn't sure there was a need to fake anything. He had a few leads on where her father might be. Now that they'd gone through photo albums and he'd picked her family's and friends' brains for their memories of Cliff Davis, she didn't see the point in continuing the relationship deceit. Still, his hand felt good cradling hers now that she'd left the warmth of the heater that had been blowing at her feet in the church tent booth.

"Sophie is my best friend, Zach," she said, trying to take her mind off her hand in his by refocusing on the conversation. "That she is also my sister is just an added bonus. Don't you feel that way about your brother?"

His face pinched. "I mentioned before that we weren't that close."

"Then you should do something about that."

AFTER A MINUTE of mulling her comment over, Zach mumbled, "Yeah, you're probably right."

Not that Zach hadn't done something about his strained relationship with his family. He'd gone home after his medical discharge, but that had been a big mistake. He'd not been able to stand the disappointment in their eyes or how they wanted to fix him and his broken life.

"My relationship with Brett is complicated." That was putting it mildly.

They'd never actually come to blows, but there had been a few scuffles over the years. Mostly when Brett had taken it upon himself to try to run Zach's life.

"Why? What's so difficult about being close to your brother?"

"Everything." Not that he expected her to understand.

If she could, she'd side with his brother, thinking Zach was the wild child. Wanting to go into the army had kept him straight enough that he hadn't strayed too far outside the law, but he'd rebelled against the restraints his high-society family had tried to shackle him with.

"Brett's always been the perfect son." His parents sure thought so, along with everyone else in their upper-crust Atlanta suburb.

Isabelle's gaze cut his way. "That implies you haven't."

"Not even close." Had wanting to follow his own dreams made him a bad son?

"I find that difficult to believe."

He stopped walking. "Did you just compliment me?"

Her cheeks glowed a bright pink. "Don't let it go to your head. That ego of yours is already big enough."

"No need to worry about my ego. Since meeting you, it's as deflated as that big ball of sunken PVC tarpaulin."

Isabelle's eyes widened. "Oh no. That's supposed to be a giant snow globe jump house filled with bouncing children. It's sponsored by the Triple B Ranch for Kids. The money raised goes toward purchasing Christmas morning goodies for each kid. The Butterflies started the charity fund after there were worries that all the kids might not have gifts last year. The fund provides a bouncy house at all our various on-the-square events."

Why did it not surprise him that the Butterflies had been up to good?

"Come on. Let's see if we can help get it going." Zach introduced himself to the volunteer running the bouncy house, then studied the setup. His brain had always worked best in fix-it mode. In under two minutes, he had air going back in to fill out the globe.

Standing, he wiped his hands on his jeans, then grinned at Isabelle. "Tell me how good I am."

Clasping her hands together, she batted her lashes. "My hero."

"I knew you'd finally catch on." Seeing her acting silly did funny things to Zach's belly, and the vision of her spinning free from her self-imposed confines ran through his mind again.

"Had you not gotten it working, I figured you'd just huff and puff and blow it up with all your hot air."

He laughed, then grabbed her hand. "Come on, Blondie.

We need to try this baby out to make sure it holds air before we let the kids jump. It's our duty to keep them safe."

Isabelle gave him a dubious look. "I'm not getting in that."

"You sure?" Grinning, he pulled her to him, not letting himself register how good she felt in his arms and scooped her up.

Wiggling, she glared. "Put me down."

"We have to do this for the kids." Pushing the flap back, he set her in the doorway, backside first with her legs hanging outside over the edge. Leaning in close, he stared into her eyes, making sure they didn't convey fear. He wanted her to let loose and have fun, not be afraid.

Excitement shined in her blue depths. "You go right ahead," she told him, "but I don't have to do this."

He grinned. "You can thank me later, Blondie."

"Thank you?" She pushed against his chest. "More like I'll be plotting on how to get even."

"I look forward to your best efforts."

Her warm breath crossed the small gap between them, drawing his gaze to her mouth. It would be so easy to close the distance between them, so easy to forget that he had no right to kiss Isabelle. He wanted to kiss her. Before he'd gotten to know her, before he'd learned how vulnerable she was, he would have. But he did know. If he made their relationship real, or any semblance thereof, she'd be hurt when he left.

So instead of the kiss he wanted, he reached for her boot and unzipped it.

"I'm not a child and can take off my own shoes." Her

protest lacked conviction, though, causing him to glance up. Curiosity shone in those big blue eyes and something that looked a lot like disappointment. She'd known that he'd wanted to kiss her but had chosen not to.

Oh, Blondie, don't tempt me any more than you already do.

Heart pounding, mind racing, hands shaking, Zach wrangled her boot free from her foot. "I wasn't taking any chances on you leaving these bad boys on in case you hoped to get in a few good kicks."

Seeming to snap out of whatever had seized her, she half smiled. "You figured me out."

In some ways. In others, he suspected that if he had the rest of his life, he still wouldn't discover all the wondrous aspects of this woman.

"Too bad this is a snow globe instead of a castle." He unzipped the second boot. "My taking off your shoes is a little Cinderella fairy tale-ish."

"Except you're no prince charming," she immediately pointed out.

"And these contraptions are no glass slippers." He pulled off the remaining shoe, smiling at her fuzzy penguin socks. "Ready to shake things up inside a giant blow-up snow globe? Pun intended."

She narrowed her eyelids to tiny slits. "I really don't like you."

Zach dropped her shoe to the ground, then met her gaze. "So you keep telling me. But for the record, I like you enough for the both of us."

Chapter Eleven

HEAD SPINNING AT Zach's comment, Isabelle leaned back into the bounce house, swinging her legs inside as she fell against the firm surface.

Don't read anything into what Zach said, she told herself. He was a flirt and hadn't meant anything by his liking her comment. Nor had he meant anything by the way his mouth had been so close, by how his warm breath had been fanning across her lips.

Which didn't explain the almost giddy bubbling in her belly. Giddiness because Zach liked her? Was she in middle school or what? Well, she was inside a bouncy house, which she hadn't been in since probably middle school or even prior to then.

"You could have waited on me," Zach called from the doorway, where he pulled off his boots.

No, she really couldn't have. Not after that comment. She'd needed a moment to think, to get her head on straight, to wonder why he'd say that when he'd chosen not to kiss her when she'd wanted him to. What had she been thinking?

There wasn't enough time in the world for her to figure out that one.

Glancing around at the inside of the inflated globe, she

took a deep breath. When in Rome—or inside a giant snow globe—a girl should just go with it, right? Managing to get to her feet, she jumped as high as she could. Floating through the air was liberating and landing on the springy floor didn't jar her back to earth, so she did it again. And again. Higher and higher.

"I'm coming after you, Blondie," Zach threatened, crawling through the opening with a grin on his face and a determined gleam in his eyes.

"Oh, really?" Launching off the bouncy floor, she waved her fingers in a bring-it-on motion as she soared upward. "Catch me if you can."

THE BUTTERFLIES, IN carefully constructed snowflake costumes they'd worn for the Miss Pine Hill Snowflake pageant, edged their way closer to the oversized snow globe, where Zach and Isabelle could be seen playing inside the curved, clear PVC outer shell.

"I'm hot." Rosie paused by the hot cocoa vendor they hid behind to dramatically place the back of her long white-and-silver-bedazzled glove onto where her forehead should be.

"We all know you're a bit flaky, Rosie." Maybelle straightened her costume. "It's just that now, you look the part."

"Don't you go talking about the way I look. You obviously got the wrong wardrobe memo." From where her eyes peered out from the costume's cut-out opening, Rosie batted her lashes. "We're supposed to be snowflakes, not icebergs."

Ruby and Claudia both snickered, then, nudging Claudia, Ruby pointed toward the snow globe. "Do you see what I see?"

"No, my costume keeps slipping over my eyes to where I can barely see a thing." Using both hands, Claudia adjusted her costume around her face. Then, eyes widening, she grabbed Ruby's arm. "Do you hear what I hear? I can't remember the last time I heard Isabelle laugh that hard."

Moving closer to the edge of the cocoa truck so she could peep around it for a closer look, Maybelle frowned. "Why is she running from him? It's not as if there's anywhere to hide in there."

"If she's smart, she'll let him catch her." Rosie waggled her brows.

"Oh!" Claudia's hand slapped against Ruby. "He's got her by the waist."

"Why is she trying to get free?" Rosie continued. "If that man's arms were around me, I'd—"

"You'd what?" Maybelle eyed Rosie.

Rosie fluffed a silvery white tentacle and replied, "Things you know nothing about, old woman."

"Shh ... you two quit." Claudia shushed, her gaze not leaving the couple playing in the bouncy snow globe. "He's got her, she's spinning, and down she goes!"

"She's still laughing," Ruby pointed out. "It's good that she's laughing."

Rosie leaned back against the truck. "Any chance there's mistletoe inside that bouncy house?"

Maybelle frowned. "There's normally children in there."

"I'm just saying that it would be nice if there was now. Mistletoe, not kids." Rosie clarified with a laugh.

Claudia clung to the edge of the vendor trailer. "Oh, do you see how she's looking at him? Why is she fighting how she feels so much?"

"For the same reasons he's fighting it, I imagine," Ruby said. "These young people complicate matters so much. Why, my Charlie—"

"We know!" the other three Butterflies said simultaneously.

"You Snowbugs aren't back here causing mischief, are you?" Clearing his throat, Bodie shined his officer's flashlight toward them.

Turning to face him, Maybelle shaded her eyes from the bright light. "Now, Bodie, do we look as if we're causing mischief?"

"Always."

Four Butterflies burst into laughter.

HER STOMACH IN knots that had grown more and more twisted as she drove toward Tennessee, Isabelle eyed the homeless shelter not too far from Fort Campbell. "I can't believe you convinced me to take off work to do this, especially when it's probably a complete waste of time."

From the passenger seat, Zach gave her an empathetic look. "Think of it as an adventure, Blondie."

"More like a nightmare," she mumbled, letting out a long sigh.

Zach studied her, something akin to pity on his face. "You sure you're ready for what we may find out?"

"No, but I'm not sitting in the car while you go in without me. I mean, wouldn't this man who says he remembers my father be more likely to talk to me than he would to you?"

"True. Let's just hope that the Cliff this guy remembers was your dad. He says it's the same guy in the photo I emailed him."

"It was a long way to drive if it wasn't." Isabelle eyed two men sitting outside the building. They leaned against the block exterior, and both had well-worn duffle bags. Had her dad once sat outside this building? Choosing to live in a homeless shelter rather than with his family? "This Mr. Simmons didn't know where Dad went from here?"

Zach shook his head. "But I got the impression during our phone conversation that he didn't tell me all he knew. We're positive your father was here at one time. This guy worked here during that time. It's logical that he could have met your father."

Nothing about this trip felt logical. Quite the opposite. Why had finding her father for Sophie's wedding felt so urgent? Sophie was marrying the man of her dreams. Why did she need their runaway father to walk her down the aisle? Their mother could do the honor. Or Sophie could walk herself to Cole. No dad needed.

"I've changed my mind. We don't need to find my father for Sophie's wedding."

"You firing me, Blondie?"

"Consider your lessons thus far as an early Christmas

gift. Besides, you've finished your table placemats."

"And that's all I need to know to make a quilt?"

"It's not as if you're really going to make a quilt, Zach. Sure, you're helping Sarah because you're staying there, but do you see yourself quilting once you leave Pine Hill?" She shook her head in answer for him. "I don't think so."

"You might be surprised."

She snorted. "The only reason you're learning to sew is to torture me into giving you lessons."

He shook his head. "That's not true. Sarah hooked my interest in becoming involved with Quilts of Valor before I'd met you, Blondie."

"Fine. I'll keep up your lessons for however long you're in town." She started the car back up. "But we're stopping this needle in a haystack search. The truth is, I don't want him found. I'm not sure I ever really did."

"Turn off the ignition, Isabelle. We're not leaving without talking to Mr. Simmons."

"Were you not listening? I no longer want to find my father. Sophie's wedding will be wonderful without Dad there to walk her down the aisle. Probably more so than if he showed up."

"I was listening. With my ears and my head." He reached over and pushed the ignition button to shut off the engine. "I know you're angry with him. Maybe you have every right to be. But maybe you need to find him to hear his side of the story."

"Why am I not surprised that you're taking his side?" She glared at him.

"I'm not taking a side, and if I were"—he lifted her hand

from the steering wheel, clasping it within his strong grasp—
"I'd always choose yours."

Isabelle trembled.

"This isn't about sides," he continued. "It's about coming to terms with your father leaving. For you and for Sophie."

"Sophie's fine."

"And you? Are you fine?"

Chin lifting, she pulled her hand free. "Are you implying I'm not?"

"You tell me."

"I'm a successful businesswoman," she reminded.

He didn't say anything.

"I'm an upstanding member of my community."

He sat in the passenger seat, staring at her.

"I graduated from high school with the highest GPA and had a full scholarship," she reminded. "All these things aren't things someone who isn't okay does."

"Good. We've established that you're fine. That means there's no reason for us not to go in and talk to Mr. Simmons. Come on." And with that, he got out of the car and headed toward the homeless shelter's entrance, pausing to talk to the people outdoors, but not once did he look back to see if she was following him.

Blasted man. It would serve him right if she restarted the engine and left him to walk back to Pine Hill.

GLANCING TOWARD THE pale woman walking next to him,

Zach fought the urge to take her into his arms. An urge he'd been fighting for the past half hour while they talked with the shelter's director, Bob Simmons. Had he been wrong to push her into going into the shelter? He hadn't thought so but seeing her so shaken had him second-guessing his belief that she was too logical to have come all this way without at least talking to the man who claimed to have known her father. Not going in would have nagged at her, possibly for forever.

Yet, who was he to have pressed when she'd wanted to leave? Wasn't that what he'd done himself rather than face his own family issues?

"You okay? What am I asking? I know you're not okay. You just found out that your dad lived in a homeless shelter less than two hours from Pine Hill on and off for several years."

"At least now we know Dad really was here."

"Yep. Bob confirmed that by how much he knew about your family and Pine Hill. It makes more sense that Bob remembered him now that we know Cliff volunteered at the shelter as well as living there. It sounded as if Bob thought a lot of him."

Isabelle nodded. "Why do you think Dad told him so much about us?"

"It's normal for a father to talk about his kids." No doubt his own father bragged about the brilliant son who'd stepped into the family business and was a *chip off the old block*. When it benefitted the business, he'd guess his old man brought up having a son in the military as well.

"Even fathers who left them?" Isabelle's voice held such a

desperate plea for reassurance that her father had loved his daughters that Zach ached.

"Sounded to me as if the man Bob remembered missed his daughters a lot." It wasn't a lie, but Zach would have said most anything to erase the pain shining in her blue gaze.

"Then why did he leave us? Why?" Isabelle demanded, giving voice to her hurt.

"I can't answer that." But he had a pretty good idea. Didn't he stay away from his own family for their own good, too? Their lives were better with him not there. "From what Bob told us, your father suffered from bouts of severe depression."

"So, he wanted the rest of us to be depressed, too?" With that, his strong, brave Isabelle began to cry and Zach's inability to do anything other than take her into his arms crumbled right along with her.

Stroking her hair, he held her close, letting his body absorb her sobs. Feeling helpless, he wanted to wave a wand and make her world right. He shouldn't have brought her today. Or, more accurately, had her bring him since he still wasn't cleared to drive. Soon, though.

Frustrations he'd been fighting from the moment he'd stepped inside the shelter hit and he held onto Isabelle a little tighter. She'd been looking around the facility and trying to imagine her father there. He'd looked around at the frail, unkempt men and women, and he'd seen people who'd once been proud, productive members of society. Some military, some mental, some just down on their luck.

He'd seen himself.

The dreaded throb in his temple started and his left eye

twitched. A sharp stab shot through the side of his head and sweat popped out on his skin. No. Not here. Not now. Not when Isabelle needed him to be strong. He did not need one of his headaches to hit. Or worse. If he blacked out, she'd tell Sarah, and then Bodie would tell Lukas. He might never get back to driving.

He must have tensed because she pulled back and swiped at her face. "I'm so embarrassed. If you tell anyone I did this, I'll never forgive you."

"No one knows we're here, Isabelle," he reminded, his vision fuzzy as he focused on her face, hanging on to her image to keep himself conscious and slowly feeling the fuzziness brighten.

"Yeah, they all think we're on some romantic Christmas shopping outing." She dug in her purse, found a tissue, and blew her nose. "That's me. Miss Romantic."

He rubbed his clammy palms over his jeans. "Someone should give you a crown and sash."

She snorted. "I'm not the beauty queen in my family."

"Sophie?" He kept his gaze trained on Isabelle's light to keep the darkness at bay.

"Sophie and Annabelle, but my Grandmother Belle is who was the true beauty queen."

Glad his head pain was dissipating, he lifted her hand to his lips and pressed a kiss there. "You're wrong, Blondie. The women in your family are beautiful, but they don't hold a candle to you."

An odd noise sounded from deep in her throat. "You don't have to say nice things just because I was crying. I'm over my boohoo moment."

Realizing she was serious, he turned her to face the car so they could see their reflection in the window. She closed her eyes.

"Look at yourself, Isabelle," he ordered. "Look and see what I see."

She kept her eyes squeezed shut. "A woman whose nose is red from the cold and crying? No thanks. I'd rather not have a visual to go with the wreck I know I am."

"Open your eyes." He rubbed his palms over her jacket sleeves in case she really was chilly. "There's so much more than what you just described. There's a woman who is strong, determined, who takes care of everyone she loves to the point of selflessness. She graduated with the highest GPA and had a full scholarship to an Ivy League school, where she kicked butt and got a dream job." Isabelle's eyes opened, staring back at him in their reflection. "She's smart and funny and has the sassiest mouth I've ever encountered and her eyes... Her eyes suck you in and drown you in their blueness."

"Suck you in and drown you? Seriously? Is that description supposed to make me feel better?"

"I never claimed to be a poet. Just a man trying to show a beautiful woman what he sees when he looks at her. Admit it, I was doing fairly well up to that point."

She stared at him in their reflection for a moment, then to his surprise, she twisted to face him and lifted her palm to his cheek. "Thank you, Zach. For being nice to me, for bringing me today, for making me go in and face what I didn't want to face, and for not judging me for crying."

"Yeah, I'm a real hero." And a huge hypocrite.

Because sometimes it really was easier to just stay away than to face one's shortcomings. Was that what had happened with Isabelle's father? He'd left and not known how to go home? Afraid of the welcome he'd receive? Convincing himself his family was better off?

BACKSTAGE AT THE high school's theater, Isabelle inspected the baggy robe's side seam. Someone must have pulled at a loose thread and undone the whole thing. Yeah, she could have that repaired prior to the concert tonight. There were a few hems that needed adjusting, as well, so she'd take those and have them back to the kids prior to time for the show to start.

Annabelle placed one of the dresses onto a hanger. "Can you even believe that Sophie's wedding is in two weeks and Christmas the week after?"

No, she couldn't. Nor was she ready for Christmas or her sister's wedding. She and Zach hadn't found her father. Sophie had mentioned having Cliff there several times over the past week. Almost to the point that Isabelle wondered if her sister knew.

Maybe she and Zach hadn't been as sly with their Tennessee trip as they'd thought. She wouldn't put it past the Butterflies to have tailed them. They probably had an entire dossier on their comings and goings. Had she hired them to find her father, he might be having coffee at Lou's with some of his old army buddies by now.

Not that she really believed that. Truth was, Zach impressed her with what he'd learned thus far. Since their Tennessee trip, he'd confirmed two additional hits as having been her father. Given time, he would locate Cliff Davis.

Time was what was rapidly ticking away, though. Time to find her father.

And time before Zach would leave Pine Hill.

He'd only been in town a few weeks. Yet, she struggled to recall what life had been like before his arrival or what it would be like when he left. He drove her crazy with his crooked grins and teasing, but he also added vivid colors to the black and white life she'd been content with, making her laugh and feel that vividness being near him filled her with. Chiding herself that a high school Christmas choir concert wasn't the time for mulling over her father's whereabouts or how, more and more, she counted time by when she'd next see Zach, she forced a smile.

"Sophie's wedding will be here before we know it, but tonight is your time to shine. I'm so excited for your Christmas concert tonight. At the shop, I've heard you practicing your solo." After Annabelle's panicked call about the nativity scene costume, she'd swung by the school to make last-minute repairs. Zach planned to ride with Sarah and Bodie and meet her there—as her pretend boyfriend, of course. What would he think of their small-town high school? What would it have been like if he'd attended their school and they'd been there together? Would he have noticed the nerdy girl who'd rather have her nose stuck in a book than go on a date?

"I'm excited." Annabelle drew her back to their conversation. "I hope I don't get nervous and forget every word. Jeff just got home from college yesterday. I've not seen him yet, but he'll be here. I may spot him in the audience and go completely blank."

"You won't," Isabelle assured, hoping it was true. Young love did funny things to a person. Not that she knew personally, but she'd watched it happen often enough. "I know you were heartbroken when his football schedule didn't allow him to come home at Thanksgiving."

"Carrie and I both were, but consoled ourselves that he was doing what he loves and would be home for a few weeks over Christmas." Her eyes, that were nearly identical to Sophie's, darkened. "Let's just hope he feels the same about me as when he left for college."

"He does. You talk to him most days," Isabelle reminded.

"Don't mind me." Annabelle gave her a quick hug. "I'm just nervous because our choir members who are also on the debate team are still competing in Louisville. We all have mixed emotions, as we want them to keep winning, but we need them back for our show."

"They have plenty of time."

But when she and Sophie got to the high school that evening and made their way to drop off the altered costume, Trevor appeared frazzled. The always neat man's hair stuck about his head in total disarray, and he flitted from one group of kids to the next.

"Is everything okay?" she and Sophie asked simultaneously when he rushed over to them.

The music teacher raked his fingers through his wavy hair, explaining the wayward locks. "Not really. The kids on the debate team aren't going to be back for the show." Stress etched itself onto his face. "No one thought they'd make it to the state championship round tonight, but they have."

"That's wonderful." At his fretful look, Isabelle added, "Unless you're their music teacher and some of them are a key part of the choir concert. In which case, their making it to the championship is terrible."

"Can't the show go on without them?" Sophie asked, her eyes full of empathy.

No doubt at any moment her sister would be offering to bake cookies to cheer him. Sophie thought cookies solved everything. They often worked.

He nodded. "It'll have to. I won't have the kids disappointed. Ever since we realized the tournament was the same weekend as the concert, I've known this scenario was a possibility. Just—"

"No one expected them to make the semifinals, much less the championship round?"

"Exactly." He sighed. "The show won't be as I'd hoped, but it'll work with tweaks and leaving off a few songs. All except the last number." His face pinched. "I could leave it off, too, or just not have our nativity scene, but it's the grand finale performance and is such a powerful way to end the show."

He told her what was planned.

"You can't leave it off," Sophie insisted. "Izzy and I can help. We sing."

Isabelle's face burned. "We aren't high school choir kids."

"No, but we sing in church, and you've always had a

beautiful voice." Sophie clasped her hands together, smiling big at Trevor. "We've got this. Just tell us what you need."

He didn't look convinced. "Thank you, but it'll take a lot more than just the two of you. There are several empty spots to fill in the original program."

Deep in thought, Sophie put her finger over her mouth. "Fine. Cole and Ben are at the firehall tonight. They'll be by but won't be able to help in case a call comes in, but we'll get volunteers."

"I'm sure Zach will help." Annabelle joined them and got caught up in Sophie's excitement. "He's always helping with something around the quilt shop."

"Zach?" Isabelle frowned at her cousin as Sophie praised, "That's brilliant. He'll definitely help."

"He doesn't sing," Isabelle insisted, not sure why it felt so imperative that Zach not be a part of the show.

Maybe because she'd just been thinking about how he'd infiltrated so much of her life, and she felt the need to protect this little part of it. Besides, he didn't sing, other than off-key in the car. Although, she guessed he'd thrown his tone on purpose, trying to cheer her during their drive from Tennessee.

"I don't need him to sing." Trevor jumped on board with Sophie's enthusiasm. "He just needs to stand there and be Joseph. Do you think he'll do it?"

"No," Isabelle said at the same time as Sophie and Annabelle replied, "Yes."

They looked at each other and laughed.

Isabelle grimaced. "Surely, we could ask someone else?"

"Nonsense. I'm sure Zach will help us. Go talk to him

and I'll find the rest of our nativity," Sophie assured.

"YOU WANT ME to do what?" Zach's expression hinted that he thought he'd heard Isabelle wrong. "I'm no Joseph."

"Part of the kids are hung up at the tournament," she explained. "They'll be missed, but the show can carry on without them, except the nativity scene. For that, they need stand-ins and Sophie thought—"

"That I should be Joseph?"

Isabelle nodded. "Cole is at the firehall, or she'd have asked him, since she's going to be Mary. You just have to stand there. It's a nativity scene, not a major production."

The glint in Zach's eyes had unease rising in Isabelle's stomach. "I'll do it on one condition."

"THANKS FOR BEING my Mary." Trevor pushed his glasses up the bridge of his nose and smiled at Isabelle. "Thanks to you and Sophie everything is covered, except the wise men and a few animals."

A burst of green bubbled to life in Zach's belly. The music teacher was sweet on Isabelle. Too bad the man was wasting his energy because he couldn't have her.

The thought had Zach taking a mental step back. Isabelle didn't belong to him. If asked, she'd say she wasn't really dating him and claim to not even like him.

She laughed at something the music teacher said that

Zach missed. More green bubbled.

You're leaving as soon as the holidays pass, he reminded himself. Isabelle would be there and deserved to be loved. The music teacher appeared to be halfway there already. They probably had a ton in common. Did Zach and Isabelle have anything in common?

Then again, they were still pretend dating so he shouldn't just stand there while Trevor Reeves made googly eyes at her.

"Actually, she's my Mary." Zach moved closer, placing his palm against Isabelle's lower back.

Frowning, Isabelle's expression seemed to ask, *what are you doing?*

"Come on, Joseph," she told him, grasping his arm. "We've got to go find some wise men."

Zach followed her back out into the half-full auditorium, not surprised when she headed toward where Lou and Rosie sat up front. Maybelle, John, her Aunt Claudia and Uncle George, and Ruby and Charlie were all already there. Great choice, he thought, when she told the guys what she needed.

Her Uncle George's eyes widened. "We got here early to get good seats not to participate. As much as I love Annabelle, I'm not an on-stage kind of man."

Nodding, Isabelle didn't seem surprised at her uncle's refusal.

"I'm not sure about standing in one place for an extended time," John claimed, rubbing his side for emphasis. "My hip fracture from last year is healed, but I try not to tempt fate."

Lou outright refused, claiming stage fright. "Christmas

choirs are spectator events."

"Now, honey, you know this is your opportunity to let the world know how brilliant you are," Rosie chided him, patting his cheek.

"They already know better than that," Maybelle stage-whispered to the others.

Rosie's gaze cut to her friend.

"He married you, didn't he?" Maybelle continued, a smile on her coral lips.

"Ha-ha." Rosie slapped her thigh. "I'm surprised you remembered that in your advanced age. Your mind seems to be slipping so much these days."

Maybelle's gaze narrowed. "I remember lots of things."

Her face failing to hide her disappointment, Isabelle sighed. "I understand you guys don't want to do this, but we can't have Annabelle's last high school Christmas choir concert be anything less than perfect."

"It won't." Maybelle stood and tugged on Ruby's sleeve. "Come on."

Ruby stared up at her friend. "Come on where?"

Rather than answer, Maybelle pointed a look at Claudia. "You, too."

"What do you think you're doing?" Rosie demanded.

Maybelle made her way out of the aisle, the other two Butterflies right behind her. "Saving the day, as usual."

Rosie jumped up to follow her friends. "Not without me, you're not."

Chapter Twelve

"THEY'RE GOING TO kill each other, aren't they?" Zach whispered ten minutes later.

Although he still wasn't crazy about how the guy made googly eyes at Isabelle, he felt sorry for the music director as the Butterflies argued over which three would be his wise men.

"Doubtful since they haven't after all these years." Meeting his gaze, Isabelle smiled impishly. "To be honest, when I went over there, I didn't think the guys would jump on board with my invitation."

Zach looked at her with admiration. "You knew they'd say no and that the Butterflies would step up?"

"I wasn't sure if they'd fill in or just find willing volunteers, but I knew I could count on them. I never doubt that they'll be there in a pinch."

"Probably with binoculars and cupid's arrows."

"Funny, but wrong holiday," Isabelle corrected, still smiling. "The Butterflies are all about Christmas. Dangling mistletoe, they lasso their victims together with garland and promises of happy-ever-afters dancing in their heads."

Zach chuckled.

"Fine. Let these old biddies be wise men." Rosie gestured

toward her friends, then fluffed her neon-blue hair. "People taking me for an old man is a far stretch, even with as great an actress as I am."

Maybelle snorted. Ruby grunted. Claudia shook her head. Zach and Isabelle exchanged looks.

"Y'all can make me the twinkling star that men follow—wise men, that is," she added with a *so-there* look at her friends.

"Ms. Hudson, we already have a star," the music teacher pointed to a large star that had been embellished with Christmas lights.

"You'd choose that over me?" Rosie's hands went to her hips.

"Yep. He would," Maybelle assured. "It's not like they have a crane readily available to hoist you above the stage so you can twinkle."

"Huh," Rosie huffed.

"I'm sure I can find you something, Ms. Hudson," Trevor attempted to appease.

"Poor guy," Zach mused. "He likes you, by the way."

Isabelle turned toward Zach. "What makes you say that?"

"My eyes." The surge of testosterone every time the guy looked her way. "He's definitely besotted."

Isabelle's gaze shifted to where the music teacher still refereed the Butterflies. "You think I should go for it?"

"No." As soon as he said it, guilt hit. "At least, not until after I find your dad."

Isabelle's gaze cut to him. "You really think you're going to find him before Sophie's wedding?"

"We know that at some point after leaving Clarksville, he

went to Florida, then on to Texas."

"Where he had a job working on a ranch. Great, we know that for a while he wasn't living at an inpatient facility or in a homeless shelter anymore, but that was still over fifteen years ago. He could be anywhere."

"True." Cliff Davis's Social Security number hadn't been used since he'd worked on the ranch.

Zach had talked with the owner in detail. The man hadn't known where Isabelle's dad had gone when he'd left the Bar T but had mentioned he'd become friends with some migrant workers and had left around the same time.

"I'll find him."

Failure wasn't an option. Neither was the man eyeing them. Zach slid his arm around Isabelle's waist.

Glancing up, her eyes widened. "Tell me you're acting."

"I'm Joseph, and you're my pregnant virgin wife. He shouldn't be looking at you that way."

Isabelle's cheeks turned a bright red. "You should come to church and let Pastor Smith educate you on the rest of the good book."

Zach wasn't religious, but he could recount Jesus's birth. "Is that an invitation to come to church with you?"

Her mouth opened, then she grimaced. "You have me there, don't you? I can't really in good conscience say no to you going to church with me."

He eyed how her cheeks flushed, how her breath had quickened, how she was twisting the hem of her sweater. "But you want to?"

"I don't think I'd pay much attention to what was being taught if you were there."

"Because?"

Sighing and not meeting his gaze, she spoke so softly that he barely heard. "You distract me."

Not allowing himself to analyze why her admission made him happy, Zach touched the tip of her nose. "You distract me, too, wifey."

ISABELLE'S HEART THUNDERED at Zach's teasing. He didn't mean a thing by it, and yet … and yet, his comment had her spinning. Or maybe it was how complicated her relationship with him was. They were a pretend couple pretending to be a married couple. No wonder she felt off-kilter.

"I am not a sit-on-the-sidelines-while-these-three-are-on-stage kind of woman," Rosie informed the music teacher.

"I hate to break it to you"—Maybelle's tone said she relished every word—"but you've been sitting on the sidelines of our lives for years."

Rosie stamped her foot. "Ooooh, you take that back, Maybelle Kirby."

"Nope. Facts are facts."

"There is another part." Trevor looked uncertain of what he was going to say. "I'd thought to have the performance without recasting that role, but if you were willing… It's a speaking part."

"Speaking?" Rosie perked up. "I'll take it. Whatever it is, I'm sure I'm perfect."

Ten minutes later and wearing her Mary costume, Isabelle slapped her hand over her mouth. She fought looking at Zach as his chest convulsed a little from suppressed laughter in response to in-costume Rosie stepping out from behind the changing area.

"Oh my." Isabelle wished she could pull the blue cloth covering her head over her face. She wasn't sure how much longer she could hold in her laughter.

"Yep." Zach's hand covered his mouth as if his half-strangled chuckle were actually a coughing spell.

Three Butterfly wise men's jaws dropped.

Isabelle wasn't sure she'd ever seen Maybelle double over with laughter before, but she cackled to the point her ribs were sure to be sore the next day. Ruby and Aunt Claudia were right there with her.

Maybelle hit her thighs. "That's priceless."

"The greatest thing I've ever seen." Ruby howled, grabbing hold of Claudia's arm as if she thought she might topple over from her amusement.

"Legendary." Aunt Claudia reached for her phone.

"Do not, and I mean do not, take a photo of me in this"—Rosie's nose curled as she glanced down at her fuzzy gray attire—"this ridiculous get-up."

"Now, Rosie, you're going to be in the spotlight for an entire song that's dedicated to you." Isabelle did her best to keep a straight face. "You look adorable."

She did, although not in her usual fashion. "Well, of course I do, dear. That's a no-brainer. But even with me tucked inside, this suit leaves a lot to be desired." Rosie lifted her chin, causing an ear to flop over.

Three Butterflies roared with laughter again.

"Who knew the concert was a comedy?"

"Sure has me laughing," Aunt Claudia agreed, with her and Ruby still clutching each other's arms in their merriment. "You think anyone will try to pin a tail on her?"

Isabelle pressed her lips tightly together, determined not to laugh. Next to her, Zach turned his head away from the women in an effort to contain his own mirth.

"Or better yet…" Maybelle's eyes twinkled. "They may think she's a piñata and give her a good whack."

Huffing, Rosie scowled. "Oh, go be wise somewhere else, you old hags."

"Okay. You're right. We need to take our places." Maybelle feigned remorse for half a second, then, practically giggling, went, "*Eeee-onk.*"

Ruby and Aunt Claudia looked at each other, then, tears running down their faces, barely able to breathe, collapsed into hysterics.

IF SOMEONE HAD bet Zach that he'd be playing Joseph in a high school Christmas concert, Zach would have lost. Why had he tossed out that he would conditionally fill in? It wasn't as if he'd expected Isabelle to say no. Whether she wanted to do something or not, she'd say yes if it meant helping someone she loved.

He liked that about her. How loyal and dependable she was.

An unfamiliar twinge seized his insides, making him swallow. Glancing at where she knelt next to a manger in the middle of the stage, he admitted that he liked a lot about his pretend girlfriend, who was currently his pretend wife.

Particularly her bent-over belly laughs at the Butterflies and again during Rosie's stellar performance. Prancing about during a rendition of a song about a Christmas donkey that shouldn't have been funny, Rosie had worked the stage with her usual gusto and earned her and the talented choir a standing ovation. Isabelle letting loose and laughing the way she had filled Zach with a happiness he couldn't explain.

Well, he could, but he shouldn't. Falling for Isabelle would be pure craziness.

"Ahem." She softly cleared her throat, drawing his attention to the fact that he was to have joined her in kneeling next to the manger beneath the bright stage lights.

Zach did so, but rather than look at the swaddled doll, he stared at Isabelle. Only her face was visible beneath her Mary costume, and he put her features to memory. He never wanted to forget a single thing about her.

Glancing up, her gaze connected with his, and he could see the question in her eyes as to why Joseph wasn't pretending awe at their newborn child. What would his Mary say if he told her the truth? That he was in awe of her? And that, not for the first time, he wondered what it would be like if they were real?

"Y'ALL WERE WONDERFUL!" Annabelle rushed over and hugged Isabelle when she and Zach entered Lou's, where everyone had gathered for an after-party. Between the cast, friends, and family, the diner was rocking.

"You are who was wonderful. Your solo of 'Mary, Did You Know?' gave me goosebumps."

"Thanks." Annabelle glanced around the diner. "Is Sophie coming?"

"Sophie, Morgan, Andrew, and Greyson went to spend time at the firehall with Ben and Cole. If it's not too late when they finish, and Greyson's not too tuckered out, they'll be by."

Jeff joined them and handed Annabelle a drink. "Here's your soda." Turning to Isabelle, he smiled proudly. "Wasn't she amazing?"

"Absolutely." Isabelle returned his smile. Carrie's son always had been a good kid and had been the single mom's pride and joy and reason for working so hard. "Jeff, this is my friend, Zach."

Jeff immediately stuck his hand out and the two men exchanged pleasantries. Isabelle and Zach stood watching when the younger couple moved on to join friends.

"She really does resemble Sophie, especially tonight when she's so bubbly."

"I've always thought they should have been sisters," Isabelle admitted.

"Sophie wouldn't trade you for anyone in the world."

Smiling, Isabelle glanced toward him. "That's a nice thing to say."

"It's an honest thing to say." He gestured toward a particularly loud group. "Speaking of nice things to say, we should tell Rosie how great she was."

"Not that she doesn't already know," Isabelle teased.

Zach grinned. "Yep. But since she and Lou are throwing

the party, it's only polite."

"And you're always polite?"

"Not always."

She eyed him curiously. "Other than your teasing, I've never seen that side of you."

"I hope you never do."

An hour later, party in full swing, Zach eyed the teens belting out the Christmas song along with the karaoke machine. "You'd think they'd have gotten enough singing earlier."

"They appear to be enjoying this more," Isabelle mused, sipping her drink.

Leaning back in his chair, Zach nodded. "It'll be a long time before I enjoy a performance more than I did Rosie's."

Isabelle snorted. "She was something else with how she sashayed around the stage, twirling her tail, wasn't she?"

Zach had never encountered anything quite like the Butterflies, particularly Rosie. "The choir was great, but my money is on her being the reason that number got a standing ovation."

Tracing her fingertip over the rim of her glass, Isabelle smiled. "She was eating it up."

"Even Maybelle was clapping," he pointed out.

After the way they'd practically been at each other's throats, he'd been surprised by how genuinely proud the older woman had appeared.

Isabelle nodded. "Don't let their bickering fool you. They're the best of friends and have been longer than we've been alive. It's just what they do. How they express their affection for one another, I guess."

"They're definitely entertaining."

"Always." Isabelle smiled, then nudged him with her elbow. "Thank you for helping tonight."

Liking the softness to her face and the happiness that shone in her eyes, Zach shrugged. "You didn't give me much choice."

She arched her brow. "You shouldn't have tossed out your condition if you weren't serious."

"I was serious."

Smiling, she poked her finger at his chest. "Then quit your whining, Joseph."

Starting at where her finger touched him and spreading, shock waves rumbled through Zach. "I wasn't whining, Mary."

Isabelle rolled her eyes. "Blondie, Cinderella, Mary ... what will you be calling me next?"

Mine. No, he'd never call Isabelle that. At least, not accurately. Feeling antsy, he took her hand. "Let's sing."

Isabelle's eyes widened. "Um, no."

He laced his fingers with hers. "Pretty sure if I was in a high school choir concert for you, then you can sing one karaoke song with me."

"Fine. One song." Frowning, Isabelle allowed him to lead her to where the karaoke had been set up in a corner of Lou's.

"Pick a song."

She shook her head. "This was your brilliant idea. You pick."

Zach skimmed the selection, then punched in a number. "Remember that I gave you the option of choosing and you declined."

She glanced down at what he'd chosen and rolled her eyes. "The guy who never wears a coat picks a song about being cold? Seriously."

"You wanted to know what I was going to call you next. Now you know."

"I'm not the kind of girl who appreciates being called baby, and I've never liked this song."

"Work with me here, Blondie."

"Fine." She sighed. "Let's get this over with, since half the room is watching us."

"Don't do it because of them. Have fun, Isabelle. Channel your inner Rosie."

She snorted, grimace-smiled, then fluffed her hair in a fair imitation of the real Rosie. "Who do you think taught her all she knows?"

Tickled at her show of sass, Zach laughed. "There you go."

The music started. Taking a deep breath, Isabelle picked up one of the microphones and half said, half sang the first line of Frank Loesser's classic about it being cold outside.

Grinning, Zach sang his line.

KEEPING HER GAZE locked with his, Isabelle jumped into the song the same way she tackled most things, by giving her all. And, if she were truthful, with a desire to throw Zach off-kilter by letting him know once and for all that she was no fuddy-duddy.

Zach took her hands. "They're like ice," he sang.

Any nervousness she'd had at singing in front of her friends and family was replaced with an intense awareness of where his fingers held hers. He was so big and strong, capable of allowing her to lean on him the way she had at the shelter, capable of pushing her outside her comfort zone, such as their current predicament.

When it came to the line about her father, she tweaked the verse to say her sister instead.

She doubted most noticed the change, but the flicker in Zach's eyes said he had. Without missing a beat, he continued the tune, though.

When they finished, clapping filled the restaurant.

Zach wrapped his arms around her, lifted her off her feet, and spun her around. "You're amazing."

Heart pounding from being in his arms, she fluffed her hair in another Rosie move. "I know."

He laughed, then put her down. "For the record, I've never really paid attention to those lyrics. Next time, I'll choose better. That song isn't who I am."

She knew that. It's why she'd agreed to sing it with him. Zach was too honorable to ply a woman with alcohol and originally, the song had been written to encourage guests to leave a house party rather than with any nefarious intent. "Next time?"

He shrugged. "Who knows? Maybe our number will come up again."

"ADMIT IT. YOU had fun tonight." Zach said later that night as Isabelle drove him home.

Tiny flecks of snow had started to fall and were hitting the windshield. The temperature had done a rapid nosedive from earlier that day, and the car's heater blew warm, thanks to his having gone outside to start it prior to their leaving Lou's. He'd offered to drive as his thirty days had finally expired without another incident, but Isabelle had declined.

"Tonight wasn't bad." She didn't take her eyes off the road. "You make a good pretend boyfriend."

Zach winced. She sure knew how to pop his euphoria bubble.

"And someday you're going to make someone a great real boyfriend."

"Probably not," he admitted. "I doubt I've ever qualified as even a mediocre boyfriend. Relationships aren't my thing."

"Mine, either."

"I wouldn't say that." Her gaze briefly cut his way, so he clarified. "You're surrounded by people who you share strong bonds with."

A soft laugh escaped her lips. "I thought you meant romantic relationships."

"There was the guy in Nashville."

"He was always staying there, and I was always coming home."

"You wouldn't leave Pine Hill for love?"

Rather than answer, she asked, "Would you stay in Pine Hill for love?"

Despite how her question tightened his throat, Zach

chuckled. "One of the many things I admire about you is that quick mind of yours. You sure turned my question back on me."

"I wasn't trying to be contrary."

"For once?"

Her lips twitched. "Is that what you think of me? That I purposely cause you angst?"

She did. On purpose, not on purpose. Isabelle twisted his insides. "I meant what I said earlier."

"Which time?"

"When I said I think you're amazing." The most amazing woman he'd ever met.

"Thank you." Isabelle drove the car into Hamilton House's drive and put it into park but didn't kill the ignition. "Thanks again for filling in at Annabelle's concert."

"No problem." He should tell her good night and get out of the car. He should, but he didn't want the night to end. "Sarah has cookies and cocoa inside."

"It's late and I should get home."

He grinned. "Seems like I've heard that before."

Her eyes crinkling with her amusement, Isabelle laughed. "It would seem so. You should get inside before you get chilly."

"Walk me to the door?"

"You afraid the abdo-abominal snowman might grab you?"

"Maybe." He eyed her, noting how her thumb tapped on the steering wheel. "Would you protect me?"

She laughed again. "I wouldn't be of much help if something grabs you that you need protecting from."

"Never underestimate yourself. A sharp mind is a powerful thing."

"That it is. I'll make you a deal," she offered, glancing his way. "I won't drive off until you're safely inside and if an abominable snowman tries to snatch you, I'll gun the gas and take him out."

"You do that." Grinning, he leaned across the console separating them and kissed her cheek. "Good night, Blondie."

"THAT IS THE most beautiful wedding dress I've ever seen." Isabelle stared in awe at her smiling sister and mentally checked *wedding dress* off Sophie's wedding checklist.

Four Butterflies beamed.

"It is quite lovely," Ruby said.

"Perfection," Aunt Claudia agreed.

Rosie glanced down at her Christmas-manicured nails. "Almost as perfect as mine."

Maybelle shook her head at her friend, then smiled at Sophie. "You are truly an exquisite bride-to-be."

"And just look at my gorgeous sister." Sophie smiled at Isabelle. "I'm so thrilled she's going to be standing by my side at my wedding next week."

"I'll always be by your side," Isabelle assured, but wasn't nearly as positive about how gorgeous she felt in her formfitting bridesmaid dress. "Any time you need me."

And with that, Sophie burst into tears, causing the Butterflies and Isabelle to rush to her.

Isabelle put her hand on her sister's shoulder. "What's wrong?"

"Nothing." Sophie swiped at her face. "Everything."

"Please tell me this doesn't have to do with Dad again."

Sophie sniffled. "Okay, I won't tell you."

"Sophie—"

"You said not to tell you."

"Honey, your father is here with you in spirit. He always has been." Maybelle's tone was so confident that Isabelle glanced her way, and to her surprise, the older woman refused to meet her eye.

Did Maybelle know something about where her father was?

It took a few minutes to console Sophie, but the moment Isabelle was able to pull Maybelle aside, she did.

"I've not seen Cliff in over twenty years," Maybelle denied.

"But you do know where he is?" Isabelle persisted, positive Maybelle wasn't saying all she knew.

Maybelle shook her head. "I don't."

"But you did at one time?" Isabelle stared at the woman. "Was it when he was hospitalized for his mental breakdown or when he lived at the homeless shelter or when he was at the Bar T?"

Maybelle's eyes widened. "How do you know Cliff was at those places?"

"Because I hired Zach to find him for Sophie's wedding." Isabelle took a deep breath. "Hired isn't really the right term. I bartered with him to find Dad. Sewing lessons in exchange for his services."

"I see." Maybelle's gaze narrowed just enough that Isabelle's confession was news and not something the woman already knew. "In the process, you've fallen in love with him?"

"No. It's all fake," she defended, not allowing memories of his kissing her cheek while sitting in Hamilton House's drive to enter her mind. If she did that, then she might have to explain why she'd dreamed of that kiss. Of why just thinking of it, thinking of Zach, made her breathy. "Every bit of it was to throw Sophie off from what we were doing. We were trying to fool the whole town."

Maybelle's brow lifted. "Are you sure you weren't just fooling yourself instead?"

"You realize that I know what you're doing? That you're just trying to put me on the defense rather than the offense?" Isabelle accused. "What do you know about the whereabouts of my father, Maybelle? I need to know everything you know."

ZACH HADN'T SPENT much time ice-skating, but back in the day he could tear up a skateboard, so had no issue with giving it a try. Isabelle, on the other hand, seemed content huddled on one of the benches, watching others skate around the man-made rink at Harvey Farm that apparently had originally been built for Rosie and Lou's wedding. Around dusk, fluffy white snow had begun to fall. The rink lights reflected off the flakes, making them shimmer on their dance to the ground. If not for their conversation, Zach would drag Isabelle out to give it a whirl. But the moment the others had taken off on their skates, she'd leaned close to tell him what she'd learned at Sophie's dress fitting.

"It's been over a year since Maybelle last heard from him?"

Tugging her hat further over her ears, Isabelle nodded. "He called her after he saw Sophie and Cole's engagement announcement online."

Which once again confirmed that her dad hadn't walked away and never given his family another thought. "Did she say why?"

"He wanted Maybelle's take on Cole, to make sure he was worthy of Sophie." Isabelle's breath made a smoky cloud in the cold night air. "Can you believe that? His nerve of wondering if Cole would make a good husband when he'd been such a horrible one to Mom? I finally talked to her, told her what Sophie had said, and that I was trying to find Dad. She just sighed, told me that if that was what Sophie wanted and what I wanted to do, then she wished me luck. How could he have just left us, Zach? What kind of man walks away from his family?"

Sophie and Cole skated by and, curious at their serious expressions, Sophie waved. Cole didn't look super comfortable on the skates, but much as Isabelle, the man lived to make Sophie happy, so skate he did.

Isabelle and Zach both waved back. When they'd passed to where their backs were to them, Zach glanced at Isabelle. The cold had her cheeks rosy, and despite her puffy down jacket and accessories, she shivered.

"Your dad did what he believed he had to do at the

time."

"Please don't defend him. Not tonight, Zach. I just can't bear it. I—" She wrung her gloved hands together. "Just don't, okay?"

Wincing at how uptight she was, he scooted closer and wrapped his arms around her, wanting to offer comfort and to shield her from anyone watching them. He'd expected her to push him away, but instead she leaned into his embrace.

"Why do I let him upset me this way?" Her voice was muffled by his jacket. "After all these years, he shouldn't have any power over me."

Glad his gloves were still poked in his jacket pocket, he stroked where her hair spilled from beneath her hat. "Because you care."

"I don't want to care. Make it stop."

Holding her close, breathing in her apple-pie scent, caring way more than he should about her, about this Christmas-crazy little town, and about his own family woes, he sighed. "If only it was that easy."

"IT'S REALLY HIM?" Isabelle's fingers tightened their hold on her cellphone. When Zach had taken off for Louisiana three days before Sophie's wedding, she'd known he might soon be coming face-to-face with her father. But that didn't prevent the nausea washing over her to the point she rested her head on her desk. "You're sure?"

"It's him, but he's not coming back to Pine Hill for Sophie's wedding."

Disappointment, anger, frustration, and emotions she had no label for had her rolling her head back and forth against the desk's cool surface. Of course, he'd said no. Why would he say anything else when he'd chosen to stay gone for over two decades?

"Make him, Zach." The request that had sounded much more like an order surprised Isabelle, but it suddenly felt imperative that he do so. "For Sophie. Please."

"You want me to tie him up and haul him back on the plane with me? I'm not sure the FAA will allow that, Blondie."

Would he think her crazy if she said yes?

"Surely you have military buddies who can pull strings to get him here? Maybe on a private plane? Something?"

There was a brief silence, then Zach's heartfelt sigh sounded in her ear. "Because kidnapping your father and forcing him back to Pine Hill will convince him to walk Sophie down the aisle two days from now?"

Isabelle counted to ten, then swallowed. "I wanted this for Sophie."

"I wanted it for you. You need to make peace with the past."

Heart shattering that they were so close and yet were going to fail, Isabelle's hand shook as it clenched her phone. "Says the man who walked away from his own family and never looked back."

"My family is different."

"Really?" The emotions she'd been trying to choke back erupted. "How are you any different from my father, Zach? You just walked away from them, too, didn't you?"

"My situation is nothing like your father's."

"Right," she snapped, knowing he was right, but lashing out even when he wasn't to blame for her father's shortcomings. "Go back inside, Zach. Please. Video call to where I can see him. I need to see him. I have to convince him to do this for Sophie."

The line was silent long enough that for a moment Isabelle thought they'd lost their connection.

Finally, he asked, "You're sure? He doesn't look the same as when you last saw him. He's older, rougher, thin."

Stop, she wanted to scream. *Stop trying to make me empathetic to him.*

"No, but I have to do this." She did, didn't she? "For Sophie."

"I'll go back in. For you."

Isabelle could barely breathe as she waited for Zach's call. She straightened the papers on her desk, pulled up her hair, untied the ribbon and let it fall back to her shoulders, put on lipstick, then wiped it off. What was she doing? What did it matter what she looked like? It wasn't as if she expected her father to see her and suddenly want to come home for Sophie's wedding.

"What is taking so long?"

Then, her phone rang with the video icon lit. Isabelle's breath caught. Her stomach clenched. Tossing the phone across the room tempted. Recalling Sophie's tears, Isabelle knew she had to at least try. If she didn't, she'd always wonder if she could have said or done something that would have convinced her father to do this one thing. Hand shaking, she slid her finger across the screen, not quite sure what she was going to see.

Cliff Davis was there.

An older version, of course, but she'd know those blue eyes anywhere. They were the same ones that reflected back at her in a mirror. Tears prickled. Anger burned. Words failed and she just stared at the phone. The man on the other side of the screen did the same, obviously uncomfortable and not knowing what to say.

"Isabelle?" Zach asked from next to her father.

She couldn't see him, but the concern in his voice was palpable. No wonder. Her vocal cords refused to function.

"This was a mistake." Her father's voice, sounding the same as she remembered, tore into her resolve and had her agreeing. This had been a horrible mistake. He attempted to stand, but Zach's hand settling on his shoulder stayed him.

"You're not going anywhere until Isabelle has her say. You owe her that and a lot more."

Zach's voice, knowing he was there, that he'd gone to Louisiana for her, eased her rattled nerves enough to free her tongue.

"Sophie wants you to walk her down the aisle," she began. Her father's eyes closed. "Her wedding is this weekend. Zach will bring you to Pine Hill. Walk Sophie down the aisle and give her the wedding she wants. I'll foot your travel expenses."

"I'm not coming back to Pine Hill."

It was the first thing he'd said directly to her in over twenty years. Goosebumps prickled her skin as the brevity of the moment hit. She was talking with her father.

"It's what Sophie wants."

His blue gaze stared at her from the screen. "Is it what you want, Isabelle?"

Her tongue stuck to the roof of her dry mouth. She swallowed. "It doesn't matter what I want. Sophie wants you to walk her down the aisle."

"That's not going to happen." He looked up at Zach. "You shouldn't have found me. Doing so was a waste of your time. I have nothing else to say."

There was a moment of silence, then Zach glanced toward the phone, his expression tight and the golden flecks in his hazel eyes glowing almost as if they were on fire. "Isabelle, is there anything else you want to say?"

Yes. No. Panic filled her. Twenty-plus years' worth of things she wanted to say flooded her. Angry things. Pleading for him to come home things. Sad things. Happy things. Now was her moment, probably the only moment she'd ever have to say any of them, and words failed her yet again.

When she still didn't speak, Cliff attempted to stand again, but Zach yet again stayed him with a pointed look that said he wasn't going anywhere until Isabelle gave the okay.

Grimacing, he repeated, "This was a mistake."

Heart beating so hard it might explode, Isabelle found her voice. "Yes, it obviously was a mistake. Because you're too selfish to do this one thing for the most amazing daughter, who, despite you abandoning her, is still heartbroken that you aren't there to walk her down the aisle." Oh, saying that felt good. Her shoulders lifted, as did her chin. "If you have one ounce of decency, if you ever loved any of us even the slightest bit, then you'll be at Sophie's wedding and give her this one thing. You owe her that and so much more."

Isabelle disconnected the call. Her bravado wilted the moment the connection ended. Her entire body sagging, she burst into full-blown sobs.

Chapter Thirteen

Feeling much as Santa must on Christmas Eve, Isabelle checked her various Sophie's wedding checklists, making sure each item was marked off or soon would be. What to do leading up to wedding. What to do on day of rehearsal. What to do on wedding day.

Flipping through her pages, she stopped at Rehearsal, then glanced around at the red, white, and blue Christmas-themed décor and quilts adding splashes of color to the church auditorium. The best Isabelle could tell, she'd created what Sophie wanted. Almost.

Her stomach clenched at the memory of her video call with her father. It was better that he'd said no. Even her mother had said so when Isabelle had told her about the call. Afterward, Isabelle had cried, long hard tears that left her gutted and in a fetal position for a while, but she was glad he'd said no. Zach had thought she needed peace. Fine, now she had it. Good riddance.

"Places, everyone." Maybelle dinged a spoon against a glass, calling the wedding rehearsal to order. "Places."

At Maybelle's bidding, Cole, Andrew, Ben, and Bodie joined Pastor Smith at the front of the church that had also been decorated with a blend of patriotic quilts and Christmas. Isabelle, Sophie, Sarah, and Annabelle moved to the back of the auditorium. A couple of the other firefighters served as ushers, and one escorted Darlene to the front. As Cole hadn't known anyone in Pine Hill other than the uncle who'd passed while Cole was serving in the Middle East, leaving him his farm, they had foregone bride-groom sides, and everyone was to sit wherever they wanted.

Pastor Smith gave a short spiel, welcoming the nonexistent guests. Then the music began, a blend of patriotic and holiday songs. Pretending to carry her bouquet, Annabelle walked toward the men, followed by Sarah. Isabelle and then Sophie did the same. They ran through the entire ceremony and when they were done, Isabelle pulled out her notebook, read through her notes, and made a few suggestions based on things Sophie had told her.

"Okay, with those tweaks, let's start from the top one more time just to be sure everyone knows when to do what," Maybelle insisted, clapping her hands.

When they were in the back of the church, Sophie gave her a big hug.

"In case I haven't told you enough, thank you." Sophie squeezed a little tighter. "I won the lottery when I got you for a sister, Izzy. I hope you know how much I love and appreciate you."

Isabelle sniffled. "I'm the lucky one having you for a sister. Can you imagine what a grump I'd be if I didn't have your constant positive attitude setting me straight?"

"Well, now you have Zach to keep you smiling. I love how happy you are when you're with him." Sophie's forehead scrunched. "I hope he makes it back from wherever he had to go in time for the rehearsal dinner."

So did Isabelle. She needed to apologize to him for her harshness when they'd talked on the phone and for not answering his later calls. After her boohoo fest, she'd shut off her ringer and had a girl's night with Sophie and her mom, getting their hair and nails done at her mom's salon. They'd laughed and had a wonderful time. Yeah, it was better that Cliff Davis wasn't coming back to Pine Hill.

But Zach should already be back. Where was he? He'd texted her that he'd meet her at the rehearsal. Had his flight been delayed? Then again, what did it matter at this point? Their relationship had been based upon finding her father.

"Let's not talk about Zach." She'd tell Sophie the truth about him, but not right before her wedding. "This weekend is about you and your dream wedding. Unless you've decided you don't want to go through with this tomorrow?" She gave her sister a teasing look. "In which case, my car is parked outside. We could take off to some quiet beach until all this blows over."

"Even if I got a case of nerves, you'd convince me to stay because you know this is where I'm supposed to be." Sophie's gaze met hers. "You wouldn't really let me run away from the most wonderful man in the world, would you?"

Isabelle shook her head. "No, but only because Cole recognizes that you are the most wonderful woman in the world and loves you with all his heart."

"He does, doesn't he?" Sophie smiled, then mouth circling into an *O,* she gave a little push. "Go, they're waiting on you."

Isabelle leaned in, kissed Sophie's cheek, then moved toward where the guys stood. Halfway there, the sound of Sophie's gasped cry had Isabelle spinning around.

"*Oof.*" She let out a strangled cry of her own.

Zach stood in the foyer. So did her father.

FEARING ISABELLE MIGHT pass out when all the color drained from her face, Zach rushed to her, placing his hand at her waist, ready to catch her if needed.

"Take a deep breath, Blondie."

Her gaze not leaving the man standing at the back of the auditorium, she whispered, "He said he wasn't coming. I told Mom he wasn't coming."

"He changed his mind." Zach hadn't given the man a choice.

One way or the other, her father had been coming to Pine Hill. The pain in Isabelle's voice, on her face, during that video call, had assured that. Only now, he wondered if he should have left the man in Louisiana.

Abandoning his position at the front of the church, Cole was now at Sophie's side, his expression tense and threatening as he eyed the older man Sophie stared at, wide-eyed.

"Cliff Davis, is that you?" Rosie screeched from where she'd twisted around to see what the commotion was about.

At her question, Maybelle, Ruby, and Claudia beelined to where Isabelle's mother sat, looking pale.

Cliff didn't say anything, just lifted his head in acknowledgement, then eyed Sophie, uncertainty on his face. Over the past two days, Zach had wavered between feeling sorry for the guy, empathy and understanding of his emotional state, and wanting to punch him for hurting his family. For hurting Isabelle.

"Daddy?" Sophie blinked, clutching Cole's arm for support. "I … you … you're here. How?"

"He brought me." He gestured toward Zach, who was grateful the man left off the details of how he'd decided it was in his best interest to go with Zach.

That he was there half-under duress wouldn't win the guy any points, and Cliff was going to need all the points he could get in Pine Hill.

Sophie's gaze went to Zach. "You brought my daddy home for my wedding? I told you I looked for him and you—Oh, Zach! Thank you."

"Thank Isabelle, not me. Your sister wanted your wedding to be all you dreamed."

Sophie's eyes widened further as they touched on Isabelle. "But … really? Oh, Izzy, I can't believe you did this." Her gaze cut back to Zach. "Or that you found him. I tried so many times…" Tears streamed down her cheeks as she turned toward the man who all eyes were now focused on. "I feel as if I'm dreaming because I have dreamed of this moment so many times. Welcome home, Daddy."

With that, Sophie threw her arms around her father.

"HOW CAN SHE just accept him as if he never left?" Isabelle's hands turned palm up as she paced back and forth in the church's nursery, where she'd pulled Zach aside the moment the actual rehearsal finished. "How? It's not right that he shows up and she's treating him like the guest of honor. And poor Mom. His showing up after I'd told her he'd said no…" Isabelle's voice trailed off.

"He's doing what you wanted," Zach reminded from where he leaned against the closed door. Sophie had been all smiles since he'd arrived with Cliff, but Isabelle had been a bundle of nerves as Maybelle had quickly gotten the group back on track to run through the rehearsal. "Were you hoping that once he got here, Sophie and the others would reject him?"

As he asked it, he couldn't help thinking there was some truth to that, that deep down, Isabelle had needed validation for her own feelings. Validation she wasn't getting, not even from her own mother, who thus far had ignored Cliff's presence once her initial shock had passed. Zach suspected she'd have a lot to say to her husband once they were away from curious eyes. He'd caught Cliff looking her way with a pained expression more than once. Hopefully, he would be honest and tell her the things he'd told Zach. He wasn't sure the man's family could ever forgive him or put his absence behind them, but it was long past time for the truth.

"No, of course not. I just…" Isabelle spun toward him. "What did he say? You sat next to him the entire flight and drive home. He had to have said something about what he's been doing all these years and why he left in the first place."

"You'll have to ask him those things." Zach wished he could say more.

It wasn't his place to share the things Cliff had told him. Zach wasn't sure Isabelle would understand, anyway. She'd not had the life experiences to understand the nightmares Cliff dealt with. That Zach did understand had him torn.

"I shouldn't have asked you to find him." She ran her fingers through her hair, then blew out a big breath. "Look at what a mess he's already made of things. I caused this chaos, hurt Mom, and I just should have left well enough alone. I didn't think this part through."

He shook his head. "I'm not buying that. You always think things through. You knew there would be chaos when he got here. So, my question is, why did you want me to find him?"

Grimacing, she covered her stomach with her hands and shook her head, as if trying to block out his question.

"Were you hoping that seeing him would remind Sophie how much it hurt to love a military man?" He hoped that wasn't it. "Maybe you were hoping she'd see your father and decide she didn't want to marry Cole?"

"No." She gasped, her eyes huge. "She loves Cole. I would never do anything to stop their wedding. Sophie would be devastated."

Zach arched a brow. "You haven't tried to change her mind?"

Her wince answered prior to her defensive, "Only in teasing."

"Sometimes we reveal a lot about our inner thoughts via humor."

Not that he believed Isabelle wanted to bust up Sophie's wedding. Far from it. But he wasn't sure she recognized that truth. Maybe deep down, she still thought she wanted Sophie to not be in love with a military man.

Her hands went to her hips. "Quit trying to make me the bad guy. I'm not the one who abandoned my family. I love Sophie and want what's best for her. That's being married to Cole."

Good. Zach agreed. "There is no bad guy here, Isabelle. Until you acknowledge that, you're not going to find peace."

Her gaze narrowed. "My father left his family. That makes him the bad guy."

"He wasn't mentally or emotionally well." Zach kept his gaze locked with hers, despite the daggers she shot his way.

Oh, how he understood how one's mind could convince you those you love were better off without you around.

"And he is now?"

Zach shrugged. "He's working full time in a shipping yard under his current alias and has been on that job for almost five years. He volunteers at a homeless shelter and regularly attends a veterans' support group. From the outside, he seems to have pieced a life together, but I'm not qualified to answer your question. You wanted him here, so I brought him."

Her eyes lit with realization. "He didn't change his mind, did he? You forced him."

Still warring with his opinions on Cliff, Zach shrugged. "Coming back to the place where you fell apart and destroyed the best parts of your life isn't an easy thing. Give your father credit that he's here."

"I'll give him nothing." Her fingers curled at her sides. "All I need is for him to walk Sophie down the aisle tomorrow and then to crawl back under whatever rock he's been living beneath."

Despite her claim, her chest flared, and pain coated each word. "You don't mean that."

"Don't tell me what I mean, Zach." She poked his chest. "You don't know me."

He captured her hand. "I know you better than you know yourself. At least, regarding this, I do." Her pain was as palpable as her hand within his.

Pulling her hand free, she snorted. "You think you're so smart, but you're wrong. I don't want him in my life, just as I don't want you in my life. Our deal is done. I gave you your lessons. You found my father. We're finished. There's no need for pretense anymore."

She was hurting and lashing out. He knew that, but her words stung.

"Our relationship isn't pretend." Was he trying to convince her or himself?

"Is that what you think?" she taunted. "Then you're wrong on that, too. All we are, all we could ever be, is pretend. You aren't someone I'd choose to have in my life. You're just like him. I don't want to see you again. Not ever."

Wondering if words had the power to leave one bleeding, Zach winced. "You're understandably upset, Blondie, but taking out your pain on me isn't going to make things better."

"Don't call me that. I've told you and told you. Do. Not. Call. Me. Blondie." With her last word, she flung her hands into the air, shook her head, and, pushing him aside, ran out of the church nursery.

THROUGH TEAR-SWOLLEN EYES, Isabelle stared into her bathroom mirror. A cold, black glob trickled onto her forehead, and she swatted at it with her plastic-covered fingers. What had she done?

Noise sounded from the front of the house, indicating either her mom, Sophie, or both had gotten home from the rehearsal. She prayed whoever it was would just go to bed. She'd known better, though.

"Izzy?" Sophie called through the door. "You okay in there?"

"I'm fine." *Not really.* "Go to bed, Soph." *Please.* "You have a big day tomorrow and need your rest." *True.* "I ... I don't feel like talking, anyway." *Very true.*

"If I went to bed, I couldn't sleep. I'll wait until you're finished."

Eyeing the wet mess on her head, Isabelle grimaced at her reflection. "That's going to be a while."

Silence. Then, "Let me in, Izzy."

Taking a deep breath and hacking as chemicals burned her throat, Isabelle twisted the lock.

Hearing the click, Sophie opened the door. Upon seeing Isabelle, her jaw dropped. "Your hair!"

Seeing Sophie's reaction unleashed the light hold Isabelle had on her tears, and a dam of them burst free. She shrugged. Sophie's arms wrapped around her.

"Be careful or you'll get dye on you," Isabelle warned between sobs, not wanting her hair to stain her sister.

"Shh." Sophie held her tighter as if she thought Isabelle

might fall apart. "After you left the church, I had a lot of questions for Zach. He told me I had to ask you."

Fighting her tears, Isabelle took another deep breath, then coughed again. "Zach and I were only pretending to be a couple to make searching for Dad easier for him. I hadn't meant to tell you until after your honeymoon, because I didn't want you to worry."

Sophie pulled back, staring into Isabelle's eyes. "I am worried. You left my rehearsal dinner and wouldn't answer my phone calls."

Yeah, she had done that. Shame hit. "I'm sorry. I—my phone is in my purse. I turned my ringer off." For the second night in a row. "I-I needed some time to think."

Sophie's brow arched. "And to change your hair color?"

"Apparently so." Isabelle half snorted, half laughed. "How's Mom? Is she with Aunt Claudia?"

Not quite meeting Isabelle's gaze, Sophie shook her head. "She's with Dad. I'm not sure where they went, but they had a lot to say to each other. Mom was upset."

Isabelle's heart spasmed. Of course, her mom was upset. Her husband had shown up after a twenty-year hiatus after Isabelle had said he'd refused to come home.

"What have I done, Sophie? What was I thinking to have Zach bring him here right before your wedding?" She'd not meant for it to come down to the final moments. Sophie should have had time to process Cliff's return. Everyone should have had time. "I've ruined everything."

"The only thing you've ruined is your hair, but Mom can fix that." Sophie gave Isabelle's head a skeptical look. "Probably not before the wedding tomorrow, but she can fix it back to your beautiful natural color. As far as the other, Izzy, don't you realize you've given me the most precious gift?"

"Dad coming home?"

Sophie shook her head. "I'm glad he's home, that he's going to walk me down the aisle, but that's not what I meant. That you set aside your feelings and went to such extraordinary measures to get him home for my wedding—I can't imagine anything you could have done that would have meant more." Sophie smiled. "Thank you for loving me so much."

Isabelle swallowed back the emotion choking her. "You'd do the same for me."

Sophie nodded. "Present moment excluded, you're always so together, and I'm the one who's always into trouble to where you never need me to do anything."

"There is something I need you to do."

"Anything," Sophie promised.

"Help me rinse my hair before Mom gets home and sees that I used discount store hair color, and her hairdresser sensibilities are offended. She's dealt with enough tonight."

"YOU CAN'T NOT go to Sophie and Cole's wedding."

Eyeing the plate of cookies Sarah put on the bar, Zach ran his fingers through his hair. "Isabelle doesn't want me there."

"Isabelle is why you have to go." Sarah gestured for him to take a cookie, but Zach shook his head.

He'd not eaten at the rehearsal dinner but wasn't hungry.

"She never wants to see me again."

Sarah gave an empathetic look. "She was upset about her father. You know that. Tomorrow is going to be difficult for her on several levels. She needs you there, Zach."

"She has you, her family, her friends."

Sarah put a glass of milk in front of him. "None of us are you."

"Don't tell me you got caught up in believing our relationship was real. You've known from the beginning it wasn't."

Sarah slid onto the barstool next to him. "The only people who didn't believe what was happening between you and Isabelle was real were the two of you."

Not true. Zach had known. But that didn't change that Isabelle would never let herself trust him. Why should she? He didn't even trust himself. How could he when he didn't know what was locked inside his head? What if memories of the explosion returned, of what had really happened that day, and knocked him back into that dark place he'd worked so hard to climb out of? What if she trusted him and then he pulled a disappearing act the way her father had?

Sighing, he picked up a cookie and stared at it. "You've been hanging out with your Butterfly friends too much."

"Nice try." Sarah laughed. "But there's no such thing as hanging out with those ladies too much. They're wonderful, and you know it."

Taking a bite of his cookie, Zach nodded. "They are, but that doesn't mean they don't meddle."

Sarah's smile lit up her eyes as bright as the twinkling lights she had strung around the house. "It's one of their most endearing qualities."

"Poor Jeannie doesn't stand a chance with them around."

Sarah laughed. "My matchmaking Butterflies won't stand a chance against her father. He swears he's not letting Jeannie date until after her thirtieth birthday. I think he means it."

Sarah's comment shouldn't have triggered anything but a smile. Instead, Zach couldn't help thinking of how Isabelle and Sophie had missed out on their father's protectiveness. Yes, they'd had the town who loved them, but they'd not had their father. He understood Isabelle's pain, wanted to make it go away, wanted to not empathize with Cliff, but Zach couldn't help doing so. In many ways, Isabelle had been right. He was a lot like her father.

Sensing where his thoughts had gone, Sarah touched his arm. "You did a good thing bringing Cliff here."

"You think?" Zach scoffed. "Because I'm not so sure that I shouldn't have just walked away when he said he wasn't coming back to Pine Hill."

Sarah patted his arm the way she did when she was comforting Jeannie. "There were a lot of unresolved emotions in Isabelle's family. Now they have a chance to heal."

"By ripping off the bandage?" Zach shook his head. "I did what Isabelle said she wanted, but I always knew she was lying to herself. Her mother didn't look too happy, either."

"Darlene is stronger than her girls give her credit for. She did what she had to do to get by. Things weren't ideal, but they never did without love or anything they needed. My dad talked to her a long time. Tonight wasn't easy, but she's going to be just fine."

"The only way Cliff would agree to come without my using bodily force"—he'd been willing and Cliff had known it—"was if no one was told ahead of time, including Isabelle." He dropped his forehead into his palm. "I should have told her, anyway."

Maybe he would have had she answered his calls.

"Not when you gave him your word you wouldn't," Sarah reminded.

Zach sighed. "Isabelle is more important."

"Than keeping your word?"

Zach thought about it a moment, didn't like how conflicted he was over his answer to her question, then shrugged. "None of it matters now. Cliff is here. Sophie is ecstatic. Isabelle will grit her teeth and bear it for Sophie's sake."

"And you?"

"I'll stay long enough to make sure Cliff shows up when he's supposed to tomorrow."

"He's sleeping in your room?"

"It is the Beds for Vets suite." Zach laughed, but without real humor. "I'm going to take the chair and keep an eye on him."

"There's a cot you can use." Sarah gave him a soft smile. "You could put it across the door. That way you can get some rest. You look as if you haven't slept much in the past few days."

He hadn't. He'd needed to ensure Cliff hadn't run. Not that the man had said or done anything to give that impression, but Zach hadn't been willing to chance it.

"I'll take you up on the cot. I'll rig the window to where it'll wake me if he attempts to open it. A few hours of sleep would be good."

He doubted he'd manage to, though. He might forever be haunted by Isabelle telling him she never wanted to see him again. She'd said it before, but tonight her gaze had held a tortured look that warned she'd never let him close again, pretend or otherwise.

"Things won't seem so bleak once you've rested," Sarah assured. "Isabelle needs you more than she realizes. Just as you need her more than you're ready to admit."

To keep from having to respond, Zach downed his milk. "Thank you for your kindness, Sarah. To me and to Bodie. He's a lucky man to have found you."

"I'm the lucky one that he found me." Sarah smiled. "Just as you're lucky to have found Isabelle."

Zach couldn't argue with her on that count. Having met Isabelle did make him feel lucky. It also made him feel guilty for what he'd done to his own family. Nothing like what Cliff had done, but he'd abandoned them and shut them out of his life. Isabelle's words rang through his head again, flaying into his resolve.

Sarah studied him a moment. "You're really leaving, aren't you? Are you headed home?"

Home? Zach scoffed at the thought, knowing he had to readjust his attitude prior to going to Georgia or nothing would change. Maybe it wouldn't, anyway. His parents' mansion had never felt like home. Not the way Pine Hill did.

Not the way Isabelle did.

Not long after, a few cookies in hand, Zach made his way to his upstairs suite. Freshly showered and shaven, Cliff sat in a wingback chair opposite of the bed, eyes closed.

"You planning to tie my wrists to the bed?"

"I didn't do that last night." Although he'd considered it.

"You also didn't sleep. I figured you'd need some shut-eye tonight."

Zach shrugged. "I've gone without longer."

"We both have. That's why we're here now." Cliff sighed, then stared at him with eyes that strongly resembled Isabelle's. "You're leaving after the wedding?"

"There's no reason for me to stay in Pine Hill."

"Other than my daughter?"

Zach snorted. "Isabelle can't stand me."

Cliff shook his head. "You can deny the way she feels if it makes leaving easier, but you know the truth."

"The truth is that regardless of how Isabelle feels, she'll never allow herself to trust me. Honestly, she shouldn't."

Cliff's blue gaze didn't waver. "Because you're like me?"

Zach wanted to deny his question, to say he was nothing like the man, but the reality was, from the beginning he'd empathized with Cliff, had understood how the man could walk away when he believed he'd had no choice and that he was doing his family a favor.

"What's your story?"

At Cliff's question, Zach's gaze lifted. "What do you mean?"

"We've done a whole lot of talking about me the past couple of days, but don't think I don't recognize the same heaviness within you that plagues me and so many others like us. What happened to put that there?"

Zach opened his mouth to tell Cliff some generic response. Instead, the truth came out with all the gory details, at least all the ones Zach recalled.

When he'd finished, he swiped at his face, realized Cliff was doing the same. The older man's gaze met his and a world of pain shined there.

"I understand why you can't stay in Pine Hill."

Yeah, Zach figured that if anyone understood, it was Cliff.

THE DRESS THE Butterflies had made Isabelle fit like a glove. One of those stretchy, clingy gloves that hugged all over. Sarah's and Annabelle's dresses were a similar color, but not nearly so curvy as Isabelle's. What had the Butterflies been thinking when they'd altered it so tightly when all they'd said they were doing was reinforcing a few seams? She tugged on the top to make sure no cleavage showed, grateful the skirt hem stayed in place just above her knees.

Staring at herself in the full-length mirror that had been set up in the church's nursery, the same room where she and Zach had argued the night before, Isabelle tugged at the dress again, trying to find some nonexistent room between her and the material. What did it matter? All eyes were going to be on the bride and if any did make it her way, well, they'd never get past her new appearance.

"You look beautiful, Izzy," Sophie assured from where Darlene made last-minute adjustments to her hair. There had never been any question that their mother would do Sophie's hair for her wedding day. Aunt Claudia fussed over

Annabelle's hair, while Ruby and Rosie *oohed and aahed* to the smiling baby in Maybelle's arms.

"You both do." Their mother slid a bobby pin over a hair strand to keep it in place in the elegant pulled-up style with its wisps about Sophie's neck. She picked up a can and sprayed Sophie's hair. "Although, the day prior to your sister's wedding was not the time to pull a stunt like dyeing your hair."

Giving herself another look in the mirror, Isabelle sighed. She'd always wanted hair the color of her mother and sister. Well, she had it. Her mother had adamantly argued that short of wearing a wig, Isabelle was stuck as a brunette for Sophie's wedding. Someday, while looking back at wedding photos, they'd probably all laugh about Isabelle's debut as a brunette. At least, that was what she kept telling herself, since she could either go with it or curl up and cry.

She pasted on a smile. "You don't think I should leave it dark?"

Every female in the room answered, "No." Even Jeannie had babbled something.

"Not that you aren't gorgeous, but you just don't look like our Isabelle." Maybelle shifted the baby.

"If you were going to color, you should have gone for a nice blue like mine."

"Or not," Aunt Claudia countered, frowning at Rosie's suggestion. "But it'll grow out. Or if you decide you like it best, then that's okay, too. Like your sister said, you're beautiful." Aunt Claudia gave one of her smiles that had always made Isabelle feel better inside. "What does Zach think of the change?"

There went her warm and fuzzies.

"He hasn't seen it." Isabelle's gaze went to where Sarah checked her reflection in another mirror.

Had Zach told Sarah about their argument? Probably so, based on the empathetic look in her friend's eyes.

Isabelle sucked in a deep breath. "What he thinks really doesn't matter. Zach and I were only pretending. Our relationship was never more than a cover for our spending time together and his interest in Dad in hopes of his gleaning information that would help find him." There. She'd admitted the truth. To her family and friends. "We were never real."

She added the last for herself to assuage any lingering doubts dancing in her head.

"You sure had me fooled," Ruby admitted.

Rosie nodded her agreement.

Annabelle looked shocked. "I can't believe it. I loved you two together, the way he looked at you and made you laugh. You were happy when you were with him."

She had been. Only she'd gotten caught up in the pretense.

"I'm sorry I didn't tell you all the truth. I didn't want Sophie disappointed if we weren't able to find Dad or if we found bad news. I told Soph everything last night."

Diamond and sapphire butterfly earrings sparkling on her earlobes, gifts from the Butterflies as her something new and blue, Sophie's eyes held empathy. Darlene didn't say anything, just toyed with Sophie's hair, despite the style being perfect. If not for the slight shake to her hands, Isabelle might have bought her mother's calm.

"So good of Zach to go to all that trouble to bring your dad here," Ruby mused, making googly faces at Jeannie.

Sarah's gaze connected with Isabelle's. "Why do you think Zach went to all that trouble?"

Isabelle shrugged. "He said he wanted to learn to sew."

"He already knew how to sew, Isabelle." Sarah looked torn a moment, then came over to stand by Isabelle, taking her hands. "While he was still inpatient at Walter Reed, he mentioned the quilt I'd given to Bodie to his occupational therapist. Wisely, she thought learning to sew would be good therapy for Zach as he regained use of his right hand. Not that you'd notice now, but he had nerve damage due to shrapnel near his spine."

Hearing about Zach's injuries, Isabelle winced. "I—he never told me."

"Maybe I shouldn't have, but I thought you should know that wasn't why Zach agreed."

Isabelle's heart thudded against her ribcage. "Why did he agree to find Dad in exchange for me teaching him something he already knew?"

Sarah gave Isabelle's hands a gentle squeeze. "That's something you'll have to ask Zach."

Chapter Fourteen

THE CLOSER IT got to two o'clock, the more Isabelle's insides jittered with anxiety. She'd mentally ticked off every item of what needed to be done prior to Sophie's walk down the aisle. She'd gone over every list, marked off every item, and committed all the couldn't-be-done-until-the-final-moments ones to memory. The only thing that wasn't as it should be was her dark hair, and that she'd have to live with. Maybe the photographer could photoshop the color. She made a mental note to ask after the ceremony.

Music played as family and close friends arrived, smiling and chatting about the various patriotic quilts draped over pew backs. After the small gathering of guests was seated, Pastor Smith, Cole, Andrew, Ben, and Bodie exited one of the side rooms at the front of the auditorium and stood near the altar. Each man wore his uniform proudly—Bodie in his army, Cole in his Marine, Andrew and Ben in their firefighter, and Pastor Smith in a navy suit.

Perfect. Perfect. Perfect. Isabelle made another mental check mark.

Well, almost perfect. The man standing by himself near the foyer water fountain kept distracting her. Did he know they could see him from their vantage point on the stairs?

Where Sophie had dug up their father's uniform was beyond Isabelle, but he'd agreed to her request for him to wear it. Based upon his pallor and the way he clenched and un-clenched his fingers, he might be regretting that decision. Isabelle knew enough about trauma to have momentary concern over his being in his uniform for the first time in over twenty years but refused to feel empathy for someone who had caused her family so much pain. She didn't want to think about him.

Or the man who stood by the doors leading into the church. Was Zach standing guard to make sure her father didn't run away?

Ugh. Isabelle moved to where she couldn't see into the foyer, turning back toward her smiling sister. That, she thought … that was why all this was worth every icky feeling inside her. Sophie was happy. Truly happy. And this day was as her sister wanted. That was all that mattered.

The music changed and they entered the foyer. Greyson, dressed in the cutest little suit, joined them. When it was time, he'd pull the wooden wagon with its gorgeous quilt and sleeping Jeannie to stand with the wedding party. One by one, Bodie and Ben escorted the Butterflies to their respective seats with John, Lou, Charlie, and Uncle George. Then, winking as he passed by his pretty redheaded wedding date, Ben came back to the foyer to collect Darlene.

Looking watery-eyed, their mom kissed Sophie's cheek. "I love you, honey. Be this happy always."

Tears prickling her own eyes, Isabelle sniffled.

"Always." Sophie gave their mom a quick hug, then smiled as Ben linked arms with Darlene to escort her down the aisle to her reserved seat in the first pew.

When her father followed Ben and her mother, Isabelle's stomach dropped. What was he doing? She reached to stop him. Did he think he was supposed to already be in the church? How could he walk Sophie down the aisle if he was already up front?

"No, don't." Sophie grabbed Isabelle's arm. "Let him go with Mom."

Panic clutched Isabelle's insides. This was not how she had things listed out on her ceremony checklist. "I don't understand."

"You went to so much trouble to get Dad here, Izzy." Sophie's eyes were soft and without a single trace of anything but joy and love. "Please don't be mad that, earlier today, I realized I didn't want him to walk me down the aisle, after all."

The floor shifted beneath Isabelle's heels. "You don't?"

Sophie shook her head. "I'm glad Dad's here but having him walk me down the aisle to give me to Cole didn't feel right. I talked with Dad about it, Mom and Cole, too, explaining how I felt, and they all agreed."

The music changed to the song that Greyson and Jeannie were to make their appearance to. Pulling the sleeping flower girl in her wagon, Greyson made his way into the auditorium.

"Aw." "How adorable." "So cute." Whispers could be heard.

With a big smile on her face and a little wave of the fingers holding her bouquet, Annabelle stepped into the auditorium, leaving Sarah, Isabelle, and Sophie in the hallway.

"I don't know what to say," Isabelle admitted, her stomach in a tight knot. "I'm not mad, just shocked that you changed your mind. But it doesn't matter, Sophie. You marrying Cole is what matters." At her words, Sophie's eyes shined, and Isabelle's tension eased. "All I've ever wanted is for today to be everything you've dreamed."

"It is," Sophie assured. "Thanks to Cole, to you, and to our friends and family sharing this with us."

"Love you," Sarah whispered from where she'd been standing next to them, watching the exchange all shiny-eyed. Then, smiling, she entered the auditorium.

Knowing she was seconds away from making her entrance, Isabelle leaned over and, careful not to wrinkle Sophie's dress, hugged her sister. "No worries, Soph. Not about anything. I agree with Mom. Be happy, always."

Sophie hugged her tightly, but didn't let go, even when the note hit that indicated Isabelle should join the others.

"Sophie?"

Her sister sniffled, loosened her hold, but still didn't let go. "I told Dad I didn't want him to walk me down the aisle, Izzy, because I told him that I wanted you to be the one to do it."

Isabelle's jaw dropped. "Me?"

Tears sparkling, Sophie nodded. "You've always been my rock, my protector, the person who loves me to pure selflessness. Who better to give me to Cole than you, Izzy? Please walk me down the aisle to my happy-ever-after."

"HAVE YOU TALKED to him yet?"

At Morgan's question, Isabelle pulled her gaze off where her father and Sophie shared a father-daughter dance. "There's no need. Sophie wanted him at her wedding and he's here. As soon as the reception is over, he can go back to Louisiana."

"I meant Zach," Morgan clarified.

Sophie laughed at something their father said as they slowly moved back and forth in the center of the reception hall, causing Isabelle's shoulders to tense.

"You mean my dad's BFF?"

Her cousin placed her hand on Isabelle's arm. "It only makes sense that Zach would stay close to Cliff, since he's the one who insisted he return to Pine Hill. He feels responsible for how uncomfortable your dad is. Honestly, I feel for him, too." At Isabelle's intake of breath, Morgan rushed on. "Over the years I've been a nurse, I've worked with several men and women with PTSD. Your dad had a really bad case, Isabelle. From what Sophie says, he blocked out everything the first few years after he left Pine Hill and when reality started hitting him, he was still such a mess that he didn't know how to reclaim his former life."

Isabelle's heart squeezed, hating how lost her father must have been, but hating how much he'd hurt them more. "He didn't even try."

"No, he didn't," Morgan agreed softly. "Now, there are a lot of programs to help our military deal with the things they've experienced. Yet many still struggle and the suicide rate is heart-wrenching. Being back here, confronted with all these memories and his own failures, can't be easy on your dad. The nurse in me wants to hug him and tell him that it's going to be okay, that he's going to be okay."

Pulse pounding in her throat, Isabelle stared at her cousin. "Do you think today should be easy on him?"

Morgan shrugged. "I know he hurt you, but you need to talk with him, tell him how you feel, and let him tell you how he feels. Otherwise, you'll never be able to forgive him."

Morgan sounded just like Zach. *Ugh.*

"I don't want to forgive him."

Morgan's brow lifted.

Isabelle took a deep breath. "I never wanted him here other than that Sophie wanted him here. There's no need for him to stay after the reception."

"Sarah and Bodie have offered to let him stay at Hamilton House in their Beds for Vets suite if he wants to spend time in Pine Hill."

Which meant Zach wouldn't be occupying the suite. Isabelle swallowed the lump in her throat. She'd known he was leaving all along. Why did her chest hurt as if his pending departure was a new revelation?

"Of course they offered." The dance ended and Isabelle took a deep breath. "I don't want to talk about Dad anymore, Morgan, or Zach. Tell me about your life in California or about Andrew being a smokejumper or about Greyson's school or anything."

"For the record, you really do need to talk to your dad and to Zach, but okay, I'll tell you something." Morgan's eyes took on a happy glow and she slid her hand low on her belly. "A secret, actually."

"Are you really?" Happiness filled Isabelle at the smile on

Morgan's face as she nodded.

"You're the first person I've told. Other than Andrew, of course. I took the test this morning and am busting to tell everyone, but we didn't want to take away from Cole and Sophie's day."

"Sophie wouldn't have minded. This is wonderful news. Aunt Claudia is going to be ecstatic to have another great. And Ruby"—Isabelle smiled—"Ruby is going to be over the moon about this baby. Andrew is her pride and joy."

The music changed to an upbeat tune as Cole, surrounded by four Butterflies, took center stage. Isabelle shook her head at what was about to take place.

"Speaking of our Butterflies, if anyone ever needed proof of how much Cole loves my sister, we're about to witness it. Where did they find those red, white, and blue boas?"

Morgan laughed. "I didn't know they were having a groom-Butterflies dance. Poor Cole. At least he's smiling."

"I'm not sure anything could wipe the smile off his face today."

"My heart melted at how he looked at Sophie while they exchanged their vows." Morgan sighed. "Every word between them was pure perfection."

Their declarations of forever love and forsaking all others had been perfect. Isabelle's heart had overflowed for her sister and new brother. Keeping her gaze on them should have been easy, and yet, she'd had to fight to keep from looking toward where Zach sat between her parents in the front pew. Had the hand he'd placed on her father's knee been a reassuring touch or one meant to keep him seated?

"Oh, Rosie!" Morgan giggled at the woman sashaying

around Cole. The other three Butterflies shook their heads, then laughed and followed suit. "I miss them so much."

"Any thoughts of moving back to Pine Hill?"

Morgan's gaze stayed on Cole and the Butterflies. "Andrew wants to work a few years as a smokejumper, but we've always planned to move back at some point. With the baby on the way, we may make the move sooner than expected, though. I'm not sure. It wasn't planned, but we're both ecstatic."

Cole took Ruby's hand, twirled her around, then did the same for the other Butterflies, coming to Rosie last. Rosie batted her lashes, then crooked her finger at him. Laughing, Cole spun her, then gave her a quick dip. When she straightened, Sophie tapped her shoulder.

The Butterflies cleared the dance floor, leaving the newlyweds to their first dance.

"Look how happy she is." Morgan leaned close. "I want that for you, too, Izzy."

Isabelle frowned. "I'm happy."

"You know what I mean. Talk to Zach."

"Why? Zach has nothing to do with my happiness." Nothing at all, she assured herself, hating that her gaze sought where he sat at a table with her father, Sarah and Bodie, and others. He looked so handsome in his dress clothes and so very far away.

"Seriously, Izzy, the two most important men of your life are at that table. Go talk to them while I go see what my husband and Ben are up to. I suspect Cole's truck may never look the same after those two get through with their JUST MARRIED additions."

As if he'd somehow heard Morgan's comment from across the room, Zach's gaze met hers. Rather than look away, he lifted his drink in a salute.

Isabelle scowled, then looked away. Zach was not one of the two most important men of her life. He was just someone who'd found the man who should have been the most important man of her life.

"WAS THAT LOOK on my account?"

"Doubtful." Although Zach could feel Cliff's gaze, he didn't shift his own from where Isabelle fiddled with the tablecloth, smoothing out the material. She'd been sitting with her cousin but was now at the table alone. He longed to go to her, but he had no right, nor did she want him to.

"What did you do?" Cliff asked from next to him.

The man had leaned close, but still spoke loud enough that Maybelle's ears had perked up.

Zach snorted. "Exist."

Cliff's sandy-gray brow lifted in question.

"Zach and Isabelle have unresolved feelings for each other," Sarah supplied from where she sat on the opposite side of Zach, proving Maybelle wasn't the only one interested in what they were saying.

Unresolved feelings? He fought laughing. From the beginning, Isabelle had looked at him with daggers. The only thing that had changed was the way he looked at her.

Cliff eyed Zach suspiciously. "Is that the real reason why you refused to leave Louisiana without me? Because you couldn't disappoint Isabelle?"

"You're here for Sophie," Zach clarified. "She wanted you here and Isabelle wants Sophie happy."

The man sat in silence a moment, then half choked on his next words. "Thank you."

Zach's heart clenched, continuing in its battle between empathy for the man and wanting to smash his face in for all the pain he'd caused Isabelle over the years. "You're welcome."

Cole and Sophie finished their dance. Maybelle and the other Butterflies rejoined them toward the front of the reception hall, calling everyone to attention.

"As many of you know, the beautiful bride heads up our local Quilts of Valor group. The quilts you see displayed around the room are all Quilts of Valor made by various members. This work is very near and dear to our Sophie's heart." Maybelle glanced toward where Sophie stood, her fingers laced with Cole's. "As part of the celebration of her marriage, Sophie requested that we do a Quilts of Valor presentation."

"And," Rosie joined in, "she made a special request on who we wrap."

Having gathered one of the quilts, Ruby and Claudia held it up, displaying the red, white, and blue pattern. Maybelle and Rosie told the history of the organization, filling Zach with pride at being a member of the foundation Catherine Roberts had started after a dream where she'd seen a dejected soldier being wrapped in a quilt and finding comfort and healing.

Maybelle glanced toward their table. "Cliff, can you and

Zach join us up front, please?" Then she turned toward where Isabelle sat. "Isabelle, you, too."

Wondering at why he needed to be up front, Zach's gaze immediately sought Isabelle. Her face had gone pale as she realized what Sophie had planned.

Sophie was going to wrap their father in a quilt to welcome him home.

NO, ISABELLE THOUGHT. Sophie wasn't doing this to her. She wasn't a part of Sophie's quilting group. She didn't need to be up front. Her sister had bride brain.

Isabelle must, too, because she made her way to the front. Avoiding looking toward her father or Zach, she kept her gaze focused on where Sophie and Cole held hands. But then Sophie was taking the microphone from the Butterflies.

"Isabelle," she said. "Come stand beside me."

Heat burned Isabelle's face as she moved to where her sister indicated. *Oh Sophie, what are you doing?*

"All of you know that my father has just returned home," Sophie addressed her guests. "Many of you wonder where he's been. Where doesn't matter. What matters is that he is here now, back in Pine Hill, where he belongs."

Isabelle closed her eyes, then took a deep, steadying breath. As she opened her eyes, she realized her father, apparently feeling just as awkward, had done the same.

"Daddy," her sister turned to him. "Today has been full of dreams come true. Every Quilts of Valor quilt I've ever made has been made with wrapping you in one filling my heart."

Aunt Claudia and Ruby stepped forward, handing off the quilt to Sophie and allowing her to wrap the patriotic material around her father's shoulders. "Thank you for your service. Welcome home, Daddy. We're so glad you're here."

Hugs were exchanged. Her father mumbled words of gratitude and regret. Isabelle's heart pounded so hard that dizziness threatened to steal her consciousness. Fortunately, before that happened, Sophie finished, and Isabelle readied to make a quick exit. She needed air.

"I want to thank the Butterflies for all their help. They made my gorgeous dress, you know. My sister's, too." Sophie gestured toward her, and more heat burned Isabelle's cheeks. "I'd planned this presentation weeks ago, before I knew my father would be here, and I already had someone in mind and knew the exact quilt he needed wrapped within."

Isabelle's gaze went beyond her sister to where Rosie and Maybelle were bringing another quilt to the stage. The quilt that had been hanging in the shop when they'd closed Thursday evening.

"I know you're a member of our great organization, but when I checked the database, I realized you'd never been presented a quilt of your own, Zach."

Her sister was going to wrap Zach in the quilt that he'd admired so much, he'd bought Sarah the kit. Isabelle just wanted this day to end so she could go home and pour her woes out to Bobbin. Maybe the cat could help her reconcile everything that had happened. Or maybe not, she thought, as Sophie turned imploring eyes her way.

"Izzy, I need your help with this one."

Isabelle gave her sister a what-are-you-doing look. "I'm not a member," she reminded in a panicked whisper.

"Actually, you are. Merry Christmas a bit early." Sophie took her hand as if she thought Isabelle might make a mad dash from the reception.

Good thinking, because that was exactly what she wanted to do. This wasn't happening. Sophie gave a short spiel about Zach's service, briefly mentioning his injuries that had ended his military career, then glanced toward where Maybelle and Rosie held the quilt. They moved closer, and Sophie took one end. "Izzy, take the other side, please."

Not moving, Isabelle stared at the quilt.

"Please, Izzy."

All her life's frustrations accumulated in that moment. Her frustrations with her father. With Zach. With everything. Isabelle shook her head. She wasn't doing this. Not even for Sophie. She shook her head again. Shock registered on her sister's face, then Sophie turned to Zach. She and the Butterflies wrapped the quilt around him and welcomed him home.

Without a word to anyone, Isabelle walked off the stage and left the reception.

STOMACH CLENCHING, ZACH glanced around the foyer, then, acting on gut instinct, headed out of the church. Where had Isabelle gone? She could have walked home, but he doubted it since she was too practical to have left her car parked at the church. Which left the quilt shop as the most likely place for her to have gone to get away for a few minutes.

Only, as he headed down the street, he paused. There she was, sitting on the bench and staring at the monument. The inscribed words ran through his mind. Goosebumps prickled his skin. What did those words mean to Isabelle? Was she thinking about the sacrifices her family had made? Not with their last breaths, but with their family unit? Her head bowed into her hands and her shoulders shook. Zach took off down the street, determined to get to her, determined to hold her until every tear had dried.

"Let me do this, son." Surprised Cliff had caught him, that his grasp was as firm as it was, Zach paused, turning to look at the pale man who wore his quilt about his shoulders. "This is my mess."

"Isabelle is not a mess. She's a beautiful and bright woman who has made a success of the life you dealt her." Even if she was currently sobbing while sitting on a courthouse lawn bench. God, he had to get to her. Only ... wouldn't she rather have her father go to her than Zach?

"I didn't mean to imply she was a mess. I'm just owning that I'm why she's sitting where she is. You wanted me here and I came. Now, give me this."

Emotions warring with logic shredded Zach's insides. Cliff was right. Her father should be the one to go to Isabelle, only ... only Zach wanted to be the one, to have a reason to wrap his arms around her and hold her one last time. But that was nothing more than selfishness on his part. He needed to do what was right for Isabelle.

"You better not hurt her," he warned, reconciling himself

that he had no rights where she was concerned. No matter how much things felt different, he was just someone who'd visited Pine Hill and would be forgotten soon enough.

Cliff inhaled sharply. "And you? Are you going to hurt her, too? Just like I did?"

Zach shook his head. "I'm not like you."

"No?" Cliff's eyes, so hauntingly similar to Isabelle's, bored into him. "You're leaving her because you're afraid of what's inside you. You worry about whether you can control the darkness if those suppressed memories ever resurface. And if you can't, everyone around you will be hurt."

Zach winced. It was why he'd stayed away from his family. That, and the fact he couldn't stand their pity.

Cliff sighed. "You know I'm right. It's why you haven't shaken my hand free and gone to her. We both know you're leaving. I'm here. Let me go to her. She and I need a chance to heal."

"She isn't going to forgive you. Not that easily."

"I never thought she would, but I need to ask her to, don't I?"

Realizing that their conversation was preventing either of them from comforting Isabelle, Zach pulled his arm free. "If you hurt her again, I'll..." He paused, not sure how to label the emotions coursing through him.

Apparently, he didn't need to, because Cliff nodded with understanding. "The last thing I want to do is hurt my little girl any more than I already have. Now, let me go to her."

Zach nodded, then watched as Cliff did just that, joining Isabelle on the bench.

He stood there for long moments, watching the father

and daughter converse, feeling guilty that he spied on them and yet struggling to walk away when he knew how precious these moments were, knowing he'd never see Isabelle again.

Not outside of his mind and heart.

Chapter Fifteen

"You ALWAYS LIKED coming here as a child."

Isabelle had heard the approaching footsteps but hadn't turned from looking up at the courthouse flag to see who'd come after her. Of all the people to have followed, why had it had to be her father?

Taking a deep breath, she winced at the memories that assailed her. She'd come here with him, sat on the bench next to him while he stared at the monument, and she ate whatever goodie he'd just bought her. Sometimes Sophie had been with them, but often, it had just been the two of them.

"I'm surprised you remember anything about my childhood being as you experienced so little of it," she accused, not looking up at him.

He sat down on the bench next to her, but rather than stare up at the flag as she'd been doing, he studied where his trembling hands held on to the quilt still wrapped around his shoulders. "I'm sorry, Isabelle. More so than I know how to express. If I could have done things differently, I would have. At the time, I did what I had to do."

"You had to leave?" Emotions assaulted her, making her want to leap from the bench and run far away, but she'd run enough for one night. It was chilly, but seriously, why was he still wearing the quilt?

He nodded. "I know you don't understand. After all this time, I'm not sure I do, so how could I ever expect anyone else to? But when I looked in the mirror, I didn't know who the man staring back at me was. I didn't like him. He scared me. I was scared by what he might do to me or to the people I loved. I operated on a thin thread, always feeling as if I could lose control of everything inside me at any moment. Then one day, I just couldn't do it anymore. I hitchhiked out of town, and don't have much recall of anything that happened for a few years."

The wind nipped at her, and Isabelle shivered. "You lived on the streets that long?"

He shrugged. "Maybe. I was in and out of homeless shelters, worked odd jobs. In Texas, I met a veteran who took me under his wing, showed me kindness, and got me into a therapy program he ran on his ranch for former service members. I found myself there, wanted to come back to Pine Hill, but too many years had passed. I convinced myself your mother, you, and Sophie were better off if I stayed gone."

"We were," she insisted, but wasn't sure how convincing she sounded.

"Probably, but I should have given you a choice." He glanced down at his hands. "Fear kept me from doing so."

"Fear?" She knew of his military service, of the brave things he'd done. If she hadn't, Sophie's recent reminder would have refreshed her memory.

"Fear of rejection." He tugged on the quilt corners. "As long as I stayed away, I had hope that someday I could come back to Pine Hill. If I came back and I was rejected, then I had nothing except regret."

"You wanted to come back?"

"Desperately, but even after your fellow showed up, I was afraid to agree."

"He's not my fellow," Isabelle insisted, wondering how long it would take for the town to accept that she and Zach had been pretend all along. Soon enough, he'd be gone, and it wouldn't matter what anyone thought.

"You sure about that?" her father interrupted her thoughts. "It took me some fast-talking to convince him to let me be the one to come after you."

"He tried to stop you?"

"It wasn't so much that he wanted to stop me as it was that he was headed after you."

Zach had been coming after her? Her father had stopped him? What was it Morgan had said about them being the two most important men in her life? They weren't ... only, they were. Leaning back against the bench, Isabelle closed her eyes, the image of the spotlight-lit flag imprinted on her eyelids taunting her.

Voice breaking, she whispered, "I don't know what I'm supposed to say."

"You're not supposed to say anything. There's no need. Just—" He took a deep breath. "I plan to stick around Pine Hill, and with time, I hope you can forgive me."

He made it sound so simple, and yet nothing could be more so. There was so much pain, so much that couldn't be undone. Looking his way, she asked, "What about Mom?"

His hands shook to where he slid them beneath the quilt's edges. "I never stopped loving her."

Isabelle's breath caught. "Have you told her?"

He shook his head. "Guess I'm afraid of doing that, as well."

"She deserves to hear it, to have the opportunity to tell you to get lost again, if that's what she wants."

"She does. That and a lot more. Do you think that's what she's going to do? Tell me to get lost again?"

"I'm not sure." Over twenty years had passed. "She's never dated, but I doubt she could ever trust you to not leave again."

Turning on the bench, the quilt wrapping him in evidence of Sophie's love, his blue gaze met hers. "What about you, Isabelle? Can you trust that I'm here to stay?"

Could she? Pain pulsed through her in hurtful waves. "I-I don't think so."

He studied her a moment, then placed his hand over hers. Isabelle's entire body zeroed in on the warmth, the first time she'd felt her father's touch in over twenty years. Tears pooled in her eyes, a few running freely down her cheeks.

"Are you willing to try?"

Swallowing her pride, her pain, her desire to pull her hand free, she fought to keep a sob at bay. "I suspect you aren't going to give me a choice."

"If by that you mean that I'm never going to quit trying to earn your trust, then you're right. I'm home, Isabelle." With that, he took hold of the quilt about his shoulders, stretched out the material to envelop her within its warmth, and held her close. "Finally, I'm home."

"I INVITED YOUR father over to stay Christmas Eve so that he could be with us Christmas morning."

Fighting to keep Bobbin off the Christmas paper of the gift she was attempting to wrap, Isabelle glanced toward her mother. What did she expect her to say? Her father had been home for a week and had wormed his way back into their lives. Who was Isabelle to argue if her mother wanted him there at Christmas?

"If that's what you want."

"Want?" Darlene sank into the chair close to where Isabelle sat cross-legged on the living room floor, surrounded by wrapping supplies. "It's a lot to take in, this past week. But I think he should be here, rather than at Sarah and Bodie's for Christmas, don't you?"

As awkward as it would be having her father there, what her mother said made sense. "You're right. This is Jeannie's first Christmas. Dad shouldn't be there."

Her mother eyed her. "You think he shouldn't be here, either?"

Bobbin swiped at Isabelle's hand as she taped the paper edges together.

"Actually, he should." Darlene's brows lifted and Isabelle shrugged. "It's Christmas. If ever someone was going to come home, that's the time."

If only she could fully open her heart to forgive him. Lord knew he'd reached out to her and her mother repeatedly over the past week. He was trying. As much as she knew she needed to keep her guard up, a part of her wanted to lower every defense and just embrace the little girl inside of her who wanted her daddy to be in her life.

"It's going to take some getting used to, your father being back in town," her mother continued, reminding Isabelle that she wasn't the only one dealing with a lot of emotional baggage. "It was good of the Harveys to hire him to work on the farm."

Despite Bobbin's sabotage attempts, Isabelle managed to get the remainder of the paper taped. "I think they were grateful he responded to their HELP WANTED ad. They've been extra busy this year with the ice-skating rink being such a success."

Isabelle stared down at the gift. Her heart fluttered and she swallowed. For the first time in a very long time, she'd wrapped presents for her father. Her mother hadn't asked who the gifts were for, but Isabelle was a planner. Her mother would know that she'd marked off every name on her gift list long ago. Every name except the one she'd added that week. The gift was nothing more than a pair of wool socks and good gloves but buying them had made Isabelle's head spin. Wrapping them, the same.

"Sophie is going to be so surprised when she gets back from her honeymoon." Her mother glanced her way. "Have you talked with her?"

Cutting off a long piece of silver ribbon so she could finish with the gift, Isabelle nodded. "She sent me selfies of her and Cole in front of the Eiffel Tower. He even took her to the Palais Garnier opera house. It all looks surreal, and yet she's there."

Picking up the package that held the gloves Isabelle had already wrapped to inspect the tag, Darlene smiled. "I got that selfie, too. Thank you for helping Cole pull that off.

We're going to be hearing about their trip all Christmas."

"At least that will give us something to talk about Christmas Day while Dad's here. That will help keep it from feeling so awkward, having him in the house again." Isabelle curled the ribbon with the edge of her scissors, pleased it twirled perfectly. Bobbin pounced, swatting at the bouncy end. Isabelle put her scissors on the floor and picked up her cat to look directly into his green eyes. "You need to stop that or you're going onto the naughty list."

Darlene reached for the gift and ribbon and tied a bow around the box. Rubbing her chin over where Bobbin had buried his head in the curve of her neck, Isabelle gestured toward the tag she'd already filled out. Darlene put the tag on, then put it under the tree.

Turning toward Isabelle, she gave a nervous laugh. "I'll take all the help I can get regarding your father. But let's not talk about him anymore. How about you? Any trips to Paris in your near future?"

Rubbing her cheek against Bobbin, Isabelle frowned. "Of course not."

Her mother's brow rose. "Then you haven't heard from Zach?"

Ugh. Not her mother, too. "What does Zach have to do with my going to Paris?"

"Sophie isn't the only one of my daughters who dreamed of a honeymoon in France."

Grateful for Bobbin's affections, Isabelle snorted. "Perhaps you've forgotten how I feel about military men in all this Dad-being-home-and-us-calling-a-semi-truce-to-take-things-one-day-at-a-time thing."

"I've not forgotten. And it really has nothing to do with how you feel about military men, but how you feel about Zach."

"Mom—"

"I saw you two together, Isabelle," her mother interrupted. "We all did. You were happier than I've ever seen you."

Bobbin squirmed in her arms, apparently deciding he'd had enough loving, but Isabelle didn't let go. "Then I should go into acting. It was all fake for Sophie's sake, remember?"

"I love you, darling, but you're not that good of an actress."

Isabelle snorted. "Thanks, Mom. I appreciate that."

Coming over to put her hand on Isabelle's shoulder, her mother sighed. "I always knew Sophie would give her whole heart to some lucky man. I'm glad it was Cole, because he'll treasure that gift. You..." her mother paused. "I always worried about you, Isabelle. I never doubted that it would take a special man to win your heart, that he'd have to have the nerves of Daniel and be as patient as Job." Her mother's dark eyes met hers. "He'd have to be tough as Samson, as wise as Solomon, to get around those seemingly impenetrable walls you've protected your heart with all these years."

"You make me sound as if I'm incapable of love." Isabelle hugged Bobbin to her, then frowned when the cat gave her a swat with its paw, causing her to loosen her hold and him to jump free.

"Far from it," her mother assured. "You're capable of great love. The kind that consumes one's very being and lasts a lifetime. Deny it all you want, but you know exactly what I'm referring to. My question is, are you going to let Zach behind those walls?"

"You may have forgotten this part, but he left. Without saying a word to me, I might add." Just like her dad had. He'd known how hurt she'd been by that, and then he'd done the same thing. "You paint a fairy-tale image of a man who could love me, but it's more a nightmare, because Zach doesn't love me."

Her mother sighed, then walked over to the Christmas tree, poked beneath it, and picked up a brightly wrapped package. "Sarah dropped this off for you. I was supposed to give it to you to open tomorrow, but everyone will be here tomorrow, so maybe tonight is better. It's from Zach."

Isabelle stared at the present. "What is it?"

Handing her the gift, Darlene shrugged. "Only one way to find out." Darlene bent and kissed the top of her head. "Tomorrow's going to be a long day, so I'm calling it a night. But before I go, know how much I love you, honey, and that I want you to be happy. If that's here, working at the quilt shop with your sister, then fine. If it's not, go find your happiness, Isabelle."

Isabelle's heart squeezed. "You mean Zach?"

"If he's your happiness."

Isabelle stared at the package for long moments after her mother had left the room. Part of her wanted to put the gift back under the tree. Another part wanted to just toss it out and never know what was inside. But a bigger part knew that if she did, she'd always wonder.

"I have to open it, don't I?" she asked the cat perched on a chair arm. At her question, Bobbin yawned, gave her a slightly annoyed look, then hopped onto the floor to inspect what she held with great curiosity.

"Sorry," she told him, giving the box a gentle shake. "This isn't for you."

Isabelle guessed what was inside, then had to know and, with shaking hands, tore off the paper. Sure enough, inside the shiny packaging, he'd wrapped the snowman placemats they'd made at his unnecessary sewing lessons. There was also a card and a smaller package with a tag that read, BOBBIN. As if he could read the tag, Bobbin gave her a so-there look.

"Okay, so perhaps it was partially for you," she relented. "I guess you want to know what's inside yours, too."

The cat might not speak human, but his expressions conveyed his thoughts quite well.

Isabelle lifted the lid from the smaller box and stared at the contents. "Does he really think you're going to wear this one? He should have learned his lesson with the last gift he bought you. You don't do cute outfits." Not that she thought the kitty soldier uniform had been cute, much, but this one ... well, it kind of was.

Pulling the outfit from the box, Isabelle held it up.

"*Meow.*" Bobbin brushed his head against the material.

Isabelle eyed the cat. "Seriously?"

"*Meow.*"

Shaking her head, Isabelle slipped Bobbin's legs through the openings, then fastened the Velcro sides together under the cat's belly. "A perfect fit."

If not for the card calling to her, Isabelle would have laughed at the sight the cat made. As it was, her smile was short-lived as her gaze returned to the red envelope with her name written on it in Zach's bold handwriting.

Rather than seal the envelope, he'd tucked the flap inside. Heart pounding and breathing shallow, Isabelle undid it and slid the card out, wondering at the thickness inside.

A jolly snowman wished her a Merry Christmas.

She opened the card. Music began playing, and a white gold chain and pendant almost fell to the floor before she could catch it.

MERRY CHRISTMAS, BLONDIE. I'LL NEVER SEE A SNOWMAN THAT I WON'T THINK OF YOU AND PINE HILL. THANK YOU FOR TEACHING ME WHAT IT MEANS TO BE A PART OF A FAMILY. LOVE, ZACH.

The pendant and chain tightly clasped in her palm, Isabelle reread the note over and over, trying to decipher any hidden meaning, then deciding there was none, despite how her gaze kept zeroing in on his LOVE, ZACH. He'd just been being his abominable self.

"He doesn't love me," she told Bobbin. "He couldn't."

"*Meow.*"

"Don't give me that," she ordered the cat, who was looking at her, smugly proud in his fuzzy snowman costume. "But he must have cared at least a little."

Otherwise, why would he have bothered with the gifts? Then again, hadn't he bought the quilt kits for Sarah? Maybe he'd just done what he considered polite. Maybe.

Her fingers shook so that she struggled with the clasp, but finally got the chain undone and around her neck. Rehooking the clasp took even longer, but she managed, tugging the chain around to where the snowman pendant fell at her throat.

As she walked to the mirror, the snowman tugged at the hole in her heart.

"He doesn't love me," she repeated to her image. "And he's ruined snowmen for me forever." Not that he hadn't already. Cradling the pendant, she sighed. "And what does it mean that I may never take this off?"

Bobbin's only answer was another "*Meow.*"

GLOWING WITH HAPPINESS and laden with presents, Sophie barely made it inside the house on Christmas morning when she froze. "Is Bobbin wearing a snowman costume? And how in this world did you get him to let you put it on him?"

Excited at seeing her sister, Isabelle enveloped her in a hug. "Would you believe he's worn it all night and won't let me take it off him?"

Sophie's eyes widened. "No way."

Bearing more gifts, Cole stepped into the house, saw Bobbin, and snickered. "I can kind of see his button nose, but where's his corncob pipe?"

"Just because you're family does not mean you can make fun of my cat." Isabelle narrowed her gaze, then gave him a hug, too. "Welcome home, *bro.*"

"Can't say as I was in a hurry to get back, *sis.* But Sophie would never have forgiven me if we weren't home for Christmas. You know how she is about her favorite holiday."

Isabelle knew.

A few minutes later, Cliff arrived. While Sophie told

them about her favorite parts of her Paris trip, Cole smiled indulgently at his wife. Their mother had gotten up early, styled her hair, put on makeup, and even a dab of perfume. Her father had been smiling at her from the time he'd arrived. Things were far from perfect. Maybe they never would be. But as Isabelle glanced around the table at the delicious breakfast they'd made together, she said a silent prayer of thanks that her family was there and safe.

After they'd cleaned up the kitchen, they opened presents. Sophie and Cole opened the first Christmas ornament with their names and wedding date on it, which Isabelle had made for them, and gushed about how much they loved it. Sophie had shopped during her honeymoon and had put together a Paris box for Isabelle with an Eiffel Tower snow globe, a scarf, and a fancy box of delicious macarons.

Isabelle sniffled at the snow globe, refused to let thoughts of Zach ruin her morning, and passed her macarons around to share with everyone. When they'd finished, and although she'd been snapping photos with her phone, Sophie pulled out her camera, the same one Isabelle had given her for her sixteenth birthday.

"Everyone huddle together in front of the Christmas tree. We need a new picture for the wall." When they were there, awkwardly huddled, Sophie added, "On the count of three, say Rudolph the red-nosed reindeer."

"Rudolph the red-nosed reindeer," they all said in unison as the camera flashed.

Sophie checked the photo, then smiled. "It's perfect."

After loading up their gifts, they headed to Aunt Claudia's for a multi-family gathering.

Isabelle smiled at all the right times. Laughed at all the right times. Was fairly positive she gave the right answers at the right times. But that didn't keep Sophie from following her into the kitchen when she went after more cider.

"Call him."

She didn't bother pretending that she didn't know who her sister meant. "No."

"You should at least thank him for Bobbin's gift and wish him a Merry Christmas." Sophie gave her a suspicious look. "If he gave the cat a costume, what did he give you?"

The pendant burned at Isabelle's throat so hotly that Sophie's gaze dropped to it.

"Not that I don't know. I noticed your necklace when we first came into the house this morning and have been dying to get you alone to get the scoop."

"It's just a necklace," Isabelle assured, trying not to reach up to touch the pendant again.

She'd fallen asleep clutching the silly snowman the night before, had dreamed Santa had stuffed Zach into her stocking, giving him to her forever. Maybe she should lay off the hot cocoa before bed on Christmas Eve.

"A necklace from Zach," Sophie clarified, emphasizing Zach.

"It doesn't matter."

"Sure, it does," Sophie countered. "You're wearing it, aren't you?"

"Sophie, I—" Isabelle paused, then gave in to touching the snowman as if it were some magic talisman that would give her the ability to go on. She met her sister's gaze, then acknowledged the truth. "I miss him." Once the words came out, they overwhelmed her. "I more than miss him. I—"

Doing a little happy dance, Sophie squeed. "I knew it!"

"It doesn't matter, Sophie. He's gone."

"So what? We live in a world filled with transportation options." Sophie's eyes twinkled. "If you want Zach, go find him."

Breathing had become difficult, but she managed to ask, "And then what am I supposed to do? Hit him over the head and inform him that he's the only thing I want for Christmas?"

Sophie giggled. "That might work. You have been extra good this year."

Adrenaline built in Isabelle, messing with logic. She met Sophie's gaze.

Her sister nodded. "Go. Take your car and go. Now. Cole and I will bring Mom and Dad back to the house. Just go get Zach."

Isabelle hesitated. "What if he doesn't want to be gotten?"

"It's Christmas Day, Izzy. The most magical day of the year. If ever there was a perfect day to tell Zach how you feel, it's today. Go."

Isabelle gave her a hug, then, not quite believing what she was about to do, headed toward her Aunt Claudia's back door.

"Hey, Izzy?" Sophie called.

Isabelle paused and turned to look at her smiling sister.

"If you end up knocking out Zach and need help getting him back to Pine Hill, call. Cole and I will head that way. I'm pretty sure most of Pine Hill would help you haul him back here. We love you."

On her drive to the house, Isabelle made a mental list of what she needed to do prior to taking off to find Zach.

Call Sarah and see if she or Bodie knew where Zach currently was.

She could call Zach's cell, but what she had to say needed to be said in person, not over the phone.

Pack an overnight bag.

Fill up her gas tank.

Surely, there was a station open somewhere because she doubted she'd make it wherever he was on half a tank, especially in the snow.

Figure out what I want to say to Zach.

That last one was the most difficult. If he was at his parents', what did she expect to do? Show up uninvited when she knew his relationship was strained? Or maybe he'd gone on to the Keys to visit his friend Matt as he'd originally intended. Or back to DC.

She voice-dialed Sarah's number.

"Merry Christmas, Isabelle," Sarah answered.

"You, too." Isabelle's mouth dried to where her tongue stuck to her upper palate. "Um, do you happen to know where Zach is?"

Sarah hesitated.

"If you know, please, tell me. I need to talk with him."

"He went to his parents when he left here, but—" There was a garbled background noise. "Sorry, Isabelle, but I have to go. Merry Christmas."

"Well, that wasn't as helpful as I'd hoped," she mumbled to herself as she turned onto Main Street, then onto her street. Pulling into her driveway, she rushed into the house, grabbed a bag, and threw a change of clothes into it.

"*Meow.*"

Isabelle paused in her packing to glance at her cat. "Sorry, Bobbin the Snowman. I'm in a rush."

But for whatever reason, seeing the cat in the snowman outfit made her think of an old Halloween costume where Sophie had dressed up as Frosty. Her sister had always chosen something happy and Christmasy to wear for the spooky holiday. It had been several years ago, but the outfit was packed in their storage building. Isabelle wasn't sure which tote, but she had each one labeled, so it shouldn't take her more than a few minutes to find it.

"Ever heard of a singing snowmanagram?" she asked the cat, who followed her outside. Snow-covered grass crunched beneath her feet as she and the cat headed to the building. "Yeah, me neither, but looks like that's what I'm going to be today." She unlocked the door, and although not warm, being in the building blocked the cool wind. "If the costume fits."

A few minutes later, staring at herself in the house's hallway mirror, Isabelle snickered at the sight she made. "Yeah, I almost wished this hadn't fit."

"*Meow.*"

"Yeah, yeah, I know," she agreed, while holding her corncob pipe in the corner of her mouth. "I look ridiculous, but do you have a better idea?"

"*Meow.*"

She stooped to pet Bobbin's tail, one of the cat's few exposed fur areas. "I'm sure that's brilliant, if I spoke cat."

A loud knock sounded at the front door, causing Isabelle to jump and Bobbin to take off to the living room.

"Yeah, I'm so not answering the door wearing this getup." It was probably just neighborhood carolers come earlier than usual. It would be better for them to come back when the others were home to enjoy their holiday cheer.

Isabelle took off her black top hat and, carrying it, turned to go to her bedroom to collect her overnight bag. She'd change back into her regular clothes and get on the road. Pine Hill to just outside Atlanta should take her roughly six hours, give or take. If she left now, she should be there before ten. That wasn't too late for a singing snowmanagram, surely?

The knocking continued, growing more persistent.

"I know you're in there, Blondie. Let me in."

Chapter Sixteen

WITH EACH KNOCK, Zach grew more concerned. Isabelle had left her car running and the driver-side door wide open. Even without her call to Sarah, that alone would have put him on alert. That she wasn't coming to the door when he knew she was inside downright had him in a panic. Was she okay? He'd give her another thirty seconds and then he was going in. It wouldn't be the first time he'd jimmied a lock and broken into somewhere, but it would be the first time he'd not had orders to do so.

When he heard movement then the deadbolt clicked out of place, he let out the breath he'd been holding. "Thank God, Isabelle. You had me wor—What are you wearing?"

She placed the top hat she was holding onto her head. "A snowman costume."

"I see that." Had Sarah forgotten to mention some Christmas show Isabelle was in? "Why are you wearing a snowman costume?"

Her lower lip disappeared between her teeth, and she shrugged a fuzzy white shoulder. "That is a long story."

One he longed to hear no matter how long. He'd missed her. Even though she was wearing the hilarious snowman costume, he'd never been happier to see anyone than he was looking into her beautiful face. "Can I come in and you tell me that story?"

Her belly jostling, she stepped aside. "Why are you here?"

"That is also a long story."

Her brow arched. "One you're going to tell me?"

He'd rehearsed what he wanted to say a thousand times in his head. Hopefully, the right words would come to him. "Yes. If you'll let me."

If she'd let him, he had a lot of things to tell her.

"Get to talking." She crossed her stick arms, making her round belly wobble again.

"You don't want to go first?" he offered as he considered where to begin in telling her all the things he wanted to say about the past week. Had it only been a week? It felt so much longer since he'd last seen her.

Her gaze narrowed. "Why do I have to go first?"

Did she have any idea how adorable she was in the costume and how absolutely distracting it was when she pursed her lips at him that way? "I thought a gentleman always let a lady go first."

"You're no gentleman," she scoffed.

Zach laughed. "Maybe not, but for the first time in my life, I've found myself wanting to be."

Her brows knitted together. "A gentleman?"

"If that's what you want, then, yes, Blondie, a gentleman."

Her throat worked and her breathing became heavy as she said, "Keep talking."

"Because you aren't going to tell me why you're wearing

a snowman costume until I do?" He couldn't resist teasing. As expected, fire lit in her blue depths, but something more was there, too. The same something that had haunted him the past week. "I've missed you, Isabelle."

"So much that you've called over and over to tell me." She bit out with more sass than a woman in a snowman costume should be able to muster.

"I couldn't call—" he began.

Her brow lifted. "Because there were no phones in Georgia?"

"Because I needed to spend time with my family, healing old wounds without being completely distracted by my feelings for you." There he'd said it. The first part of what he'd rehearsed. "Believe me, partially distracted was more than enough."

"I'm glad you went to see your family." Not taking her gaze off him, she bent to pick up her cat.

Despite all the tension coiling inside him, Zach laughed at how she had to angle herself in the costume to accomplish the task. "Blondie the Snowman holding her snowman cat. I'm glad your hair is back to its natural color, by the way."

"Don't laugh at me and my cat," she ordered, lightly stomping the floor with a black boot and causing Bobbin to want down.

She let the cat go and he scurried over to the sofa.

"Or?" Zach pressed, taking a step closer to where he stood as close as her snowman belly allowed.

The costume failed to mask her apple-pie scent. Inhaling, Zach smiled. This. This was why he'd arranged for an iSecure plane to fly him to Louisville, rented a car, and driven like a maniac to Pine Hill.

Isabelle's eyes glittering up at him, she put her stick fists on what he supposed were her snowman hips. "Or I'll toss you out."

"I love you, Isabelle Davis."

Her face otherwise as frozen as if she really were a snowman, she blinked. "What did you say?"

"That hat blocking your ears?" he countered to buy himself a moment.

He'd had a week to figure out what he wanted to say, had it all rehearsed in his head, on how he'd come by later that night to wish her a Merry Christmas and to ask her to go on a date with him. A real date. One where he could hold her hand to his content and not need mistletoe as an excuse to kiss her perfect mouth. How could he have known she'd call Sarah, put him in a panicked tizzy to get to her, answer the door wearing a snowman suit, and completely throw all his preconceived plans right out the door? He'd sure not meant to blurt out that he'd fallen head over heels for her before giving her time to adjust to the idea of dating him for real.

She took off the hat and tossed it onto the sofa, yet again startling Bobbin, who let out an unhappy screech. Eyeing her with displeasure, the cat stalked over to beneath the twinkling Christmas tree, knocked off an ornament with his tail, then plopped down.

Tilting her chin upward, Isabelle locked gazes with him. Zach's breath caught at the beauty of her face, at the beauty of her spirit, and what shined so evidently in her eyes as she slid her fingers beneath the suit's collar and lifted out the snowman pendant.

She was wearing his gift.

She was his gift.

Not that he deserved anything so precious as Isabelle. But if it took him the rest of his life, he'd get this right with her. It might take him the rest of his life to convince her to let him, to convince her that, although he didn't know what was locked inside his head, he knew exactly what filled his heart. Her.

ISABELLE LIFTED THE snowman away from her neck with shaky fingers. "Okay, maybe I heard wrong, so let's try a different question. Why did you give me this, Zach?"

Why was he smiling so goofily at her? For a moment, she'd thought he said he loved her, but that couldn't be right. Could it? If it was, why was he so hesitant to say it again?

"Because it's Christmas." He covered her hand with his, tracing his thumb over where her fingers held the snowman, sending shivers down her spine. "My turn for a question. Why are you wearing it?"

She lifted her chin. "Because it's Christmas."

Cupping her face, Zach chuckled. "I've never met any- one like you my whole life, Blondie. You're stubborn and fierce and love with all your heart, and I've missed you with all of mine. When I realized it was you on the phone with Sarah, I—"

"You were at Sarah's when I called?" she interrupted,

pulling out of his embrace.

"How do you think I got here so fast, Frosty?"

"I thought you stopped by to make fun of my snowman suit." Standing on her tiptoes, she leaned toward him, her stuffed belly pressing against him as she stared up into his laughing eyes.

"I think you look *snow* good," he teased. "Where were you headed in this?"

Keeping her gaze locked with his, she took a deep breath. "To find you."

"Because you missed me, too?" His hand was back, cradling her face.

"I thought you were at your parents. I was coming there and—"

"And thought they'd welcome you with open arms if you were dressed as a snowman?"

"And wasn't sure how things were going with them," she continued as if he hadn't interrupted. "I thought if I showed up as a singing snowman telegram, it would give you the option of sending me away if things weren't going well or if you didn't want me there."

"Or inviting you in for after dinner entertainment if it was and I did?"

"Something like that. How did things go?"

"Brett and I will never be as close as you and Sophie, but we were civil." His palm tensed against her cheek. "More than that, really. I shared a lot of things with them, some of which I'm not sure they wanted to hear, but they listened. I apologized for shutting them out of my life and tried to explain how I thought I was protecting them by doing so, when in reality, all I was doing was trying to hide behind the walls I'd built after my accident." He paused, took a breath. "They want to meet you, but I told them it might be a while, as I had my work cut out to convince someone as wonderful as you to choose to be with a messed-up guy like me."

"You're not messed up."

"I wish that were true, Blondie, but I am. On the surface, my wounds are scarred over, but deep inside, the wounds to my mind and heart"—he took a deep breath—"I'm not sure they've ever stopped bleeding, or if they ever will. There's this part of me who feels so unworthy to be here, asking you to choose to be with me when you deserve so much better."

"I've never thought of you as unworthy, Zach. Not once."

"That means you'd give me a second chance, even though I don't meet any criteria on your ideal guy list?"

"I don't have an ideal guy list," she countered, barely able to believe they were having their conversation. "But if the new me who jumps in bouncy houses and dresses as a snowman on a whim wrote a list describing her ideal man, well, I'd be listing out all my favorite things about you."

"Such as?"

Isabelle bit into her lower lip. "How you look at me and really see me, who I am deep inside, and yet you like me, anyway."

The corner of Zach's mouth lifted, digging his dimple deep. "I love all of you, Blondie, the past, the present, and every future you."

Joy filled her to where she thought it might overflow. "Really?"

Staring into her eyes, he traced a fingertip across her bottom lip, causing a tingle to shoot through her. "I know it's going to take me years to convince you that I'm sticking around wherever you are, that no matter what inner demons I may battle in the future, I won't run from them or you. Not ever. Maybe by the time we're John and Maybelle's age, you'll believe me."

Isabelle's breath caught at the sincerity in his gaze, in what he was saying. Zach loved her and was telling her he wouldn't leave her and would fight anything that attempted to pull him away from her.

Her knees threatened to buckle as she said, "Or I could just believe you now."

The golden flecks in his eyes softened and he brushed his thumb across her cheek. "You could, but you'd never make things that easy on me. Nor do I expect you to. There's a lot I have to tell you about my past, my injuries, my rehab, how low I felt, and my fear that the darkness might return someday. Part of me wonders how I can ever expect you to trust in me when I think of all the reasons you shouldn't."

"True," she admitted. "But if I told you I believed you now, that despite all those reasons I shouldn't trust you, there's even more that say I should." She turned her face to press a kiss into his palm. "Believing you now might come with rewards."

His eyes sparkled. "It definitely would, Blondie."

"Then," her breath heavy, she told him, "I believe you now."

Zach leaned across the gap between them created by her belly and pressed his lips to hers. Firm, and yet so gentle.

Sweet, and yet spicy. Every Christmas morning rolled into one perfect moment.

When he pulled back, she smiled. "Does this mean you want to be my guy?"

"This means I am your guy. With every fiber of my being, I love you, and I always will."

Giddy inside, Isabelle pulled away, went to her purse, and pulled out the new journal her Aunt Claudia had given her for Christmas earlier that day.

"What are you doing, Blondie?"

"Making a new list." At the top she wrote, LOVE ZACH WITH ALL MY HEART FOR THE REST OF MY LIFE.

She drew a heart at the end.

"Great list, but it's not done." He took the journal and her pen and wrote out a second, longer item, then handed them back to her.

Glancing down at the page, Isabelle smiled as she read, BE LOVED BY ZACH WITH ALL HIS HEART FOR THE REST OF HIS LIFE, KNOWING HE WILL NEVER LEAVE, BUT WILL FIGHT FOR ME AND OUR LOVE ALWAYS.

Isabelle hugged the journal to her snowman chest. "I'm going to hold you to this forever. You know that, right?"

Grinning, Zach nodded. "I'm counting on it. Merry Christmas, Blondie."

The End

If you enjoyed *Wrapped Up in Christmas Love,*
you'll love the next book in....

Wrapped Up in Christmas series

Book 1: *Wrapped Up in Christmas*

Book 2: *Wrapped Up in Christmas Joy*

Book 3: *Wrapped Up in Christmas Hope*

Book 4: *Wrapped Up in Christmas Love*

Available now at your favorite online retailer!

More About The Quilts of Valor Foundation

Although described quite eloquently in Janice Lynn's fictional series "Wrapped Up In Christmas" the Quilts of Valor foundation is a real organization and I am honored to have the opportunity to share our mission with her readers.

The Quilts of Valor foundation is a national organization founded in 2003 by Blue Star Mom, Catherine Roberts whose son, Nat, was deployed to Iraq. It began with a dream, literally a dream. According to Catherine "The dream was as vivid as real life. I saw a young man sitting on the side of his bed in the middle of the night, hunched over. The permeating feeling was one of utter despair. I could see his war demons clustered around, dragging him down into an emotional gutter. Then, as if viewing a movie, I saw him in the next scene wrapped in a quilt. His whole demeanor changed from one of despair to one of hope and well-being. The quilt had made this dramatic change. The message of my dream was: **Quilts = Healing."**

The First QOV was awarded in November 2003 at Walter Reed Medical Center to a young Soldier from Minnesota who lost his leg in Iraq. Chaplin Kallerson saw the value of awarding quilts to his wounded service members because of the message they carried that someone cares. Chaplin Kallerson has remained a part of our foundation ever since.

His remarkable speech, given at our 20th anniversary conference in September 2023, can be found on the Quilts of Valor Youtube channel.

Quilts of Valor have been awarded in all 50 states, and in several countries such as Germany, Iraq and Afghanistan. **Our Mission is to cover Service Members and Veterans touched by war with comforting and healing Quilts of Valor.** The quilt says unequivocally "Thank you for your service, sacrifice and valor in serving our nation." To date, we have awarded over 387,000 quilts. Before the end of 2024, we will award our 400,000 quilt!

We have over 11,300 members who are our unsung heroes. These selfless volunteers bring their unique talents to inspire beautiful quilt making, coordinate award ceremonies, manage donations and fundraising, and meet the record keeping requirements of the foundation. Many of our members are veterans, others have family members who served. We join Quilts of Valor to continue serving and honoring the servicemembers and veterans we hold dear.

The Quilt of Valor Foundation maintains a website (www.qovf.org) where you can learn more about the Quilts of Valor organization, our history, our core values and most importantly how you can nominate someone to receive a Quilt of Valor. Nominations of quilt awards are sent to over 690 groups across the country so that every effort is made to present the award in person.

The Quilts of Valor Foundation extends a heartfelt thank you to Janice Lynn for being a valuable member of Quilts of Valor and for including us in her marvelous and entertaining books!

I personally invite each of you to visit us at www.qovf.org

Respectfully,

Lauri Leirdahl,
President, Quilts of Valor Board of Directors

Chasing Time   by Nancy Cann

Overall Size: 63.00 by 81.00 inches

Hourglass block 6" finished

For each star you will need 4 red/white hourglass blocks for a total of 24 red/white hourglass blocks).

For each pinwheel block you will need 4 red/white/blue hourglass blocks

White : 12 – 7 ½" squares

Red: 12 – 7 ½" squares

1. Draw a line across one diagonal of each white square.
2. Place a white square on top of a red square, right sides together. Sew ¼" from each side of drawn line.
3. Cut on drawn line.
4. Open hst and press to red. You have 2 pieces
5. Right sides together, place half square triangles on top of each other, opposing colors facing each other. Draw a line from upper left to lower right dissecting the hst. Sew ¼" on each side of drawn line.
6. Cut apart on drawn line. Press open to make two hourglass blocks. Square to 6 ½".
7. Make a total of 12 pair following instructions 1 - 6.

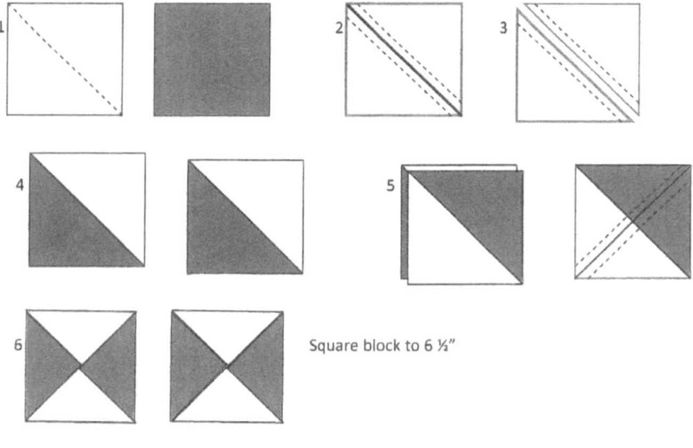

Square block to 6 ½"

Hourglass block 6" finished

For each pinwheel block you will need 2 red/white hourglass blocks and 2 blue/white hourglass blocks.

White : 12 – 7 ½" squares

Red: 6 – 7 ½" squares   Blue: 6 – 7 ½" squares

1. Draw a line across one diagonal of each white square.
2. Place a white square on top of each of 6 red squares, right sides together. Sew ¼" from each side of drawn line. Repeat for each of 6 blue squares.
3. Cut on drawn line.
4. Open hst and press to red or press to the blue. You will have 12 each red/white and blue/white hst triangle blocks.
5. Right sides together, place half square triangles on top of each other, opposing colors facing each other. Draw a line from upper left to lower right dissecting the hst. Sew ¼" on each side of drawn line.
6. Cut apart on drawn line. Press open to make two hourglass blocks. Square to 6 ½".
7. Make a total of 12 blocks following instructions 1 - 6.

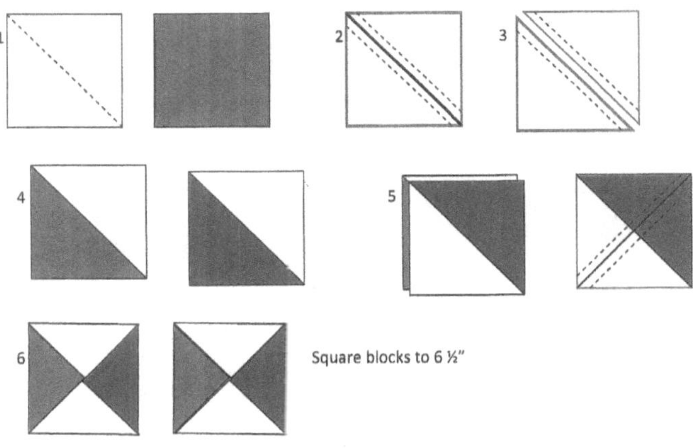

Making the blocks:

Ohio Star: Place block pieces according to diagram shown below left. Sew across Row 1, Row 2, Row 3. Press in the direction of the arrows. Join Row 1 to Row 2. Join Row ½ unit to Row 3. Press both seams toward Row 2.

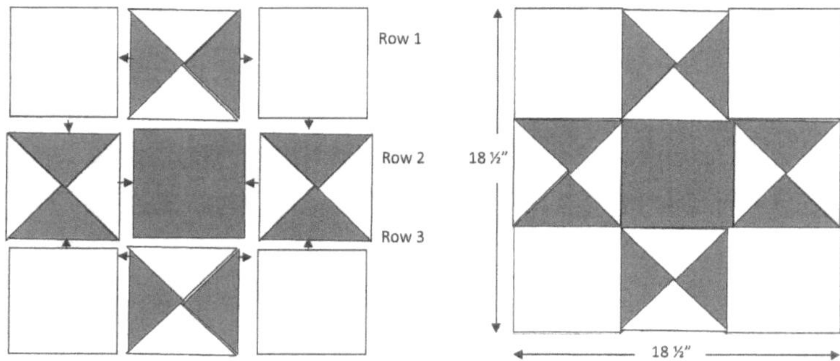

Bordered Pinwheel:
Place hourglass blocks as shown below. Sew block 1 to block 2. Press to block 1. Sew block 3 to block 4. Press to block 4. Press according to arrows. Block measures 15 ½" at this time.
Cut 12 – 3 ½" X 15 ½" block side border strips. Sew one 15 ½"strip to each side of pinwheel block.
Cut 12 – 3 ½" X 18 ½" block top and bottom border strips. Sew one 18 ½" strip to top and one to block bottom.

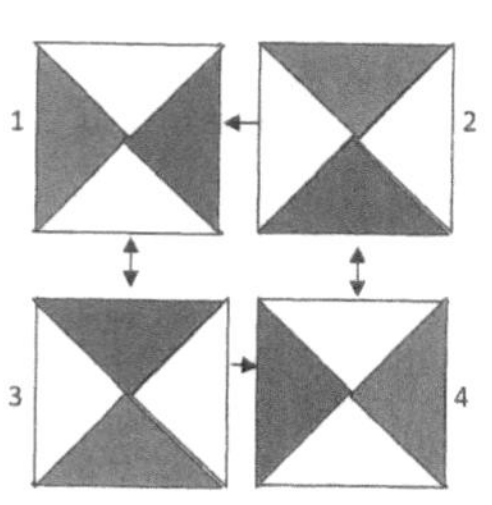

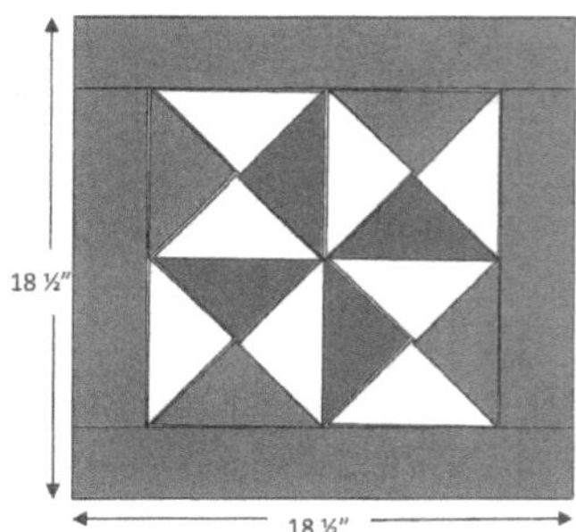

<u>**Adding borders to your quilt.**</u>

1. Sew blocks together in rows following diagram provided.
2. To add borders, measure the length of your quilt through the center (a1 – a1), the length of quilt along the left about 3 " in from the edge (a2 – a2), and length of the quilt along the right about 3" in (a3 – a 3).
3. Add these three measurements together then divide by 3 and this will be the size to cut your side borders.
4. Mark center of quilt and center offside borders. Pin left border to quilt top at center, top, and bottom. Sew in place. Repeat to add the right border.
5. Repeat this same process for top and bottom borders (b – b).
6. Repeat for second border.

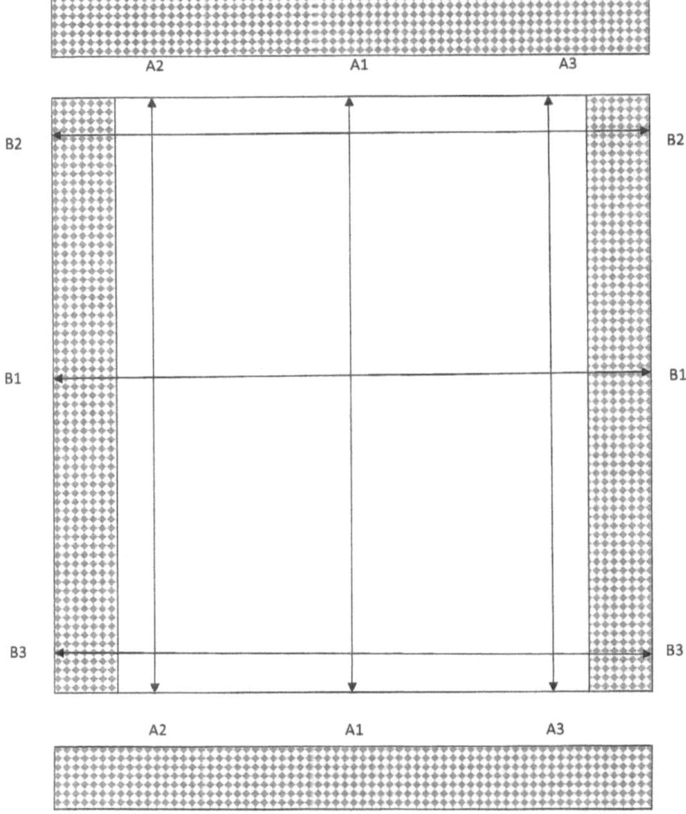

About the Author

USA Today bestselling author Janice Lynn lives in Tennessee with her Prince Charming, her vivid imagination, an adorable Maltese named Halo who's the true princess of the house and a bunch of unnamed dust bunnies who took up permanent residence after Janice started her writing career.

After writing more than thirty books for Harlequin, Janice began writing heartwarming sweet romance stories featuring the Quilts of Valor Foundation. As a Blue Star Mom, the organization is dear to her heart.

Janice's stories have won numerous awards including the National Readers Choice Award, The Golden Quill, The Golden Pen, the Holt Medallion Award of Merit, and RT Book Club's The American Title Contest. She's a Wall Street Journal, USA Today, and Publishers Weekly best-selling author.

In addition to writing romance novels, Janice has a Master's in Nursing degree and works as a nurse practitioner. She's a quilter, an exercise queen, a military mama, and a member of and supporter of the Quilts of Valor Foundation. Just kidding on the exercise queen.

Thank you for reading

Wrapped Up in Christmas Love

If you enjoyed this book, you can find more from all our great authors at TulePublishing.com, or from your favorite online retailer.

Made in United States
Troutdale, OR
12/16/2024